Cat's Paw

L. A. TAYLOR

ACE BOOKS, NEW YORK

This book is an Ace original edition,
and has never been previously published.

CAT'S PAW

An Ace Book / published by arrangement with
the author

PRINTING HISTORY
Ace edition / March 1995

All rights reserved.
Copyright © 1995 by L. A. Taylor.
Cover art by Gary Overacre.
This book may not be reproduced in whole or in part,
by mimeograph or any other means, without permission.
For information address: The Berkley Publishing Group,
200 Madison Avenue, New York, New York 10016.

ISBN: 0-441-00181-5

ACE®
Ace Books are published by The Berkley Publishing Group,
200 Madison Avenue, New York, New York 10016.
ACE and the "A" design are trademarks
belonging to Charter Communications, Inc.

PRINTED IN THE UNITED STATES OF AMERICA

10 9 8 7 6 5 4 3 2 1

For Cathy

Cat's Paw

GWYNNHEAD

1

A ragged yellow cat was crouched on the library steps when Miranda leaned the door open against the wind.

The cat stood up and fixed its silver-eyed gaze on Miranda's face while she maneuvered herself and her books around the heavy oak door, then, seeming almost to nod, it trotted down the steps beside her. She turned toward home, heartened at the sight of the animal: a beast the color of polished brass, a streak of something like sunlight in the gloomy afternoon.

She needed that brightness, any brightness. Miranda pressed her lips together and faced the long black line of flagstones beside the road. Above it, the bare-branched elms made a tunnel of the narrow lane, their gray bark seeming almost to yearn toward the ground. Somehow the image drained her of spirit.

She had taken only a few steps away from the library when she heard a soft mew. Glancing back, she saw the cat staring after her with an intensity that struck her as more canine than feline. A brush of pity became a thought: *Poor thing, it's homeless.*

She abandoned the idea of rescue before it had a chance
to shape itself. Her life had no room for another problem,
not even the relatively minor one of settling a strange cat
in with her own two resident royalty. She shrugged her
hood forward, pulled her wool cloak more closely around
herself and the books she carried, and trudged on. Dry
leaves skittered past her ankles. A few snowflakes drifted
out of the sky, whipped about or let hover until they touched
the walk to lie poised an instant before melting.

Even snow would help brighten things up, Miranda
thought, looking at the drab dead landscape, and felt a
chill creep into her heart. No, snow wouldn't help. Snow
wouldn't help at all.

From beyond the squat stone houses hunkered close beside
the lane to her left she could hear the boom of surf and the
clack and rattle of the pebble beach as the waves withdrew.
The sound, as familiar as the pulse of her own blood, only
darkened her mood. Three weeks, a month at most, and
then ice would begin to gather wherever the spray landed,
the rocky shore become a gallery of fantastic blue-white
sculpture.

And Alexi had not yet returned.

The road ended. The last of the houses beside it was dark:
her good friend Evelyn wasn't home. Unfair, really, to bring
her sorrows to Evelyn's door so often. . . . Telling herself
she had no time to stop for a chat anyway, Miranda blinked
away her disappointment. She passed by the house into the
less effective shelter of the junipers that now bordered her
path. Sparrows and chickadees had taken noisy refuge in
the tangled branches, but Miranda scarcely noticed. She was
too consumed with her thoughts.

A newly lean woman, no taller than average, she bent
to the blustery wind with the hem of her cloak flapping
unheeded. Her long face, with its angled planes, high cheek-
bones, and forthright nose was typical of this coastal province, as were her dark gray eyes and the hair once as golden
as the cat that still followed her. With middle age she had
become handsome. At the moment the wind had slapped her
cheeks pink, making her almost beautiful. Had she known,

Miranda would not have cared. Not without Alexi here to see her.

As she rounded the end of the juniper hedge a gust swirled her cloak out of her clutching fingers. The sea became abruptly louder: she had reached the end of the lane, where it turned into a broad-stepped path to the tower where she lived. Eyes drawn upward as always, Miranda saw the lighthouse beacon still unlit and hurried up the steps. Now she noticed the unusual silence of the gulls. They must be close to the water, expecting bad weather. The tide was high, the wind off the sea laden with spray. By the time she had climbed the fifty yards to her door, her cloak was heavy with damp and her face stinging. She shut the ancient slab of carved chestnut, grateful for warmth.

"Up, you, and move," she said to her younger son as she passed through the sitting room. "Your blood wants stirring, or it will all sink to your seat. Then where will your brain be?"

"In my head," Steth said mildly, his eyes still on his book.

"Up, up, up! You've been there all afternoon!" Miranda set the library books on the table under the kitchen window and took off her wet cloak. She draped it over a chair to dry and combed her hair with her fingers, going back to the sitting room door to ask, "Where's your brother?"

"Gone up to light the beacon."

"It wasn't lit when I came up the path."

Steth yawned and put a finger on his place. "That's what he said he was doing," he said. "What's for supper?"

"I'll think about that in a minute. First I'd better see to the beacon. I think we're in for a storm." She opened the door at the bottom of the winding tower stairs to call, "Hathden?"

An incomprehensible reply floated down to her.

Miranda sighed and started up the steps. As she climbed, the stairwell suddenly brightened and a low whirring noise began: Hathden had turned on the light. One of Miranda's newest problems was that the beacon's automatic switch had failed last week, meaning that someone had to be home when dusk fell or when storms darkened the sky. She had examined the failed switch, had even taken the casing off and seen what controlled it. An arrangement of thin, overlapping metal leaves formed an open circle that *should* adjust to let a constant amount of light fall on a sensor plate behind, much like the pupil of an eye. When the leaves opened widest, the switch was tripped. But Miranda had seen nothing wrong with the workings. To be honest, she had not understood exactly how the thing was supposed to work. Alexi was the one who knew how to fix the lighthouse gadgets. A twinge of worry cramped her belly at the thought.

She reached the top of the steps. Over her head the beacon rotated on well-oiled gears, its brilliance shielded from her eyes. Huge windows began just above waist level and angled outward to the roof, held in place by narrow strips of stonework reinforced with steel—and, legend had it, a good dose of magic. Miranda trusted the steel. She was inclined to chuckle at the very idea of the magic. Even if such a thing did exist—a possibility she was not prepared to entertain seriously even for a moment—didn't the old tales say that a spell did not long outlive its caster? And no one could have renewed this magic lately . . . although, Miranda reminded herself with an echo of her usual humor, Lexi did seem to have a magic touch with the workings of the beacon!

She found Hathden kneeling at the broad windowsill, his chin on his folded arms, looking out to sea.

"Hi," she said. "What's up?"

"Nothing."

"Thanks for lighting the beacon."

Hathden said nothing for a moment. Then he stirred and said softly, "It's mine to light now."

"Hathden, no! It's just until your father comes home."

Without turning, Hathden said, "He hasn't been home since midsummer. He said the job was dangerous the day the letter came from the Governor asking him to do it— whatever it was. We've had no word from him or anyone since long before the leaves turned and now it's winter, or nearly."

"Your father will come home," Miranda told him fiercely. "I *know* it."

"You wish it," Hathden said, still gazing out the window. Tarnished pewter sky and peened pewter water merged in a horizon made uncertain by dimness and distance. Closer at hand, the white scum of seafoam and gulls danced over the waves. Closer still, the intense beam of light turned the sparse snow into a whirling glitter. Miranda, grasping the handrail, backed down two steps instead of going up to the windows to peer down at the foundation of rock beneath her as she usually did. The stone wall was cold beside her.

"I wish it, too," Hathden went on. "But we have to be sensible. I'm keeper of the beacon now."

"Can *you* fix the switch?" A vicious question. Miranda was sorry the moment it left her mouth.

"I'll find out how. Someone must know." Hathden stood up, at last, and looked down at her. His face was his father's made young. So very, very young—but older than Alexi's had been when they had first met. "It's not as if the trade were secret, like the dyer's or jewelsmith's." Hathden shrugged. "It's just ours."

Ours. Hathden's and Alexi's and the men of the Glivven line, back and back for so many generations Miranda always felt a kind of awe at the thought of them, back even as far as the days before what some people thought had been magic was outlawed, when some poor fool might have mouthed a rhyme in the Elder Speech and thought that by doing so he had put a spell on the tower to keep it safe in a wind like this. *If* it was still the same tower, as Alexi maintained and Miranda doubted—although she had to admit that the stone steps had developed dips in their centers that suggested centuries of use.

"I'm going to start supper," she said, to bypass whatever Hathden might have to say next. *Seventeen years old, a lightkeeper?* "We'll talk about this later." Her feet striking an even beat on the worn steps as she descended, Miranda tried to imagine Hathden grown to manhood, and could think only that it was impossible for so many years to have passed since she had first seen him, red and wrinkled and bawling and streaked with her own blood. She had been twenty, Alexi three years older.

"Take your nose *out* of that book, Steth, and come give me a hand with that supper you're so anxious about," Miranda ordered when she reached the bottom of the stairs. She went into the kitchen, took a skillet off its hook, set it on the stove, and stared at it.

No matter that I haven't learned to cook for three instead of four, she told herself. *The boys eat everything but the bones, and the cats gnaw those.*

"Steth!" she called, turning angrily toward the sitting room. The boy was standing right behind her. As he began to protest, she heard Hathden coming down the stairs.

Somehow, she and her sons would manage. Until Alexi came home.

2

For years, Miranda had slept with the pulse of the beacon at her shutters, but this night the regular brightening and dimming of the room made her restless. Again and again she rolled drowsily toward Alexi's side of the bed, waking when she found it cold. Nights were when she missed him most.

The wind muttered in the chinks of the stone tower, phrases in which Miranda could almost make out words, as years before she had almost been able to hear a child crying distantly, although he slept in the cradle at her side. First one cat, then the other, came and curled up on Alexi's side of the bed. Reaching for the nearest, she curled herself around the warm fur, getting a half-hearted purr in response. No cat could substitute for the warmth of Alexi's back against her own. Still, she must have slept, because what seemed a moment later she stretched to find both cats at the foot of the bed.

As had happened so often since his letters had stopped coming, she dreamed of Alexi. But this time she dreamed that she *was* Alexi, crouched on all fours in a space too low to allow him to stand, looking out upon a bleak world of cold stone and dead flowers. Again she woke, again she lay listening to the dark wind blowing with the cry of a child, or a cat, and she shivered.

Snow spattered against the glass beyond the shutters; the room softly brightened and softly dimmed. Morning would come. Morning always came. And Alexi?

Miranda remembered his wry smile the day he left, his comment that she'd find this job—what was his exact word? Not *silly*. *Preposterous*, that was it. Preposterous, but dangerous. He hadn't said why: like other, smaller "jobs" he'd done for the Governor, this one was secret. Alexi was good at some kind of investigation, Miranda had gathered over the years, and once in a while he was needed.

As always, he had checked all the mechanisms of the beacon, before leaving her and the boys in charge of it, so that it would need no great attention from them. The windows would have to be cleaned inside and out—a balcony around the tower could be reached from a door on the landward side, although whether one could properly speak of a "landward side" on a narrow promontory like Gwynnhead was something Miranda had teased Alexi about for years. Hadn't Alexi said that he'd hoped to be home in time to help? But they'd washed the windows four times since he'd left.

Letters had come twice a week for almost two months, reassuring and humorous as only her Lexi could be. Then nothing. *In the morning I'll get his letters out again,* Miranda thought, *and read every last one yet again for a clue, a code,* something *to tell me what has happened.*

She slept again, and woke in the fresh light of dawn.

Steth, as always, was hard to wake, but Hathden wasn't even in bed. Miranda found him in the kitchen, stirring oatmeal into a pot of boiling water.

"Good morning," she said. "You're up early."

"Couldn't sleep." Hathden set the spoon down and put the lid on the pot. "It snowed a little last night," he said. "Did you see?"

"No, I haven't looked out yet."

"Want me to sweep the steps before school?"

"Leave them for me," Miranda said. "I need the exercise."

Hathden gave her an odd glance. "That's right." He nodded. "It helps settle me, too. But I'll have a walk, I guess, going to school." Miranda hugged him as he stood at the stove, wishing guiltily that it could be his father she hugged instead—or rather, in addition.

"Steth up yet?" Hathden asked.

Miranda went back to the kitchen door to call her fourteen-year-old. She didn't quite know what to make of Hathden in his new, somberly adult frame of mind. *It'll work out*, she told herself, bellowing, "Steth?"

Hearing the jingle of the bells on the postman's horse later that morning, Miranda went to the door. The steps had garnered a thin shell of snow overnight. In it, she saw catprints: not from one of her own cats, but from one with an extra toe on each foot. She put on her cloak and grabbed the broom to sweep her way down the many steps to the base of the hill. The catprints were only on the top two steps. Miranda recalled the crying wind of the night before. Had it really been a cat, freezing in the storm and pleading for warmth?

The idea saddened her as she worked down the hill. Nothing in the mailbox at the bottom of the hill improved her mood: a bill for lights and one for water, a notice from the library about the overdue book she had returned the afternoon before. No answer to the letter she'd written to the Governor, asking for any news. Above all, nothing from Lexi.

She climbed the steps to the house feeling weary, early in the day as it was. The gulls were crying today, the air salty but neither well-worn sound nor well-worn scent lightened her heart as they usually did. She opened the door. A streak of gold shot past her into the house. That cat!

"Hi!" she shouted. "Come back here!" Tail high, the beast vanished into her kitchen. Expecting an instant explosion of snarls and shrieks from her own cats, she ran after it, and then stopped, astonished. Mrs. Putz and Tomtom sat, one at each side of the mat on which the cat food dishes lay, while the golden cat ate. They gazed at the invader with interest, but no animosity.

Miranda plunked down at the table, still holding the broom. "Well," she said, after watching the beast polish both dishes with an eager tongue, "I guess you have a home, after all."

The cat turned at her voice, came toward her, and rubbed its head against her shins. Miranda could have sworn it was smiling.

Over the next week and some, winter, having given fair warning, retreated. Hathden took over the lighting of the beacon.

Miranda watched her son's absorption in his self-imposed task with a mixture of pride and panic. Even at seventeen he was a responsible lightkeeper: the day after their conversation in the tower, Steth came home from school alone, saying that Hathden had stopped at the library to see what he could find out about automatic switches. Just before dusk Hathden arrived and went up the tower steps after the briefest of greetings.

"Did you find anything?" Miranda asked when he came down.

"No."

"I guess we'll just have to keep turning the switch by hand, then," she sighed.

"I'm going to ask Andreu if he can do anything," Hathden said. "I'll stop by his house on the way to school tomorrow."

Old Andreu, the village handyman, came to the door the next day. He went up the tower steps, grumbling at the long climb. Still grumbling, he took the casing off the switch to poke at the innards, knotted his shaggy gray eyebrows together for at least half an hour while Miranda waited with clasped hands for his verdict, and went away scratching his head.

"Did Andreu come?" Hathden asked the moment he walked through the door that afternoon.

Miranda nodded. "He couldn't fix the switch, though. He couldn't figure out how it worked."

"Andreu couldn't?" Hathden echoed, sounding as surprised and disappointed as Miranda had been. She shook her head. "I guess I'll have to think of something else, then," Hathden said.

Miranda, hearing a mew at the back door, opened it. A parade of three cats entered. She stood in the doorway a moment, watching the flash of the beacon on the narrow band of coarse grass between herself and the fenced edge of the cliff. "What about asking Master Craffid to look at it?" she suggested.

"I guess I could do that," Hathden agreed. Miranda closed the door against the cool air and returned to the kitchen table to help Steth draw some geometry problems.

The next day Master Craffid, the science teacher, came home with Hathden to look at the automatic switch, examined the instrument carefully, and declared that not only did it not work now, it had never worked in the first place.

"That's absurd," Miranda said. "It's been working perfectly well for years."

"How?"

"I don't know. That's why we asked you to help."

"I'm sorry, Mrs. Glivven. There's just no way on earth that switch could have operated," the man insisted. "Not as it is now. You're sure you haven't removed some part?"

"Quite sure," Miranda said, looking thoughtfully at Hathden, who shook his head. Maybe Andreu had left something out when he reassembled it? Dare she insult him by asking? The science teacher went home, and at twilight Hathden climbed the stairs to turn the beacon on, refusing Miranda's offer to do it.

When she went down for the mail the next morning, to find nothing in the box but a card from a friend who had moved to the mainland a few years before, Miranda knocked on Evelyn's back door.

"Come in," Evelyn said, searching her face. "I'll put on the kettle."

"Oh, that would be wonderful." Miranda sat at the kitchen table and showed Evelyn the card.

"Did you get the switch fixed?" Evelyn asked, nodding and handing the card back. "I saw Mikkel Craffid coming down your steps yesterday afternoon."

Miranda shook her head. "And Hathden insists on turning the beacon on himself," she said. "Oh, Evvie! He thinks Lexi's dead—that it's his job now, forever."

"Shh," Evelyn soothed.

"It's hard to see him grow up so young," Miranda continued. "And I *won't* believe that Alexi's dead!"

Evelyn looked out her kitchen window to the hill and the tower rising above the village. "Still nothing, then."

"You'd have heard," Miranda assured her. "I wouldn't even go up to the tower from the mailbox! I'd run straight over here."

The kettle began to sing on the big iron stove. Evelyn fetched it and poured boiling water into the teapot. "Where was he, last you heard?" she asked, returning the kettle to the edge of the stove. "Bierdsey, wasn't it?"

Miranda nodded.

Evelyn got two mugs down from a shelf and set them on the table. "Why not go look for him?"

"It's so far!" Miranda sighed. "Two days by train, with a change overnight at Clunn. That's four days just traveling there and back, and who knows how long to look for him?"

Her friend sat down and poured tea into the mugs. "If it's money . . ." she said slowly.

"No, no. It's the light," Miranda said hastily. "Someone has to see to it, every day."

"Hathden's doing that," Evelyn pointed out.

"Evelyn, people's *lives*—"

"Depend on the light, I know. Don't you think Hathden does, too?"

Miranda sipped at the hot lemony tea.

"Would Hathden let down the whole line of Glivvens?" Evelyn asked. "Not for a moment. You know it, Miranda."

"True."

"Besides, David and I are here, a stone's throw away. One of us can always run up to the tower and prod the boys." Evelyn gave her a sideways look. "We come of sailors, remember," she added, an oblique way of assuring Miranda she wouldn't forget.

Miranda nodded.

"If it's housework and eating and such that worries you, they can eat here, or I'll make sure they have food in the house. How much of a mess could they make in just a few days?"

"Oh, they're neat enough, for boys." Miranda sat looking at her mug, worrying. Suppose she did go? Would Steth do his schoolwork? Would the beacon *always* be lit? Would . . .

"I could look in on them," Evelyn went on. "Make sure they have clean clothes, if you're gone that long, and nag Steth about his homework—"

"That would be a help," Miranda admitted.

"Good heavens, Miranda, they're fourteen and seventeen! In the old days they'd have been out on their own at their ages. They can manage without you, or me either, for that matter, though I'm glad to keep an eye on them."

"I suppose you're right," she said unhappily.

"You're afraid of what you might find in Bierdsey, aren't you?" Evelyn reached across the table and clasped Miranda's hand. *Her fingers feel so warm, my own hands must be icy,* Miranda thought. She nodded.

"But isn't it worse to wait here, day after day, hoping for some word and knowing nothing?" Evelyn pursued.

After a moment of anguish Miranda nodded again.

"Think about it," Evelyn said.

She didn't want to think about it. She didn't want to think about anything ever again. But somehow, half an hour later Miranda had decided to go. She climbed the hill to the beacon house clutching the edges of her cloak to pull it snug. Two years had passed—or was it three?—since she had crossed the causeway from the village to the mainland on her own. Too long. Time for an adventure. But her adventures had always been shared with Alexi . . .

She waited until after supper to announce to her sons that she was going to search for their father. Hathden looked almost relieved. Steth was openmouthed with surprise.

"Where will you look?" Steth asked.

"I'll start by going to Bierdsey, since that's where his letters came from." Miranda scraped a plate into one of the cat food dishes. Three small heads crowded around it, munching contentedly. The golden tomcat glanced up at her. It had plumped up well since adopting her, she noticed. Its coat was thick and sleek, and the bumps of its backbone hidden.

"Then what?" Steth asked.

"I'll go to the inns and see if he stayed in any of them, and if I find that he did, I'll ask whether he said where he was going when he moved on, I guess."

"That sounds like a good plan," Hathden agreed.

"I'll be gone at least five days, probably a lot longer." Miranda shoved Mrs. Putz out of the way with one foot and scraped the last plate into the dish. The cats moved back into position. "Are you sure you can tend the light absolutely without fail and keep up with your schoolwork?"

Hathden made a faint sound of assent. Steth groaned, "Oh, Mother!"

"Evelyn says she'll feed you, if you want, or help you with the marketing," Miranda went on. "I'll have to catch the train at Gwynn-on-the-Main, and change at Clunn. Perhaps Andreu would be willing to drive me over the causeway."

"When will you go?" Steth asked.

Miranda hesitated. She hadn't thought that far ahead.

"Tomorrow," Hathden said.

"Tomorrow! Oh, no, not that soon. I'd never get packed in time," Miranda protested. "I haven't stocked the pantry for you, or—"

"I'll go right now and ask Andreu if he's willing to drive." Hathden took his cloak from its peg beside the kitchen door. "We can shop for ourselves, if you'll leave us some money. The bank will be open before you have to leave, so you can get some cash and some letters of credit."

"Hathden," Miranda said suspiciously. "How have you thought of all this so quickly?"

The boy shrugged into his cloak and fastened the closure. "I've been wanting you to go look for Father for weeks, but I was afraid you'd say no. So I thought it all out, but I didn't know how to go by myself without stealing the money."

"I see."

"And there's the light. I can't leave it." Hathden opened the door and stepped out.

"We'll be fine," Steth said. As if to prove it, he went into the sitting room and fetched his sack of schoolbooks. Miranda sank into a chair at the kitchen table. The golden cat leaped into her lap and settled down. She stroked it absently.

Funny that it never purrs, she thought.

3

The next morning was a whirl of arrangements—friends to be told she was going and farewells to be said, the bank, a visit to the school to tell the provost Hathden and Steth were on their own for a few days. *They'll be all right,* Miranda admonished her doubtful self, looking back at the school after saying good-bye to her boys. In a village of three hundred seagoing people, everyone was sure to look out for the lightkeeper's sons.

Miranda returned home, breathless from her fast climb

up the steps, and finished packing under the eye of the nameless yellow cat. She lugged her case to the front door and looked around the sitting room flooded with sunlight, sunlight that picked out the loose threads of the worn chair cushions on which she and Alexi had sat so many evenings, sunlight that glinted from the touch-polished wood of the chair arms. *Twelve good years spent here,* Miranda thought. Ever since Alexi's father had drowned when he was out in that storm with the lifeboat, trying to save four sailors who had also drowned. . . .

She shuddered. And even before that, she had known this room well. Had known it almost as long as she could remember. How could she bear to leave it?

A knock interrupted her melancholy thoughts. She opened the door to Andreu. "Morning, Miranda," he said. "Ready to go?"

"Yes, my case is right here." She pushed it forward.

"I'll carry it down for you."

"Thanks." Miranda took one more long look around the room. As she did, the yellow cat trod deliberately out of the kitchen and across the sitting room. She let it go through the door. With its fine thick coat of fur it wouldn't be chilled before the boys got home from school to let it in, and it could always find itself a sunny spot to lie in.

Andreu had already reached the wagon that was sitting at the end of the lane. Miranda closed the door with an extra caress of farewell, saw Evelyn standing beside the horses ready to wish her good-bye and good luck, and swallowed her panic.

As she started down the steps, the yellow cat appeared from around the corner of the house and twined between her feet, looking up at her as she tried to avoid stepping on it. She bent to pat it and went on down the hill to join Andreu and Evelyn at the wagon.

"My, you look wonderful," Evelyn said. "This is doing you a world of good, Miranda."

"I suppose so."

"You *know* it is." Evelyn squeezed her tightly. "Good-bye, sweet, and good luck."

Miranda climbed onto the wagon, blinking away tears and trying to smile. She looked down at her knees: she was wearing her very best winter clothes, a pair of dark green wool trousers embroidered with flowers in pale blue and purple, a long-sleeved purple tunic with a band of embroidery around each cuff to match the trousers, and her best high leather boots. She'd thought the clothes, even as loose as they'd become recently, would give her confidence, but now she could only think that in Bierdsey they would look horribly provincial.

Andreu shook the reins and she was on her way. The wagon jangled down the street, past the library, the three shops at the heart of the village, and on past the school. A gust of wind caught at her cloak as they started onto the causeway.

The golden cat darted ahead of them. "Looks as if Gwynnhead is losing a citizen," Andreu remarked. "B'longs to someone, by the look of it, though I can't just bring to mind who."

"Oh, dear," Miranda said. "It's mine—that is, it strayed into my house a week or more ago, and no one's claimed it."

"Pretty creature," Andreu said. "Should we stop and take 'im back?"

Miranda pulled her watch from her tunic pocket and cast a worried glance at it. "No," she said. "I might miss the train. If we can get it into the wagon, would you mind taking it back?"

"Glad to. Hold the reins and I'll see if he'll come to me."

It crossed Miranda's mind that if Andreu didn't recognize the cat, then it might have wandered onto Gwynnhead from the mainland and now simply be on its way home. But, to her surprise, when the horses pulled up the animal jumped onto the wagon and into her lap, where it settled down and craned its neck to see forward.

Gwynn-on-the-Main was a half-hour drive inland over a gravel road, protected from the sea wind by a line of low hills. The trees here struggled less than those on the headland:

a group of oaks beside the road grew straight and tall, and the archway of elm branches over them as they approached the town was far taller than the one over Gwynnhead's single street. Blooming snapdragons still stood in some dooryards. Even a few chrysanthemums flaunted their bright rusts and yellows here and there, despite the hard frost of three weeks before. A woman pulling the last of her garden beets waved to them as they passed, and the sun was warm on their backs.

Miranda felt her anxiety changing to anticipation as Andreu turned the horses toward the train station. The low stone platform, half roofed over, and the little box of a ticket office soon came into view. Andreu drew up close to the platform and hitched the horses to a ring set into the stone.

"We'll be just in time," he said, reaching up to give Miranda a hand down from the wagon. The cat shifted, but wouldn't leave her lap. She scooped it up with one arm and climbed down, the cat clinging to her shoulder with one spread paw. "You'd best run and buy your ticket," Andreu told her. "I just heard a whistle."

Miranda hurried into the tiny station and bought a ticket for Clunn. She met Andreu on the platform and looked down the track for the train. "Yes, there it is," she said. "We weren't a moment too soon."

"Good thing we didn't go back," Andreu agreed. The train chuffed into the station and stopped with a clanging of metal and a loud hiss of steam, the bell at its side ringing. Miranda held tightly to the cat to keep it from dashing under the huge iron wheels.

"Good luck, then, M'randa," the handyman said.

"Thanks. I think I'll need a lot of good luck," she replied rather forlornly. The idea of going to a town as large as Bierdsey scared her. How lucky she was to live in a tiny village where she had a place in life without asking! She smiled at old Andreu, feeling a flash of affection, and stood on tiptoe to brush a quick kiss across his cheek. The golden cat twisted and slipped from her hands.

"Hi," she yelled. "Come back here!" A streak of gold

disappeared behind a luggage cart. The trainman was calling for passengers.

"Never mind that," Andreu said. "I'll catch 'im and take
'im home for you, don't fear. You board that train, or it'll
leave without you!"

Miranda climbed the steps. Andreu had to trot beside
the already moving car to hand up her case. The trainman
helped her get it aboard and settled in the luggage rack
at one end of the car. Miranda balanced herself carefully
to move along the aisle of the car and find a seat near a
window. Andreu was already too far behind to wave to.

One step at a time, Miranda told herself. She was on her
way to Clunn. There, she'd find a room for the night and
take the morning train to Bierdsey, and then . . . what?

About fifteen minutes later, while she was watching the
landscape glide past at five times the speed of old Andreu's
wagon, she heard a *prrrt* beside her and looked over. The
golden cat had jumped onto the empty seat and now stepped
a tentative paw onto her thigh.

"Well!" Miranda exclaimed. "How did you do that?"

The cat, by this time in her lap, merely folded its paws
beneath itself and let its eyes close. Miranda stroked its
ears. "You seem to have chosen to go wherever I go," she
remarked. No doubt at all, it was nice to be chosen, even
by a cat. *I should name it,* she thought. But its coat was the
color of her husband's hair, its eyes were almost the same
iridescent gray as her husband's eyes. The only name that
came to mind was his.

Rational skeptic she might be, but coincidence still had
the power to send a shiver down Miranda's back. The cat
glanced up at her with its odd appearance of smiling, fitted
its head to its forepaws, and went to sleep.

CLUNN

1

At Clunn, an unpleasant incident occurred, made all the
more disagreeable by her weariness and the late hour.

Miranda woke as the train slowed to pull into the station.
The side of her forehead ached from leaning against the
cold window. Sometime after she'd dozed off, the cat had
left her lap and had curled up close beside her leg. Now
it woke too, stretching and yawning as completely as only
cats and infants seem able to do.

A door slammed at the end of the car, and the trainman
came through shouting that this was Clunn. Miranda got
to her feet to retrieve her cloak from the hook beside the
window. Five or six other people in the car also rose. The
train stopped with a series of jolts, and she heard the stairs
bang down into place.

She pulled on her cloak and her gloves, picked up the
sleepy cat, and made her way to the end of the car to
exchange the stub of her ticket for her suitcase. When she
descended the folding steps she found the platform wet: a
fine chilly rain was falling. The steam of the locomotive
swirled thickly around her legs as Miranda stopped to get
her bearings. She spotted, across the road from the station,

the sign of an inn beneath a streetlamp.

The golden cat, clinging to the fabric of her cloak as it had in the station at Gwynn-on-the-Main, stayed on her arm when she hefted her suitcase. She hoped it wouldn't get away from her as it had before. Lugging the heavy leather case, Miranda crossed the narrow street with several other train passengers and waited patiently in line to see whether there would be a room left for her.

She was in luck. One single room remained. "I've got my cat with me," she said. "Will that be all right? It's housebroken."

"I don't like it, missus," the landlord said. At the sag of her shoulders he seemed to take pity. "But if you promise it won't spray, or you'll pay for the cleaning, you can keep it one night." He added, "Be sure it doesn't get out of the room."

With some misgivings—how far could she trust this beast after so few days?—Miranda promised that her cat would behave. She signed the register and paid for one night's lodging. Turning from the landlord's desk, the cat tucked into the crook of her elbow, she found herself facing a haggard old woman in a ratty brown cloak.

"That's a magicked cat," the woman half-hissed.

"Magicked?" Miranda laughed. "Hardly." The cat shifted on her arm and she automatically reached up to steady it. It tucked its paws under her cloak.

"See?" the old woman shrieked, pointing. "See how it hides its paws! You, woman. Are you the magician?"

A magician! Could even an old crone like this believe that such people had ever existed? Miranda chuckled. "Only on alternate full moons," she said.

The old woman's nostrils flared. She drew back to glare at Miranda. "Once is treason!"

Miranda shook her head and grinned at the woman. She bought a newspaper from a boy hawking them to the inn's new customers, picked up her leather case, and followed the landlord's directions up to her room. There she let the cat jump from her arm to the bed so she could spread the newspaper on the floor for it. Humming a bit, she unpacked her soap and cloth and washed up, hoping that the dining room could still give her a decent supper.

She stopped wiping her face and looked into the mirror over the washstand. Now, there was another problem. What would she feed the cat? The landlord might have some idea.

Miranda went down to the dining room and ate a meal so hastily served she was certain the inn's staff had merely been waiting for the train passengers to arrive before closing the kitchen. But they provided her with a large helping of a hearty mutton stew. She saved some meat and a chunk of potato for the cat, and carried the meal up to her room on a borrowed saucer. With the cat fed, she prepared to settle down for the night.

The animal had scarcely licked the saucer clean when someone knocked on her door so loudly it seemed he intended to break the stout panel. Miranda rushed to find out what the noise meant and was flung back against the wall as three men burst into the room.

"There she is!" cried the old lady who had accused her of being a magician. "That's the one with the magicked cat! Seize her!"

One of the men grabbed Miranda by her forearms and pulled her hands behind her back, squeezing so hard that she gasped with pain. A second man strolled across the room to the bed and felt the hollow where the cat had been lying when Miranda had brought its supper. "Gone cold," he observed. Turning to Miranda, he asked, "The cat?" in an oddly calm voice.

She swallowed against the pain in her wrists, determined not to cry out. "It's only a pet."

"Sit her down."

The third man remained in the doorway. The old woman stood behind him, first on tiptoe and then trying to peer under his braced arms. The man who held Miranda marched her to the chair beside the bed and roughly pushed her onto it, shifting his grip to keep hold of her arms.

"Has the beast vanished itself?" he asked the man by the bed, his voice shaking with awe.

"I don't know." The man tossed his cloak over the foot rail of the bed. "Possible, I suppose."

"*Vanished* itself? It's just an ordinary house cat," Miranda protested. "It's just hiding. You frightened it, coming in with all that noise."

She was frightened herself, confused by the intrusion but relieved that the door was still open and that the hostile old woman was now being joined by others trying to see past the man standing in the opening. Surely no one would let them do . . . anything?

Now Miranda realized that the two younger men were wearing the dark blue and purple uniforms of the Governor's Public Guard. Dear heaven, was she to be arrested? *Jailed?* Because of a crazy old woman?

The other man, the calm one who had felt the bed, wasn't a uniformed guard. A distinguished-looking man of perhaps fifty, he seemed to be in charge despite his civilian dress. Miranda blinked away tears of pain and looked at him. "Please, can't the guard let go of my arms?" she begged.

"You say your cat is just hiding?" The man gazed at her a moment, nodded slightly, and went down on one knee to look under the bed. "So it is," he agreed, standing.

"Do we take her?" asked the guard in the doorway.

"Yes, yes!" insisted the old woman. "I've told you what she is! Every other full moon . . . she said so herself."

"Did you?" the finely dressed man asked Miranda.

"It was only a joke," she said weakly. The pain in her wrists was making her sick.

"And why would you joke about treason?"

"I've no patience with sillies who believe in magic," Miranda said. "Please, the guard's hurting me. I swear to you, it's all a lot of nonsense."

The civilian nodded. "Let her go." To the guard in the doorway he added, "Shut that door. We'll test her here."

Miranda rubbed her aching wrists, watching the second guard pull the door firmly shut. Both were now inside. Someone pounded on the door—the old hag, wanting to be let in to watch this test they planned, no doubt—but the older man shook his head and the guard stood against the door with his hands clasped behind him.

Reaching into a pocket of his stylish tunic, the stranger pulled out a pale red crystal threaded on a gold chain. "Look at this," he said to Miranda as he sat down on the edge of the bed and raised the crystal to her eye level.

"Why?"

"Do you want to prove your innocence?"

Miranda cradled her aching arms against her belly. How casual the man sounded! He might have been asking her to pass the salt, or whether she preferred to cross the street here or a little farther on.

"Well?" he prompted.

Miranda nodded.

"Then do as I say."

She looked at the crystal. The man rolled the chain between his fingers and thumb to make the clear red stone glitter in the light of the wall lamp over the bed. "Look quite steadily," he instructed her in that same calm voice. "Breathe evenly, and listen to me."

Miranda stared at the crystal, trying to breathe evenly. Pain lingered in her arms. *Treason,* the old woman had said. Wasn't the penalty for treason death? What if she failed this test by crystal?

Fear coursed through her. *Who'll look after my boys?* she asked herself, trying to swallow her panic. After a moment or two she began to sob. She shut her eyes and buried her face in her hands. The guard standing beside her grabbed at her arm.

"Not needed," the man with the crystal said. The guard let go as if burned.

"What is your name?" the man asked now. He sounded deliberately gentle.

"Miranda Glivven," she gasped.

"Mmm!" he said, as if he recognized her name. But that was impossible: she was only a lightkeeper's wife.

"Miranda Glivven, stop crying," the man said, still calm, still gentle. "You are in no danger. Look at the crystal and listen to me. You are breathing very softly, aren't you? Breathing softly and surely and looking at the crystal, which now seems to grow in your vision . . ."

And it did seem to grow, to brighten. She wanted to look away but somehow could not. "Miranda Glivven, you are listening to my voice," the man droned. "And you feel just a little sleepy, don't you? It's late, you've had a long train ride, and you just feel that you must sleep . . ."

She woke with a snap. When she opened her eyes, the man was just tucking the crystal into his pocket. "She's innocent, as you heard," he said to the guards. "I thought as much."

While she had slept that strange, brief sleep, the guard had clasped her shoulder so tightly Miranda thought his fingers might have left bruises. The man in charge nodded to him to let go of her and cocked his head on one side.

"Well, Mrs. Glivven," he said. "What brings you to Clunn?"

Miranda swallowed and rubbed her still-painful arms. "I'm just going to stay overnight." She wasn't used to sounding quite that timid.

"To—?"

"I came on the train from Gwynn-on-the-Main, and I'm"—she hesitated a split second, realizing that she should try to be politic—"I was planning to take the train to Bierdsey in the morning."

"What business have you in Bierdsey?"

"My husband . . ." She drew a deep breath. "My husband's the lightkeeper at Gwynnhead. Last summer he went to Bierdsey, and he hasn't come home, and his letters have stopped coming—I haven't had one since the first of October—"

"Ah." The man nodded. "So you're going to look for him?"

Miranda cleared her throat. "I know it sounds silly, but what else can I do? We need him at home."

"Who's tending the light?"

"I did, until today. And now it's my eldest son, Hathden. He's only seventeen, but he's quite mature, really. The beacon will be lit every night, I can promise you that."

"Bierdsey's a long way from Gwynnhead," the man observed. He curled long, well-kept fingers around his sharp chin and stroked his cheek with his thumb.

Now that the pain in her arms was fading, Miranda could look at him with a clear head. He was a man of high position, that much was obvious. She'd seen that his clothing was fine, but hadn't realized how fine: she was looking at real wealth, real power. The leather of his short boots was the color of butter and looked almost as soft. No dirt marked even the toes, despite the rain that still ticked against the windowpane behind his head. His brown wool trousers were cut in the latest style. The brown tunic over them emphasized his wide shoulders, yet skimmed over his thickening waistline as no garment could unless made to his exact measure. The darker brown embroidery of the deep yoke was expertly done, and shone like silk; the matching purse at his waist was slung from a chain that was surely real gold. His dark blond hair was pulled back from his face in a golden clip, showing wings of gray at the temples, and the cloak flung carelessly onto the end of her bed was lined in a glossy fur. Who could he be?

Now his hazel eyes narrowed. "Why did your husband think it necessary to go to Bierdsey, do you suppose?" he asked.

"I don't know, sir. A letter came from His Grace the Governor last summer, giving Lexi a job—he's done other small jobs for the Governor, but I don't know what they are. State secrets, all of them." She took a shaky breath. "I know it's not my business what the Governor wanted of him, and I don't really care if I never know, but I want to find . . . I even wrote to His Grace a few weeks ago, but he didn't . . ."

"Shh," the elegant stranger said. "Don't upset yourself. Lexi would be Alexi Glivven?" She nodded. The man appeared to mull over this information. Miranda folded her hands in her lap and sat looking at them. What had she stumbled into? Something even worse than staying home, waiting and waiting?

"Why is the cat with you?" the stranger asked suddenly.

She told him how the cat had run ahead of Andreu's wagon onto the causeway, how they'd decided to take it with them so it wouldn't get lost and she wouldn't miss her train, how it had escaped her in the station and reappeared on the train after they had already started to move.

"I suppose you've had it since it was a tiny kitten and have come to feel some affection for it," the man remarked.

"Actually, no," Miranda replied, and instantly cursed herself for her truthfulness. "That is, it—" He lifted an eyebrow.

Well, she'd started, she might as well finish. "It was a stray," she said. "It moved in with us and we, we've come to be used to it." No need to say how recently the cat had moved in. "And once it was on the train . . ."

"Yes, of course." The man turned to the guards. "Go back to your duties, men. I'll finish up this business and make a final report myself." As the two left, the old woman, still vigilant in the corridor, began to protest. The guards bundled her out of the way. The stranger watched the door shut behind them with his mouth bunched in thought.

Miranda waited. After a moment his gaze turned toward her. "Tell me, Miranda Glivven, what do you think of these charges against you?" he asked.

"Charges? I don't even know what they are!"

The stranger smiled broadly. He looked much less forbidding with an amused glint in his eyes. "The old lady thinks you're a practicing magician. Since that's treason, she reported her suspicions to us."

"Treason!" Miranda laughed in disbelief. "The whole idea is absurd." She touched her arms and winced. Bruises, for sure, and her shoulder still ached. All that pain, over some old hag's delusions? "There's no such thing as magic," she added, more heatedly than she'd intended. "It's just a stupid ruse somebody thought up to get other people to do what he wanted, out of fear or their own guilty consciences or—or whatever he could make use of. Anyone with half a brain can see that!" She found herself gesturing and folded her arms. "Why would some old woman accuse a perfect stranger of magic?"

The man flipped a hand toward the floor. "The cat has extra toes."

The cat, Miranda noticed, had crept out from under the bed and was contemplating the stranger. "Lots of cats have extra toes. Some have six! Eight! So what if the cat has extra toes?"

"Superstitious people *will* believe a five-toed cat must be under a magic spell," the man told her. He sounded very patient. Maybe she wasn't the first the old woman had pointed at. "Especially if the forepaws have no dewclaws. Magical practice is strictly against the law," he went on, "and has been for two hundred years. We have made a point of teaching the people exactly that, so loyal subjects report even a suspicion of treason. Usually there's nothing to it, but sometimes we do find people who don't care about the law. I'm sorry we frightened you."

Miranda laid her hand on her aching shoulder. "Hurt me, as well."

"For that, I also apologize."

"It's a bit late for regrets," Miranda said, pushing up one sleeve. Half of her forearm was reddened. Shadows of bruises already showed. "Look at that!"

"Yes, I see." He sighed. "The guards *were* a little too rough. Fear of what you might do, I suppose. A reprimand will be issued."

Of course! They thought I might put a spell on them! Now they'd be in trouble just for doing their jobs. Miranda put her face into her hands and rubbed at her eyes.

"Try to remember that the law was made because the belief of the common people in magic is often a serious detriment to the smooth functioning of the government." The stranger sighed. "Since we can't seem to shake their belief, the best we can do is forbid the *use* of magic. I'll give you a letter of conduct, so this won't happen again." Still sitting on the bed, he reached into his cloak for a leather folder, from which he extracted a piece of paper and a fountain pen. He leaned across the bed to use the wide windowsill as a desk to write a brief note.

Finished, he pulled the curtain aside and looked through the window for a moment before turning to hold the paper out to her.

Miranda took it and glanced at it: *Be it known that Miranda Glivven has been tested for magical practice and found innocent of that despicable crime. The yellow cat she owns I have personally found to be an ordinary animal.* The crest was the eagle and orb of the government; the signature, *Landers Bikthen,* one she knew well: she saw it every month on the bank orders that paid for the beacon and its keeper and family. She scrambled to her feet to make a deep bow. "I thank you, sir," she said, feeling a little breathless. "I'm sorry not to have bowed to you earlier, but I didn't know who you were."

"Why would you?" the provincial prefect asked. "I'm quite sure we've never met. Please sit down, Mrs. Glivven. There's no need for ceremony between us. What we do need, most urgently, is to talk over this little project of yours. I presume you still intend to go to Bierdsey?"

"Where else would I go?"

"Home."

That had not occurred to her. "No." Miranda shook her head to convince herself. "No. Now that I've started, I'm going all the way to Bierdsey."

"Excellent."

2

The golden cat jumped onto the bed and regarded the prefect with a cool silver gaze. Miranda still held the man's note, which she now flattened on her lap and read again. "You didn't test the cat, sir," she pointed out.

"I'm not worried about the cat!" Bikthen grinned and reached out to scratch lightly under the animal's chin. "Think, Mrs. Glivven! If magic doesn't exist, the beast can scarcely be enchanted, can it?"

"Of course not," Miranda agreed, a little confused. "But I thought—"

Bikthen leaned his elbows on his thighs and clasped his hands between his knees to stare at her with as much intensity as she'd ever seen from a cat. "I have duties which must be carried out in prescribed ways, Mrs. Glivven," he said. "One of them is to investigate all claims of magical practice. Note that I say magical practice and not the practice of magic. What matters to the Governor is what the accused *believes* himself or herself to be doing."

"And you don't believe magic works any more than I do, do you?" Miranda found the courage to ask.

The prefect chuckled. "Please, Mrs. Glivven. I am a rational man. I go by the evidence of my senses and experience, just as you do yourself."

"But I don't understand. The crystal—wasn't that some kind of . . . magical practice?"

"No. Not at all."

"What was it?"

"Simple hypnosis."

Miranda nodded slowly. She'd heard of hypnosis, but had never encountered it before.

"I put you into a hypnotic trance, told you that you must be perfectly truthful with me, and asked whether you had ever performed any magical spells or knew of anyone who had," Bikthen explained. Miranda eyed him doubtfully.

"You denied the allegations with great force. One of the guards almost fainted when you questioned the sanity and intelligence of a provincial prefect in such terms. The other one"—he smiled again, charmingly—"the other one was envious of your freedom to speak so openly, I think."

"I beg your pardon for whatever I said, sir."

"None is given because none is needed. Now. Tell me why you are going to Bierdsey just now to look for your husband. Was there some particular event that made you decide?"

"No, not really." Miranda sighed. She doubted whether this powerful man, clothed as richly as he was, could have the slightest idea what life was like for people like the lightkeeper's family. "It just built up, and then a good friend suggested that I ought to go . . . because he's been gone such a long time, and the waiting is just *awful* . . ."

"Yes." His voice was soft, rather sad. Maybe he did understand.

Someone knocked at the door, far more gently than the Guard had. Bikthen got up and opened it. The landlord stretched his neck to look into the room, caught Miranda's eye with a frown, and turned to the prefect. "Sir, there's a crowd downstairs," he said. "Come to see whether the charges of magic are true." Alarmed, Miranda stood up.

"Yes, I saw them gathering outside a few minutes ago," the prefect said. "Tell them on my authority that the woman is innocent. If they won't go away, then call the Guard. The two men who were here before witnessed the test."

"Sir, they're angry."

"As they should be," Bikthen said smoothly. "Go tell them what I just said."

He shut the door and returned to sit on the bed, motioning to Miranda to sit down again.

"Mrs. Glivven, I must be open with you," the prefect said. "We've been looking for your husband, too." He caressed the cat's sleek fur with a somber expression. "It seems most likely that someone has captured him and is holding him prisoner for some purpose. What that might be, I couldn't begin to say."

Miranda twisted her wedding ring around her finger. "Why hasn't anyone said anything to me? I'm his wife!"

"When did you write to the Governor?"

She stopped to think. "About three weeks ago. Maybe not quite that long."

"The letter may not have reached his desk," Bikthen told her. "Messages from the public pass through layer upon layer of subordinates. Then, too, he might delay a response in hope of having some kind of news to give you."

In despair, Miranda pressed her hands to her mouth. If the Governor's men had been searching for Alexi and not found him, what hope did she have?

"It's a good thing old lady Mirk went to the Guard about you." Miranda clasped her hands over her aching wrists. "You see, Miranda—may I call you Miranda?—I think you may be able to accomplish what the Governor and the Guard could not."

She glanced at him, surprised.

"Your dress is unsophisticated, for one thing," Bikthen said. "That's a nice enough tunic and the trousers are quite fine, but the cut is a bit old-fashioned and many-colored embroidery went out of style in Bierdsey years ago. And you have a look about you that's . . . what shall I say? Somewhat naive?"

Miranda blinked at him.

"Inexperienced, perhaps. Fresh-faced, although not young. I fear people may try to take advantage of you because of it, vendors and innkeepers and such, so you must be on the lookout for that. But people may also be more helpful to a middle-aged woman from the North Coast looking for a strayed husband—"

She shook her head violently.

"You must realize that's the explanation most city dwellers will think of first."

"Leave *me,* yes, that's remotely possible," Miranda allowed. "But Alexi would never leave the lighthouse."

"No, I agree. That's just not in the Alexi Glivven I know." *He knows him?* Miranda thought, startled.

"I'm very concerned about his disappearance," Bikthen continued. "I only wish it had taken place in my own province so that I would be free to help you investigate." Frowning, the prefect pressed his lips together for a moment. "Still," he went on, "I was about to say that people might be more helpful to you—a woman wronged, but loyal— than to a Public Guard sent to ask questions."

"I see," Miranda remarked. She thought she did: the prefect planned to make some kind of use of her himself—like the monkey that got the cat to pull chestnuts out of the fire in the old story. But she didn't care if her paws got burned. Not if it would help to find Alexi.

"Try not to be so guileless, Miranda." Bikthen's hand rested on the cat's back. "For instance, you could have told me you'd had your pet from when it was a kitten, and not given me the slightest suspicion that you might wonder if it *is* a magicked cat."

"Yes," she said. "I did think of that, sir. Too late."

"Call me Landers; that's my name. If I were you, I'd try to keep the beast out of sight."

She nodded. Even if he did know her husband, she couldn't bring herself to call a provincial prefect—a stranger—by his first name. "What should I do when I get to Bierdsey?"

"I won't tell you that. I want you to act naturally, and you might not if I give you suggestions. So do whatever you've planned to do." He stopped to stroke the cat. He was obviously a man who liked animals. "If you find your husband," he said, "or find a way to get to him, either telegraph me immediately or go to Jon Welkin, the senior assistant to the provincial prefect there. You can reach him through the Province House. The Bierdsey prefect himself, Morten Shells, is a rather self-important man, so don't go straight to him. Still, I'd better tell him you'll be in his district—he might prove useful, though he probably won't want to be bothered." He and the cat seemed to have established a rapport, which Bikthen seemed reluctant to break. "No, Welkin's your best bet in an emergency," he said in a musing tone.

"Thank you." *For not very much*, Miranda thought.

"If you get into any serious trouble, do go to Welkin for help. But I think you may have more success if you show no one that you have any connections to the government, so stay away from the prefect's office altogether unless the need is urgent. How much money do you have?"

"I've a little cash and a letter of credit for seven hundred lukers."

"That's not as much as you think." The prefect stood up and pulled his purse from the chain at his waist. "You'll need more," he said, opening the purse and peering into it. "Here's what I've got with me. Consider it salary for doing a job the government ought to do on its own." He folded a number of banknotes in half and handed them to her.

"Sir, I—"

"Landers." The corners of Bikthen's eyes took on a slight crinkle, as if he were pleased with himself. "Alexi Glivven is a very lucky man," he said. "A safe journey to you, Miranda. Courage." With a small smile and a nod, the prefect went into the hall and closed the door silently behind him.

"Well!" Miranda sat down suddenly with the folded banknotes still in her hand. The cat roused itself from the bed to climb into her lap. She let her hand run along its sleek back.

"Conceal you, he says." *As if that were easy!* "A sensible woman would abandon you."

The yellow cat responded with a small distressed mew, as if it had understood her words. She thought of the cat standing in the snow-spangled wind on the steps of the library, the night's worth of footprints on her snowy step the following morning, the tentative touch of the cat's paw on her thigh when it had found her on the train that afternoon.

"No," she said.

The cat purred faintly and folded its legs under itself, still looking into her face.

Miranda sighed. "No. I'll surely need a friend, even if it is only a cat."

Besides, getting rid of the beast might be seen as the act of a guilty woman. Who knew what that old hag might stir up then? Even a friendly prefect couldn't control everything that happened in his province. And she would have to come back to Clunn, if only for one night, in order to get back home.

3

Next morning Miranda started early, with breakfast in the inn's dining room. She returned the borrowed saucer and took a dish of scrambled eggs and a small cup of milk up to the room for the cat, packing up the few things she had taken out of her suitcase while it ate.

The rain had stopped during the night, leaving a cold gray day. Following the desk clerk's directions, she located a shop near the station that sold luggage. There she found a brown leather case meant to carry a pet, one that opened at the top and was pierced with small holes for air and a tiny screen to look through—horribly expensive. But when she'd gotten over the shock of having had the Prefect of Clunn Province sitting on her bed, she had counted the money in her hand and been shocked again: Bikthen had given her over three hundred lukers. Miranda bought the carrier. Once she had the animal where she was sure it could not be lost—and where its abnormal feet could not be seen at a casual glance—she felt very much relieved.

As was the landlord. "I won't pretend I'm unhappy to see you leave, Mrs. Glivven," he said, as she carried her two cases to the door. "That was a most annoying incident last night."

"You can scarcely blame me for it," Miranda replied.

The man looked uncomfortable. "Well, no. But to have the Guard at the door of my inn the whole night long? It's never happened before. We're a reputable establishment."

"I'm sure you are, and I do hope it never happens again," Miranda said, smiling: there was the night's stay on the way home to think of.

The landlord had a good point. Stepping through the door of the inn, Miranda had half-expected to be confronted by the old woman and a bunch of frenzied good citizens, but the street was almost deserted both times she ventured out, and when she crossed the street to the train station only a few people stood on the platform, none showing the slightest interest in her. Then, as she turned away from the ticket window, she found herself faced by a uniformed provincial guard. Her heart jumped.

"Miranda Glivven?" he asked.

"I am she."

"Message for you," the guard said, and handed her a long, ivory-colored envelope. While she waited for the train, the cat carrier tucked between her feet, she read the brief letter from Bikthen: he had sent Welkin an official notice to tell him that she would be searching for Alexi in Bierdsey and might come to him for assistance. Bikthen had also checked the official reports: as of yesterday evening, the search for her husband had uncovered nothing. It was thought that he had left Bierdsey around the middle of September. No further trace of him had been found. Bikthen wished her better luck, hoping that "her loving heart might uncover" what the Governor's inquiry agents could not.

Miranda put the letter back into the envelope and folded the envelope into her purse. Bikthen's meaning could not be clearer. She was very much on her own.

BIERDSEY

1

The train ride to Bierdsey was quite a bit longer than the one from Gwynn-on-the-Main to Clunn. Two hours past sundown, Miranda stepped onto the platform with the feeling of having launched herself upon an unfamiliar sea in the least reliable of boats. She soon found a room in the Railway Inn: even smaller than the room at Clunn—and far more expensive—but adequate for one woman and one semi-clandestine cat, with the advantage of being located in the heart of the town. Settled in, she went out again and bought two meat pies from a street vendor—one for herself and one for her companion—and a newspaper, partly for the news and partly for the use of the cat.

Where to begin?

While she and the cat ate their suppers, Miranda spread out the newspaper to look for a list of inns. None was supplied, but an inside page reported something that made her heart sink: the local prefect, Morten Shells, had left that morning for a visit to a western province, taking his senior assistant with him. Something about trade negotiations, during which Shells hoped to extend the influence of the Province of Bierdsey with respect to agricultural something or others. Miranda didn't read the whole story. The important information was that Jon Welkin was out of town. She was even more on her own than Bikthen had thought he had left her.

The cat used the newspaper as intended. Miranda carried the result down the hall to the sanitary facilities before going to bed. When she returned, the cat was curled up beside her pillow. It yawned widely and looked at her as she entered the room.

I should give it a name, she thought again, and again the only name that came to mind was her husband's.

Shuddering as she had on the train from Gwynn-on-the-Main, Miranda washed her face and hands and changed into a nightdress. Within five minutes the room was dark and she was lying in a cold bed, slowly growing warmer under a fat down comforter. She stared at the dark ceiling, twisting the ivy-chased gold ring on the middle finger of her left hand, the ring that almost matched the one she had given Alexi. Ivy, the ancient symbol of faithful love. The designs of the rings had been their own: the one on her finger Alexi's; the one he wore, drawn carefully by herself and given to the goldsmith with love and hope. How long ago that was. And yet, how short a time!

The next morning Miranda considered asking her landlord for a list of inns, but decided that might leave an unfortunate impression. Instead, after scribbling a quick note to Hathden to tell him where she was staying and dropping it into the mail, she went back to the train station to see whether a list of hostelries might be posted there. None was. The ticket seller suggested she try the City House. So, after a breakfast of pickled eggs from the stall just inside the station entrance—the cat had some meat pie left from last night—she followed the man's directions and, after half an hour of walking, found herself lost.

Wouldn't you know! Miranda looked about for a Public Guard, or even just a friendly face, and saw none. She

retraced her steps, walking slowly to be sure of her way,
her cloak snugged tight against the cold wind that had
sprung up overnight. A fur lining like the one Bikthen
enjoyed would be most welcome. Obstructed by the stone
buildings, gusts seemed to come from every quarter. At
each corner she found the wind again in her face, making
her eyes water. *At least it blurs the sight of filth*, she
thought, disgusted by the scraps of paper blown against
her boots and the smashed rims of meat pies ground into
the paving wherever a vendor had paused his barrow. In
Gwynnhead, no one would dream of dropping trash just
wherever he happened to be—but then, in Gwynnhead,
Miranda reflected, no one would hesitate to scold anyone
who did.

She had almost reached the Railway Inn before she spotted a man in purple and blue and asked for new directions,
only to discover that she had missed one turn and had
passed a block from the City House. Thanking the guard,
she turned back, glad to move briskly.

To Miranda, Bierdsey seemed grim and spiritless. The
idea surprised her: Alexi's letters, with their little word-
pictures, had given her the impression that this was a town
filled with vitality. Maybe each of them had endowed the
town with something of their own states of mind, or maybe
it was just that the gray sky over the dirty gray stone
buildings gave no contrast to the eye. Or, if the lines
of trees down the centers of the wider streets were leafy
instead of bare-branched, if the circles of dusty ivy around
their bases were outlined in flowers as Alexi had described,
if the people were less pinched with cold and in less of a
hurry to get out of the wind, then maybe the town would
attract her more . . .

The City House, when she caught sight of it, was a great
contrast. The building was white stone, very ornate and
formal. Miranda thought it a little intimidating. Perhaps
it was meant to be. She took a breath for courage before
climbing the broad steps. Inside the tall bronze doors a
large entrance hall led to a high rotunda, bright with daylight streaming through windows under the dome. To her

annoyance, not one sign offered to tell her where to find anyone or anything. Even Gwynnhead was better marked than this! Miranda stood just inside the entrance, deflated, wondering what to do next.

"Something you need, mistress?" asked a light voice. Miranda turned and saw a dark-haired young woman looking out of an office door at one side of the entrance hall.

"Yes," she said. "I—ah—I wondered if someone here might be able to give me a list of the inns in Bierdsey?"

"A list?" The girl frowned. "I don't know about a list. But the Railway Inn's quite good. You might try that. Or the Sun. They've a good quality clientele."

"No, no. I'm not looking for a place to stay." Miranda moved closer. "I'm trying to find someone who was here last summer. I don't know where he was staying, so I thought if I went round to all the inns and asked—" She broke off with a shrug and a timid smile.

"You'll have a long day," the woman said. "Or several. I can think of a dozen inns just here in town."

"Oh, if you could tell me their names?" Miranda said in a rush. She felt in the pocket of her cloak for a pen but had no paper.

"Who are you looking for?" the young woman asked.

"My husband."

She got an incredulous stare. "And you don't even know where he was staying?"

"No, he wasn't supposed to—that is, the job he—I'm just going by the postmarks on the envelopes of his letters, you see? But he stopped writing without a word of warning, and that's just not like him. We've been married eighteen years, and he never—" Feeling like the idiot the girl obviously thought her to be, Miranda stopped. The young woman's face had turned somber.

"Have you asked at the hospital?"

"No," Miranda confessed.

"Or checked with the Guard?"

Miranda felt the courage drain out of her, as if a plug had been pulled somewhere just below her navel. "No." She scarcely recognized her own voice.

"Here," her questioner said. "I'll write out a list of the inns I know about." She went into the room and sat down at a table. "But I really do think you should check with the hospital and the Guard," she continued, taking a sheet of paper from a pile on the table and beginning to write.

But the Guard would have checked the hospital, Miranda thought, with relief. And Landers Bikthen would have known if they'd found Alexi there.

"You might save yourself a lot of time and walking," the young woman said, holding out her list.

Suppose they just didn't know who he was? Miranda took the list and managed to thank the girl. The paper trembled so violently in her hands that she couldn't read it, so she folded it and put it into her cloak.

"I'm sorry," the woman said softly. "But I really do think—"

"That's all right." Miranda cleared her throat. "It's a good idea. Where is the office for the Guard?"

"Headquarters, it's called. Straight back through the rotunda. You'll see the sign."

"Thanks." Miranda turned from the doorway and looked across the rotunda. A short hallway led to a door with something written on it in small black letters. As she neared, the words "Municipal Guard, Bierdsey" became clear. Miranda pushed at the door. It yielded, and she went in.

Two men in uniform looked up from their desks. To the one who asked, she stated her business. Twenty minutes later, she walked back across the rotunda, not certain whether to be relieved or not: no unidentified man with golden hair and silver-gray eyes had been found either dead or injured in Bierdsey late that summer, or since.

"I'm sorry," the senior officer had said, when she asked. "But a grown man can travel as he pleases, missus, and just because he doesn't tell his wife where he's gone is no reason to have the Guard out looking for him."

"But I'm sure he's—"

The man had smiled, a smile she had wanted to shove behind his teeth. "Now, missus, all wives feel that way, don't they? But that doesn't keep their men from chasing after a new bit of fun, now, does it?"

Miranda had flashed him her darkest glance, which had made him laugh, and slammed the door behind her. As she passed through the entrance, she looked for the helpful young woman to tell her that at least her husband hadn't been killed or injured in Bierdsey, but the room the girl had been working in was empty.

2

The list was short enough, but the inns were very far apart. A woman less patient than Miranda might have begun to feel that the population of Bierdsey was determined to hide the fate of her husband from her. But just as her imagination had failed to acknowledge the possibility of his death—or to bring that notion out where she would be forced to look at it—it also failed to provide any but a surface acceptance of each word as it was spoken. No one remembered Alexi Glivven, or any other North Coaster, from two months before. Miranda headed back toward the Railway Inn at dusk, chilled to the bone, a blister rubbed up on her left heel from all the walking, and with only three inns investigated.

She was also hungry. After the third fruitless interview, she bought two cold pork turnovers from a street vendor and ate one as she walked back to the inn. The other turnover she fed to the cat. At least she had one more task for that evening: she disposed of the newspaper she'd left on the floor, went down to the street to buy another, and returned to the room.

Now what?

The inns tomorrow, of course. If only she could shorten the task somehow!

She got out Alexi's letters to read again but found nothing to tell her what might have become of him. The best she could think to do was to finish up the list the young woman had provided. If nothing resulted from that, then she would search out the places Alexi had sketched with such vivid words, and wait at one of them hoping for *something*. . . .

Perhaps she should do that first? Or maybe the landlord could help her? Miranda gathered the letters, shut the cat into the room, and went downstairs only to find the man's wife in his place helping someone to register for a room. *Better yet*, she thought. The woman looked kindly enough, plump and grandmotherly, and her voice remained pleasant although the man registering had a thousand complaints and demands.

"Mistress?" Miranda said, when the guest had been sent upstairs, key in hand. "I'd be glad of your help, if you can give it."

"Certainly, lamb." The woman clasped her dimpled hands on the desk with an amiable smile. "What's the trouble?"

Miranda produced the letters and explained her search.

"Oh, poor dear!" the woman said. "Come sit down with a cup of tea, and we'll see what we can do. Lavran?" she hollered. "That's my husband," she explained in a loud whisper behind one hand. "Lavran!"

The landlord came out of the ale room, his eyebrows high with inquiry. His wife explained Miranda's problem.

"Let's go into the office, then," the man said. "It's a bit more private, and we can leave the door open in case someone wants us."

"Bring us a pot of tea from the kitchen, dear, there's a love," the wife said. She beckoned to Miranda. "Nothing like tea for comfort, now, is there, lamb?"

Miranda managed a smile. *I should write to Evelyn*, she thought, recalling her neighbor's warm kitchen.

The office was a tiny room reached through the door behind the registration desk. Another door, with a drapery to one side, seemed to lead into private quarters. When the landlord came in with the pot of tea and three mugs on a tray, he quietly closed the curtain. His wife busily questioned Miranda about her search while setting two more chairs to join the one at a square oak table. Another chair, two low cupboards, and a shelf full of ledgers were all the furnishings in the room, but to Miranda it looked like a home.

They spread the letters out on the table and drew up the chairs. The landlord poured out the tea while his wife picked up a page at random and began to read.

"Here, now," she said, sounding pleased. "He's been to the market. This would be Dames' Alley—such a way with words your husband has, lamb! I can see the clock on that corner just as plain as I can with my own two eyes!" A small glow of pride in Alexi offset Miranda's discomfort at sharing something as intimate as the paper he had touched, the words he had meant for her.

The landlord's wife dropped the letter onto the table and picked up another, which she read all the way through. Miranda saw which letter it was and felt herself redden as the older woman smiled. *Why didn't I leave that one upstairs?* she thought, and then was glad it was the wife, and not the landlord himself, who'd read it. The woman folded the pages and passed the letter quietly to Miranda while reaching for a third. "Ah," she exclaimed, after a moment. "Here, now. He doesn't say, lamb, but he stayed at the Blue Swan."

Blue Swan? Not one of the inns on her list.

"Wouldn't you say so, Lavran?" the landlord's wife asked. "Look, where he describes the door."

The landlord frowned at the passage his wife pointed out and nodded. "Yes, that's the Swan, all right," he agreed.

"So you could ask after him there, lamb," the wife said. "Mind you, two months is a long time in an innkeeper's life." The landlord nodded. "They might not remember him, even if he did stay, especially if it was only a night or two before moving on." Sucking in her mouth, she read more, with quick darting brown eyes that made Miranda think of a small voracious animal.

"I might go down to the Blue Swan yet this evening," she said. "If you can give me directions."

"Oh, no. No, no." The landlord flashed a concerned glance at her. "Not you, missus. That is, I don't wish to appear to run down a competitor, but the Bruised Goo—I mean, the

Swan—is down near the river. That neighborhood's no place for a lady like you to walk in the evening."

"Still—"

"No, I can*not* recommend it." His eyes flicked sideways as his wife picked up another page. "What did your husband look like?"

"He's a little taller than you, and thinner." *A lot thinner.* "Forty years old, with bright butter-gold hair and gray eyes."

"Ah. A North Coaster like yourself."

Miranda nodded.

"Can't say I've seen 'im here—and we've a *good* dining hall, best in the city if I say so myself." He raised his eyebrows at her as if to ask why she hadn't yet tried the inn's food. "But I can't say I haven't seen 'im, either. Two months is a long time, as the wife said."

"Yes," Miranda agreed. "A very long time."

She stayed long enough to be polite, drinking the landlord's tea and chatting with his wife, and then excused herself and went up to her room.

"News, cat." At the sound of her voice, the yellow cat lifted its head from its paws and looked at her.

"I've found out where he was staying. Oh, *bless* Lexi for wanting to share with me!"

Miranda checked the cat's newspaper, found it unused, and sat stroking the faintly purring animal for a minute or two before taking her cloak from the hook behind the door. If the Blue Swan was well-enough known that an innkeeper's wife could recognize it from just the description of the front door carvings, then surely almost anyone could give her directions!

3

The door of the Blue Swan was exactly as Alexi had described it, down to the chips in the paint and the rain-curdled dirt on the window. Miranda pushed it open.

A sharp odor of beer and sweat had drifted into the entrance from the rowdy ale room to the left. To the right was a darkened dining room with chairs upended on tables and a mop standing in a bucket in the doorway. Straight ahead, a tall desk commanded a view of the entrance. Somebody sat there—arms folded on the desktop and his head on his arms—snoring. Miranda crossed the tiled floor and woke the somebody up. He didn't look any older than Hathden.

"Room?" he said dubiously, peering around her as if expecting someone else.

"No. I'm looking for somebody who stayed here late last summer," Miranda said.

"Last summer!" The boy yawned. "And you've only got around to looking now?"

"My husband was staying here in September," she explained. "He's disappeared, and I'm looking for him."

This brought a stare she didn't quite understand. "You'll have to talk to the landlord," the boy said. "He's in the ale room." He put his head back down on his arms. Miranda resisted the impulse to give his dark curls a sympathetic touch and turned to her left.

She had been in ale rooms a few times before—always with Alexi. Never one nearly this noisy. She stood just inside the doorway, wondering how to tell which of the crowd of men was the landlord. After a moment, the man beside the ale kegs glanced at her and his eyebrows twitched in surprise. *Yes, of course,* Miranda thought. *If he's tending the kegs, he'll know.*

"I'm looking for the landlord," she said to the man, after she'd managed to cross the crowded room, avoiding one man's grasp and the legs of a very drunk woman sitting on somebody's lap.

"That's me."

"I'm looking for my husband, Alexi Glivven."

She could see the man chuckle. The room was too loud to hear him, and now somebody started singing in a nasal off-key voice, something bawdy enough to make Miranda blush.

"Look all you like, missus," the landlord bawled at her, with a wave to include all the men in the room.

"He's not here now," she explained, leaning over him to make herself heard. "He stayed here last summer. A North Coaster, like me, bright blond hair and gray eyes, pretty tall?"

"Summer was a long time ago." The landlord gave her a look that made her feel half-undressed. "But I do recall somebody like that." His voice had a sardonic undertone Miranda could see no reason for. "Come back in the morning and I'll have him looked up." He smiled—nastily. "What name?"

"Glivven. Alexi Glivven," Miranda told him. "Can't you check now?"

The man guffawed. "Look around you, woman! Can't you see I'm busy? What's a few hours more or less without the man? Go on home and come back in the morning." He looked past her to a waiter with a tray of empty beer mugs.

"Oh, please," Miranda begged. "I've come so far—"

The man's face hardened. "Look, you want help finding out where he's shacked up? Don't bother me when I've got better things to do. Tomorrow, I said."

"But—"

He stood tall to look over her head. "Jambo," he called. "Come throw this woman out."

Miranda went quietly, preferring that to being wrestled to the door. The crowd parted for Jambo. Having the huge man two steps ahead didn't prevent a few hands snatching her cloak aside, and worse. Outside, she sighed with relief. No wonder the place had been nicknamed the Bruised Goose!

A few lamps on posts cast pools of light like beacons on a treacherous shore. Even so, fewer people walked the streets than she had seen when going the opposite way just a little while ago. Wisps of fog rolled out of the alleys that led to the river. A rancid odor she hadn't noticed in her earlier excitement permeated the air. Miranda clutched at her cloak. A longing for the clean salty scent of Gwynnhead brought a prickle of tears to her eyes.

The Blue Swan. Try as she might, Miranda could not imagine her sedate Alexi spending an evening in a room like the one she had just left. *What about those mysterious jobs?* an imp of suspicion whispered to her. What if Alexi had another side, one she had never seen, that needed to be exercised at times? Some "secret mission" would be a convenient fiction, wouldn't it?

No. Official envelopes *had* come. Landers Bikthen *had* seemed to know all about the jobs. So they must have been real.

So? asked the imp.

Why hadn't she waited until morning, as the landlord of the Railway Inn had urged?

The doors of the darkened shops were deep with shadow. As she passed, Miranda thought she heard a chink of unseen metal from one of them. Years of living in Gwynnhead had softened her sparse memories of cities, but now they all returned at once, hard-edged and glaring. Her stomach recalled the realities of crime, the reasons for patrolling guards. Frightened, she scuttled toward the inn where the cat would be sleeping curled on the bed. Oh, to climb into that bed, with its one warm spot where the cat had lain, even without Alexi!

"Hey, not so fast!" The male voice sounded warm and pleased with itself. Miranda glanced over her shoulder but kept going.

"A luker for you, sweet," the man continued, coming after her. "I've got a good place. Warmer than a doorway."

She quickened her pace, saying nothing.

"Come on, come on, you haven't even had a good look at me."

Running, Miranda gained the high street. Still no one else about. Footsteps followed after her.

"You don't want to sell it, I can always take it," the man shouted. She tried for more speed, her left heel burning where the blister had torn. *Shouldn't have come, shouldn't have come*, beat her feet on the cobbles. The man behind her lost interest, or decided to look for easier game—his steps slowed and faded—but Miranda kept running and almost cried out when a new voice called, "Hi! Missus! Where so fast?"

But this was a man in a purple and dark blue uniform. She ran up to him, gabbling about the one who had propositioned her.

"Nobody there now," said the guard. He walked her to one of the lamps and took a good look at her face. "What are you doing out by yourself so late, then, missus? Shouldn't you be at home, tending your fire?"

Defeated, still panting after her run, Miranda shook her hanging head. "Oh, if only I could!" she groaned. "But no, I've just got to get back to the inn."

"Where's that?"

"The Railway Inn."

"I'll walk with you," the guard offered. "It's a fair distance. You really shouldn't be in this neighborhood alone after dark, missus. Only certain women—" He broke off and glanced at her, head to foot and back.

"I'm looking for my husband," Miranda said.

"If he's with one of them, you don't want to know. Why not just wait for him to come home?"

"I've waited almost two months, that's why," she said. "And I'm not going to sit still and wait any longer. So if you can't find him, I will."

"If *I* can't find him?" the guard echoed, sounding perplexed.

"Not you, yourself. The Public Guard. You've been looking for him and can't find him, the prefect at Clunn told me, and now I'm going to find him myself."

"Who is he?"

"Alexi Glivven."

The guard walked beside her in silence for several seconds. "I don't recall—this way, missus, it's shorter—I don't recall any search for a man named Glivven. That's a North Coast name, isn't it?"

"Yes," Miranda said. She had almost caught her breath. "He disappeared at the end of September, and the Guard was set to look for him—"

"Wait a minute," the guard said. "I don't remember the name, but maybe I'd remember a description."

She glanced at the man. Somewhere in his mid-twenties, he was blue-eyed and fairly tall. "He's not quite so tall as you," she said. "And a little thinner, I think. He's got bright gold hair and gray eyes, very North Coast. He's the lightkeeper at Gwynnhead, in fact."

The guard frowned at her, twirling his stick as they walked. "Lightkeeper at Gwynnhead? A lightkeeper, hey? Is it true about them?"

"Is what true about them?"

The guard looked down at her. "Nothing. I don't remember any memorandum on a lightkeeper, or any other North Coaster."

"Maybe it's slipped your mind."

"In less than two months? Not likely." He stopped walking. Miranda looked up and saw that they were in front of the Railway Inn.

"Thank you for helping me," she said formally, putting out her hand. The guard looked surprised, but he clasped it briefly and smiled.

"All part of my job," he told her. "But after this, try to be more careful."

"No fear," Miranda sighed. She waved a farewell and walked into the inn.

"No luck, cat," she reported. The beast stretched out one foreleg with its five toes spread wide, glanced at her, yawned, and tucked its nose under the leg.

Cats, she thought, envious.

Miranda was back at the Blue Swan in the cheerful light of a crisp sunny morning. The whole mood of the place had changed: she felt quite comfortable eating a breakfast of buns and eggs in the dining room that had been closed and dark the night before. Looking around the pleasant room, at the curtains white with sunshine and the gleaming red tile floor, she could easily imagine Alexi across the table from her. The raucous ale room of the evening before—now closed—seemed the stuff of nightmare.

The man at the landlord's tall desk this morning knew nothing of anyone to be looked up, so once again Miranda explained why she had come to Bierdsey.

This man smiled, not the leer she had come to expect, and nodded. "No trouble, mistress," he said. "Middle of September, I think you said?" He hopped down from his high stool and took a large book from a shelf behind the desk.

"Here we are," he said, after turning several pages. "Alexi Glivven, Gwynnhead. Come to us on . . . mmm . . ." He turned more pages. "Sixth day of August, left us . . . the nineteenth of September. I remember him, a blond man, very courteous and pleasant to pass the time of day with. A quieter type than we usually get."

"The nineteenth of September," Miranda repeated, suddenly hopeless. Two of Alexi's letters had been dated after that. "Did he say where he was going when he left you?"

The clerk blinked at her.

"I mean, leave any address for things to be sent on?"

"Not here," he said. "Of course, we don't usually provide that service—this isn't the Sun, mistress. But if he'd left a deposit against charges, maybe."

"Could you check?"

The clerk glanced back at the registration book. "I don't see that he did, mistress, no."

"Well." Miranda forced a smile. "Thank you. You've been very helpful." It took her a moment to understand why he extended his hand so casually over the desk, palm upward. Sighing, she opened her purse and dropped a couple of large coins into the hand, which closed over them.

In the cold morning sunlight the street outside the Blue Swan was less frightening but no more appealing than it had been the night before. Her breath was just as white on the frosty air. Barrels of trash that had been hidden under darkness by day could be seen oozing a slimy-looking liquid, and the street was littered with scraps of garbage and dog and horse droppings. How she'd reached the high street last night without stepping in something that left her stinking to high heaven was a mystery.

September nineteenth, Miranda thought, avoiding a small child running ahead of its mother, a worn young woman dressed as if she might have worked the whole night— one luker at a time. *September nineteenth.* But Alexi had written a letter both dated and postmarked in Bierdsey on the twenty-second, and another on the twenty-sixth. So he had still been in town, but staying somewhere else. *Why?*

No way of telling. What she needed was a *complete* list of the inns of Bierdsey. Where could she get that? *Not from the host at the Railway Inn,* she thought. He'd already lectured her on getting in so late last night—with his wife at his side calling her "lamb" as if she had no name of her own and carefully laying out the dangers of city life for idiot women who came alone on the train from the boondocks.

Still nine left to check from yesterday's list, Miranda reminded herself. *Back to the room to change the bandage on this blister,* she thought, *and then find a map to plot the most efficient route from one inn to the next.* Remembering the cat's needs, she bought a newspaper from the boy just outside the inn, dragged open the door, and forced her weary legs up the stairs.

Consulting the map she had drawn, Miranda tried to decide which way to turn as she left the third inn she had visited that day. It seemed she could go a long way around in either direction; but here, straight ahead of her, was a small alley that hadn't appeared on the large map of the main features of Bierdsey posted at the Railway Inn, which she was sure she had copied exactly. A shortcut?

She crossed the street, looked down the alley, and saw light at the opposite end.

Miranda had all but memorized Alexi's letters. As she walked through the alley, she had an odd sense of having been there before. Yesterday, perhaps, one of the times she'd been lost? No. *Ah,* she thought, spotting a staircase close against one brick wall. *That's it.* Surely that odd wrought iron railing was the one Alexi had described in his next to last letter, each curl of the design filled with a roosting sparrow? Though only one bird sat there now, fluffed against the cold . . . And there, had those chopped-down barrels held scarlet geraniums two months ago and caught Alexi's eye?

At the end of the alley, she saw a sign to her left marking an inn not on her list. The place had a welcoming air about it. The gray stone walls were a warmer shade than she'd grown used to in Bierdsey—or was that the sunlight?—and the hands that had set containers of geraniums on either side of the doorstep last summer were surely the same that had hung a beribboned wreath of holly and yew on each side of the entrance come winter. The Red Door Inn. Miranda mounted the step and pushed open the red door.

Ah, yes, she thought, looking about. This was a place she could imagine Alexi living in—far more readily than the Blue Swan, even given that establishment's friendlier daylight aspect. Whitewashed walls like the ones at home, a floor of large square yellow clay tiles; the woodwork all dark with age and polishing, just like her own. A thin elderly woman sat on a high stool behind the slab of a desk. Her glance darted to Miranda's side. Looking for a suitcase, Miranda had finally figured out. Seeing none, the woman raised her eyebrows inquiringly.

"Hello, mistress." Miranda pushed the hood of her cloak back. "I'm trying to locate someone who may have stayed here toward the end of September." Practice had polished her speech so thoroughly, she had to be careful not to rush through it. "A North Coaster, about so tall, with blond hair and gray eyes—"

The old woman relaxed. "Givvens, Gribben, something like that?" she asked.

Miranda's heart skipped a beat. "Alexi Glivven."

"Got his stuff in the back room," the woman said. "Friend of yours?"

"My husband."

The stern lines of the woman's face softened a bit more. "Never come home, did he? That's a sore trial, I'm sure."

"Yes. I'm trying to trace—"

" 'Course you are. I would myself, missus," the old lady interrupted. "Come just in time, you did. Another couple of weeks, and the time would have been up."

"The time would have been up?" Miranda repeated.

"We're bound to keep left belongings ten full weeks," the woman explained. "Then we're free to sell the stuff to put toward the unpaid bill, you see?"

"Oh." How much could a week's lodging be? "I'll pay the bill," Miranda said. "In exchange for his things."

This brightened the woman's face considerably. "Let's see," she said. She got down from the stool stiffly and turned to a shelf behind her where a number of ledgers had been stacked. "September, September. Here it is." She opened the book out on the desk. "Came on the nineteenth. Didn't see him after the twenty-seventh. Held the room till the end of the month, then put his things into storage."

Miranda, looking at the book from the other side of the desk, had to clench her fists to keep from reaching out to caress Alexi's signature.

"So that's, um, let's see, twelve days' lodging," the old woman calculated with a finger on the desktop. "Plus the storage fee . . ."

The sum left Miranda with less than the price of an apple in her pocket, but she paid it. The old woman shouted into the ale room for someone to keep an eye out for customers, sorted out a key from a bunch hanging on a nail behind the desk, and led Miranda through a door into a dingy back hall.

"He didn't have much," the woman said. "Just the one case. I packed everything into it"—she cast a shame-faced glance over her shoulder—"a bit higgledy-piggledy, I'm sorry to say. Didn't expect anyone to come looking for it. Or him."

"You didn't report him missing?" Miranda asked. The old woman shook her head and smiled as she unlocked a door. A moment later, Miranda understood: the tiny room was choked with unclaimed belongings.

"The things people leave behind," the woman said, pointing at a mounted deer's head with a fine set of antlers. "I expect *that* one thought she'd made a deposit on the room." She started poking through the things on the floor. "When

the time's up I'm going to hang it in the ale room. Don't
you think that will look fine? Here we are." She reached
into the jumble and extracted a brown leather case, the mate
to Miranda's own.

"I locked it." The woman handed the case over. "There's
no key, but it can lock on its own, I suppose you know."

"I think mine will fit." Miranda wanted to set the case on
the floor and open it that instant, but instead trailed the old
lady back to the entrance, holding it in both arms. "No one
else ever came looking for him?" she asked, as the woman
hoisted herself back onto the stool.

"Nup."

"Not the Public Guard, even?"

The woman's eyes widened. "Nup."

"I was told there was an investigation," Miranda protested, hugging Alexi's suitcase even tighter.

"Then it didn't catch up with him, did it?"

"No, I guess not," Miranda sighed.

"He wanted by the Guard for something, um, wrong?"

"No."

The woman nodded. "I wouldn't have thought it. Nice
quiet gentleman, your husband, a nice sense of humor. You
got any kids?"

"Two boys. Fourteen and seventeen."

"Ah! Then I'm sorry for you, missus, truly I am. But at
least you've got his belongings back."

"Yes," Miranda agreed bleakly. "I've got his belongings." She pushed out into the cold street, fighting despair.

But how puzzling, she thought, frowning as she began
the long walk back to the Railway Inn. She was *sure*
Bikthen had said the government had searched for Alexi.
She couldn't bring to mind his exact words, but it hadn't
been a matter of implying half a dozen things and letting
her conclude what she liked. He'd *said* they'd looked for
Alexi, and that she might have more luck. . . . He'd even
put it in writing.

Maybe the young guard who had walked with her last
night had been away from his job for some reason. Miranda
tried to recall whether she'd said *when* the search had been

made. Maybe that particular guard hadn't been part of the unit that had made the search. Of course. And because they didn't have Alexi's letters—which he wasn't even supposed to have written, really—the Guard wouldn't have known he'd stayed in Bierdsey after leaving the Blue Swan. So if they stumbled upon that record first, as she had, they'd think he'd just left town and stop there. Yes, that would explain it all.

Nobody had told them how important it was, that was it. Because the job was a state secret. So they'd made a cursory search for a missing man, found he'd moved out of the local inn where he'd been staying for well over a month, and assumed it was no longer their business. And, of course, if questions came down from above later on, whoever had been in charge would look out for his own neck before admitting anything of the kind. Curse bureaucracy!

But *why* had Alexi moved?

She had reached the inn. With Alexi's valise dragging at her arms, she climbed the stairs and let herself into her room.

The yellow cat raised a sleepy head and came alert. "No good, cat," Miranda told it. "I've found his belongings, but I haven't found him." She laid the case on the bed and used her own key to open it. *Higgledy-piggledy* didn't begin to describe the careless job of packing. Tears ran slowly down her cheeks as she took each piece of wrinkled clothing out, shook it, and laid it on the bed beside the case. The cat climbed into the lid and sat watching her with interest.

Clothes. A few sheets of crumpled paper. One, the start of a letter to her, dated the twenty-seventh of September: "My lovely Miranda," and not a line more. The tears fell faster.

Nothing else. She forced herself to search all the pockets, ousted the cat from the lid and felt in the pockets there, and then began to smooth and fold the clothes. His shaving kit was missing. The elegant leather case, her gift to him before he left, might have tempted someone at the inn. Or had he gone somewhere for one night? Wearing his dark blue trousers, tan shirt, and the blue sleeveless tunic she'd embroidered two winters ago, his best pair of shoes and his ring—

Where?

Miranda could see no hope of ever finding out. She had come to the end. Now she would have to go home.

Alexi's case was larger than hers and not at all full. She could pack her own tightly, put it in his, and pack what she'd need the next night in Clunn around it to make tomorrow's journey easier. She had only two hands, after all, and the cat to carry, too.

She sighed. "I guess we'll never know," she said to the cat. It sat looking at her until she snatched it up, just to have something alive to cradle in her arms. When it touched her face lightly with one deformed paw, she could not swallow a sob.

A few minutes later, Miranda stopped crying and put the cat down in its favorite spot on her pillow. She had just had another idea.

BIERDSEY, STILL

1

Maybe the citizens of Bierdsey just liked its public buildings to be imposing. The library, two streets and a park
away from the City House, certainly lacked nothing in
that respect. Comparing it with the cozy little library in
Gwynnhead, Miranda was hard-pressed to think of the two
buildings as housing the same kind of service.

She stopped in the echoing main hall to look around. To
her right, a rather grand marble staircase led upward, lit
by tall leaded-glass windows behind her. If she tilted her
head far back, she could just make out ranks of bookcases
beyond a balcony railing. But she thought the newspapers
were more likely to be kept on the ground floor. In the
middle distance, she saw tables with three or four people
seated at them, reading; beyond that were doors standing
open. Closer at hand, a sign promised information, but no
one sat at the desk beside it. Miranda walked toward the
open doors.

As she moved forward, the corridor revealed itself to
be L-shaped, with a stubby extension to her left. At the
end of the extension were racks of newspapers and, to her
delight, a man at a desk, looking very busy and official. Or

officious, at any rate. Just as good.

"May I help you?" this man asked when Miranda approached. Something about his nostrils and upper lip made him look as if he didn't think such a thing could be even remotely within the bounds of probability.

"I'd like to see some newspapers from the end of September," she said. "Is that possible?"

"Over there." He waved at the racks she'd already seen.

Miranda stood her ground. "Where would I find September?"

"They're in order," the man said.

Sighing, she gave up and walked over to inspect the racks. Yes, in order by date and, apparently, by city; the first ones she looked at were from Andrevver. Perhaps she should read through those, too, but Bierdsey first.

What she was looking for was some event on the twenty-seventh of September that could explain why Alexi had interrupted a letter after writing no more than the greeting; and why he had never returned to finish it. What that event might be, she had no idea.

We have to be sensible, Hathden had said. The idea turned her stomach, but she would also look for any reports of unidentified dead men fished from the river, perhaps, or found after many days of lying unnoticed. *Here.* Miranda stopped in front of a rack holding ten days' newspapers clipped to long bamboo rods from which they could hang. She'd start a few days early, on the idea that Alexi might only just have heard of something that had happened several days before. Maybe start with the day before he'd left the Blue Swan, in fact. She lifted the top newspaper out of its place and moved to one of the tables to begin her search.

September seventeenth. Two days before Alexi had left the Blue Swan. With no idea of what to look for, she would have to skim every word. Miranda felt the thickness of the paper with dismay and draped her cloak over a neighboring chair.

An hour or more later, the officious gentleman tapped her shoulder. Miranda looked up.

"Closing time, mistress."

"Oh."

"You'll have to leave," the man told her, as if he doubted she could figure that out for herself. Miranda got to her feet. And after scanning only five days' news!

"I'll put this away for you," the man said, picking up the newspaper she had not quite finished reading. "I've let you stay to the last possible moment as it is. You'll have to go out the side door."

"Where? . . ." Miranda began revising her opinion of this person. He pointed to the end of the L. She saw a normal-sized door in the corner beyond his desk. "Thank you."

"Did you find what you were looking for?"

"I don't know." She smiled slightly. "I don't know what it is. I'm just hoping I'll know it when I see it."

The man nodded. Not a new idea to him, obviously. Miranda settled her cloak on her shoulders and went out to the street.

Nothing she had seen in the newspapers had struck her particularly. Welkin had been reported as leaving Bierdsey on one of the days she'd looked at, but she wouldn't have noted his name if the Prefect of Clunn Province hadn't mentioned it. He could have nothing to do with Alexi, unless . . .

Maybe Welkin had been Alexi's local contact with the Governor's office, too? And had gone out of town, so that when some kind of trouble arose, he wasn't available? And Alexi, rather than stay in some kind of danger—*What* kind *of danger?*—had moved to another inn?

Certainly possible, Miranda thought, hurrying toward the good dinner she had promised herself. She cut across a small park at the center of town. A train was just pulling into the station, so she took the footbridge over the railroad tracks and the staircase down to the platform, planning to cross the lane to the Railway Inn from the station entrance.

Think of a witch! Wasn't that Landers Bikthen?

Twilight had fallen. In the irregular lamplight of the station, she couldn't be sure. The man Miranda had seen descend from a high-class car now pulled the hood of his cloak over his light-colored hair and hurried away from her, while a man at his side struggled to carry two huge pieces of luggage. Should she call to him?

Mouth open, lungs filled, she hesitated. What if it wasn't the prefect at all? Shouting to some other important citizen might prove embarrassing.

The man turned left and disappeared around the corner of the station, his companion at his heels. By the time Miranda reached the corner, neither was anywhere to be seen.

Well, and what would she have said or done if she had been right? Miranda couldn't imagine. She turned back to the station to buy supper for her cat, crossed the lane, and went into the Railway Inn.

Upstairs in her room, she dropped her cloak over the end of the bed and unwrapped the meat pie. "Food, cat," she said, setting the pie down on its wrappings. "Food, but no news, I'm afraid."

Cleaned up, her hair combed, Miranda went down to the dining hall. She followed the waiter to a small table. Odd, that the simple act of sitting down should be so welcome; after all, she'd just spent over an hour sitting futilely at another table. Adding up the cash she had left in her purse and hidden in the cat's carrier, she ordered a supper of baked chicken and salad. In a couple of days she would have to find a bank and cash one of her letters of credit: even with the generous gift from Bikthen, she was running low.

She had only just finished her meal—hadn't yet been given the bill—when the landlord came looking for her. Something about his face alarmed her.

"If you'd come with me, Mrs. Glivven?" he said.

"I haven't paid for my meal."

"I'll have it put on the bill for your lodging," he said. Miranda glimpsed his wife at the doorway to the dining hall, her hands clasped tightly at her waist and a troubled scowl on her face.

Something's happened to the boys, Miranda thought, trailing after her corpulent host. *I should never have left them alone—*

They reached the doorway. The landlord's wife shot her a glance in which there was nothing congenial at all. *Or they've found Alexi dead somewhere—*

"Come into the office," the landlord said.

In the office, one of the inn's housekeepers was waiting. She let out a little squeak when Miranda followed the landlord's wife into the room. The landlord shut the door. All three of them faced her.

They're afraid! Miranda could scent it.

"About your cat," the landlord said.

A sense of reprieve almost loosened her knees. Only the cat. That she could handle. *Ask something innocent.* "Oh, dear," she managed. "Did it spray?" She let her anxiety surface, hoping it looked natural. "I was in the room less than an hour ago, and I didn't smell anything then."

"It's the feet," the landlord's wife said, glancing nervously at the maid. "We've looked at the feet. Jorja was cleaning, you see, and petted it—"

"Oh. It's got an extra toe on each hind foot. That's all right."

The landlord cleared his throat, but his wife, her hands massaging each other as if by their own will, spoke first. "And the front paws are, well, funny-looking. You see, we don't know whether we ought—"

"I'll call the Guard, if you don't." The maid eyed Miranda defiantly.

Miranda sighed. "I suppose I should have known better than to try to keep the cat with me," she said, with what she hoped would look like a regretful shake of her head. Thinking of Bikthen's comment about her honesty, she went on, "But you know how it is with a favorite pet, and I've had this cat since it was born. I left it home, of course, but when my friend drove me to the mainland it followed the wagon. Then somehow it managed to get on the train at Gwynn-on-the-Main—and then what was I to do? I couldn't abandon it."

"There, Lavran." The landlord's wife smiled feebly. "I knew it was something like that."

"However—" the husband began.

"A terrible thing happened at Clunn," Miranda interrupted. "Some old woman there thought the cat was magicked, which it absolutely is not, and she went to the prefect to accuse me." She smiled at the housekeeper, who seemed to flinch. "I was examined and found innocent. The prefect gave me a paper to say so."

"May I see it?" the landlord asked, still forbidding.

"It's upstairs."

They all trooped up to her room, the landlord in the lead, then Miranda, and then the wife and the housekeeper giving each other moral support. When she opened the door, the cat was lying on the bed, but the arrival of the small army sent it to seek shelter in the darkness underneath.

"See how it hides," gasped the maid.

"Most cats hide from strangers," Miranda pointed out. She sorted through the papers in her cloak pocket and found, first the letter from Bikthen delivered to her in the station at Clunn, then, after scrambling four times through the rest with rising panic, the letter of conduct.

The landlord ran his fingers over the eagle and orb of the government crest, turned the page over to see the back of the embossing, and read the note. "Well, there's a comfort," he exclaimed.

"Let's see." His wife took the letter out of his hand, read it, and passed it on to the maid. "Oh, wonderful! I'm sorry to trouble you so, lamb—and what's more, in the middle of all your other troubles," she said, with all of her usual friendliness. "It's just, you see, the cat does have *five* toes."

"It was born that way," Miranda said.

"So Prefect Bikthen's letter says," the wife agreed. "So that's that. My, what a relief!"

"I'm sorry, missus," the housekeeper mumbled, not meeting Miranda's eye.

"Oh, please, don't apologize," Miranda told her. "You were just doing what's right. Though I wouldn't want to have the Guard come for me again on such a charge. You see what they did to me at Clunn." She pushed up her sleeves to show them her bruises, already beginning to yellow.

"Oh, lamb, how dreadful for you!"

"I suppose they were frightened," Miranda said. Inspired, she added, "I know I would have been."

Even Jorja smiled then, and the landlord invited "My good lodger, Mrs. Glivven" down to the dining hall to join them for dessert. "At house expense, of course," he added, so overly cordial she knew he must have been badly shaken.

Nevertheless, Miranda was careful to put Bikthen's letter of conduct into her purse and carry it with her. That was one piece of paper she did *not* want to lose.

2

When she returned to her room with the evening newspaper in hand, the cat was on the prowl. Poor thing. Cooped up in this tiny room, it was getting almost no exercise, when it was used to roaming wherever it pleased. *I'll have to take it out to the park on a string,* Miranda thought. But not now; the hour was far too late. She sat on the bed to scan the newspaper before putting it down for the cat.

As she read, the effects of her earlier panic and vast relief subsided, and a question occurred to her: why had the maid been cleaning her room during the dinner hour? Wasn't morning a far more usual time?

What *had* the woman been up to? Miranda looked at the cat, now placidly gnawing at what was left of the kidney pie. Usually it kept its feet tucked under it, and it did seem shy of strangers, now that it had ventured this far from Gwynnhead. Had someone recognized her from Clunn—one of those people who'd crowded the hall while the prefect was questioning her?—and put the maid up to examining the cat? Out of sheer curiosity, perhaps?

Miranda wondered whether she might somehow befriend the housekeeper and induce her to explain herself without causing any further trouble. But money didn't go far in Bierdsey, so her time was shorter than she'd have liked. And if she approached the woman too quickly, she'd never get any information out of her. Better leave her alone.

Not that it mattered. Nothing Jorja could have to say would speed her search for Alexi. Miranda returned her attention to the newspaper.

She was looking for reports of unidentified bodies, trying to distance her heart as much from her mind as she could. But the distance proved unnecessary; no such report had been printed today. Nor did she see anything else that suggested a possible new direction for her search. "I'll just have to keep pushing wherever I can until something gives, cat," she sighed, and spread the newspaper out on the floor.

When a bored-looking young man unlocked the main door of the Central Library the next morning, Miranda was the first one through it. She went straight back to the newspaper racks, fanned her damp cloak out over a chair—it was drizzling again—and found the *Bierdsey Record* she hadn't finished examining the afternoon before.

Like the others, it had nothing for her that she recognized. Many of the stories made no sense to someone new to Bierdsey life. Most that did, she found of little interest. A fight at the Blue Swan was reported on the twenty-second, but Alexi was gone from the place by then. Reading on, Miranda surmised that fights at the Blue Swan were not exactly unusual; and this one, over a woman whose relationship to either of the young men who had started the melee was unclear, was typical. *Poor Alexi,* she thought. *Staying so long in a place like that!* Instantly the imp that had plagued her on her flight from the Blue Swan the night before last came back to life, full of suggestions. She closed her eyes and shook her head. Her beloved Alexi—loyal, affectionate, tender, imperturbable Alexi—brawling over a trollop? Unthinkable! Yet she had just thought it.

What is happening to me? Miranda wondered. She hastily flipped the page over, then turned it back when she remembered that she'd read only the smallest corner.

Much later, as she turned away from the rack with the newspaper for the twenty-sixth of September in her hands, she discovered the man who had let her stay late yesterday standing beside her.

He rocked onto his toes and back. "Good day, mistress."

Wary, Miranda replied, "Good day."

He raised his eyebrows at her. "Having any luck?"

Miranda sighed and shook her head.

"Maybe I can be of assistance? I've some free time at the moment."

She smiled. "Oh, it's nice of you to offer, but I'm afraid I really don't quite know what I'm looking for."

"Perhaps if you explained the circumstances?"

Not quite sure what to say, Miranda held onto the bamboo spine of the newspaper and looked at the man. A skinny man ten or fifteen years older than herself, with graying hair and dull blue eyes beginning to be obscured by drooping flesh, just now he didn't look the least bit officious.

"You've piqued my curiosity, mistress." He gestured toward the reading area. "You've been working so intensely, all day—even the scholars take rest breaks."

"Perhaps I've got more at stake than they do." She moved toward the reading table where she'd left her cloak. The man came with her.

"Do you mind if I ask what? I can see that you're from the North Coast," he added rapidly. "Your clothes and your coloring. We don't get many North Coasters here, let alone women working by themselves."

Miranda put the newspaper on the table and sat down. Somewhat to her surprise, the man took the chair on the other side of the one holding her cloak. Maybe if she explained what she was doing, he'd see that he couldn't help and leave her alone to get on with it.

"My husband was in Bierdsey on business last summer," she told him. "Then, at the end of September, he just disappeared."

"Vanished?" the man asked, with a trace of alarm.

"Oh, no, no, nothing like that!" That someone presumably well-educated should assume the existence of magic—just like that ragged old woman in Clunn—shocked her. "I mean, his letters stopped coming, and I've discovered that he never came back to the inn where he was staying. So I thought if I looked through the newspapers I might see something that would explain—" She stopped, hearing in her own voice to how slim a reed she had anchored her hopes.

"You don't know the date?"

"The twenty-seventh of September."

His face transfigured, he exclaimed with apparent joy, "Oh, yes, the night of the bolide."

"Bolide?"

"A huge meteor, mistress. No one who saw it will ever forget that sight, I do assure you. I happened to be out rather late that night, myself." For some reason, the man flushed and looked away. He flicked a glance at her and continued, "The whole sky was lit. Just *white,* mistress, blinding white, then dying to the softest of pinks!" He spread his arms, a look of rapture on his faded face. "They say it passed far above, but the sound was like the most enormous of thunderclaps right over one's head. *In* mine, I did think at the instant. You ought to read the stories in the newspaper, mistress."

"I don't know that I've got the time," Miranda said.

"Oh, but you must make time!" The man's eyes shone. *Poor fellow,* Miranda thought. *So little must happen in his life.*

"Such a phenomenon!" he went on. "It can't have had anything to do with your husband, of course, having come from beyond the atmosphere and burned up without trace before reaching the ground, but it is worth reading about, even so. I'm surprised you haven't heard of it. I suppose our news doesn't reach the North Coast."

"We're rather isolated in Gwynnhead," Miranda agreed. "But now that you mention it, I do recall some comment about a large meteor to the south. What was that you called it?"

"Bolide. That just means a very large, very bright meteor, mistress, particularly one that explodes. This one surely deserved that title."

On another day, Miranda might have been fascinated to hear all about this "bolide." Now her eyes strayed from the man's eager face toward the newspaper published the day before the meteor had come.

"Did you say Gwynnhead?" the man asked.

"Yes." Hope leaped. Had Alexi come to check newspapers, too? "My husband's the lightkeeper there."

"How interesting." Her heart plunged. "Someday, if you should find the time, you must tell me what it's like to live in a lighthouse," the man said, sounding a lot more reserved than he had about the meteor. "I so enjoy learning about others' peculiar ways of living."

"There's nothing *peculiar* about it at all!" Miranda turned away pointedly and straightened the newspaper in front of her. "Living in Bierdsey's peculiar, if you ask me."

"I beg your pardon, mistress." The man sighed and got up, resuming his officious air. "If I can be of any help to you, just let me know." He went back to his desk. Despite a twinge of guilt, Miranda was glad to see him go. Gwynnhead peculiar, indeed!

When she got to the newspaper of the twenty-eighth— where the meteor was not said to have "burned up without trace" but to have passed out to sea—she read every last word. Nothing she read gave her the faintest clue to Alexi's fate: no bodies, no brawls, no accidents, nothing.

By closing time that afternoon, Miranda had worked through the news to the middle of October. Still nothing. On one count she was, she supposed, reassured: in the second to last newspaper she had checked, she'd found the report of a badly decomposed body cast up by the river. Hand at her throat, she'd read enough to discover that it had been in the river at least a month—and that it was a woman's— so couldn't be Alexi.

"The whole idea is useless," she caught herself muttering as she racked the *Bierdsey Record* for October fourteenth. But what else was there? She was tired and hungry and despairing when she went out the small door in the corner of the L.

While she had been studying old news, the drizzle of the morning had become a fine snow that now blew into the crannies of the sidewalk. The Central Library was almost a half-hour's walk from the Railway Inn. With the cold wind whipping her cloak around her knees, Miranda suddenly realized that she wasn't just hungry, she was famished.

The small inn where Alexi had stayed last was much closer, even if not precisely on her way. Miranda considered seeing what sort of supper the inn might provide. She might find occasion to ask about Alexi, and the meteor. She glanced about. The neighborhood, still twilit, didn't seem nearly as seedy as the one near the Blue Swan, and plenty of people were walking along the streets. A Public Guard strolling far ahead decided her.

She turned to her right. After two days of wandering about Bierdsey, Miranda felt fairly sure of her bearings despite the haphazard pattern of the town's older streets. Inside ten minutes' brisk walk, the brightly lit red door of the inn appeared across the road. Pleased with herself, she made for it and went in.

The dining room was small, but several people were eating there even though the hour was rather early. A good sign, Miranda hoped: people who'd stopped between their workplaces and home, perhaps, or staying guests not tempted away by the Sun or the Railway Inn. Miranda was told to find her own place to sit—another good sign; dinner would be cheap—and, after studying the menu chalked up on a board, ordered roast beef with potatoes and cabbage. Nobody could go far wrong cooking that.

"Why, Mrs. Glivven!" The elderly woman who'd sat at the desk in the entry the last time Miranda had been here stopped by her seat, a tray balanced on her shoulder. "Come to see how well we fed your man, have you?"

Miranda tried to smile. The woman placed her dinner before her: a huge slab of beef—*Some for the cat,* she thought—done perfectly, mashed potatoes swimming in butter, and a fine green cabbage slaw cooked with caraway seeds.

"Very well, it looks like," she managed to say.

The woman set the tray on a nearby table and drew up a chair beside her. "Go ahead and eat," she said. "But I'm glad to see you, I must say. I got to wondering after you left. Would you like to talk to my son? I think he was the last of us to see your husband."

"Oh, could I?" Miranda's pulse seemed to flutter in her throat. "If he's not too busy?"

"I'm sure he's not," the woman said. "I'm just sorry I didn't think of it sooner. I'll send him right over. Shall I have him bring you a glass of ale or wine?"

"A small glass of wine," Miranda said. "Thank you."

She was still starving, so she started to eat although already filled with apprehension. But fate was merciful. Before she'd eaten half a dozen mouthfuls the son came to her table and set a small glass of red wine by her plate. He had his mother's fine bones, thinness, quickness, and the same way of cocking his head. "Hello," he said. "I'm Steth Fastel. My mother said you'd like to talk with me about your husband."

"Yes! Oh, yes. Please do sit down." When he had, she said, "We have a son named Steth."

"Yes, I know. Your husband told me."

Miranda crossed knife and fork on her plate and looked at the man. He and Alexi were about the same age. The warmth in his tone suggested they'd gotten on well for the few days Lexi had stayed. Suddenly she realized that this might be the last person who had ever seen her husband and known his name. The thought knocked any idea of what to ask him clean out of her brain, and there he sat with his head still cocked, waiting for her to speak. "I don't know what to say," she confessed.

"When the Guard come around asking, as occasionally they move themselves to do, they usually begin with, 'When did you see so-and-so last?' "

"All right," Miranda said breathlessly. "When did you?"

"September twenty-seventh. I remember particularly because that was the night of the meteor. Broke every window in the building and quite a few others, besides."

"Really! Was Alexi here to see that?"

"No. The meteor came just before midnight, and he'd left early that evening."

"Alone?"

Fastel shook his head. "I was at the desk, that evening. A man came in and asked for Alexi Glivven, so I sent one of the maids up to tell him he had company. He came down, greeted his visitor, and they went into the ale room. They were there long enough for about one glass of beer, and then they came out and left together. Seemed friendly enough, so I didn't think anything of it until your husband didn't come back."

"What did this man look like that Lexi went out with?"

"A tallish man, I'd say. Not fat and not thin. Dark hair. I didn't especially notice his eyes, so they were probably dark, but they might have been hazel."

Not Landers Bikthen, Miranda surprised herself by thinking. She looked down at her plate and cut another bite of meat. "Nothing else to distinguish him?" she asked, before putting the fork in her mouth.

Her informant frowned. "Not really. Even his dress was average—that was a warm day, so a shirt and a sleeveless tunic, worn open. I'm sorry, I don't remember the color. I'm not good at noticing." He flashed a grin. "Only if they look as if they couldn't pay for their lodging."

Judging by that room full of abandoned junk, not even too good at that. Miranda kept this thought to herself and sipped at the wine. Too sweet.

"Would you know him again?"

"Not to be certain, no." Fastel sighed. "A very ordinary man."

She'd hoped for better than that. *One* distinguishing feature didn't seem so much to ask! "Did they seem to know each other?"

"Oh, yes."

"Alexi didn't greet him by name, by any chance?"

"Not that I remember."

That would have been far too much luck. "Lexi had started to write me a letter," she said. "I guess that's when whoever this was came, because he only got as far as the greeting."

" 'My lovely Miranda,' " Fastel quoted. "I've been curious to see you ever since. The letter was lying on the desk when we decided he wasn't coming back and went to inspect the room," he explained. "So I read it."

"And you didn't call the Guard to report him gone?"

"I did, yes, but so long as all he had stolen was the use of a room, they weren't interested. What it is about the Guard lately, I don't know. They seem to think people just walk out of their lives on the spur of the moment, and as long as they aren't wanted for a crime and seem to have gone willingly, given no one's found a—er, no one's seen any sign of, um, trouble, as far as they're concerned it's no business of theirs."

"Yes, I talked to a sergeant like that over at the City House," Miranda agreed.

"Then you know."

"Of course, when I talked to the sergeant I didn't know Alexi had started a letter to me and just left it. I wonder if it's worth going back?"

"You could try." Fastel sounded as if he thought the effort not worth so much as two seconds' consideration.

"Well." Miranda tried to smile. "Thanks for talking to me."

"Glad to. Good luck with your search, Mrs. Glivven."

"I'll need a lot more than I've had, I fear." She watched Fastel start across the dining room, get stopped first by a waiter, then by his mother, and finally leave. When she'd paid for her dinner and was ready to go herself, he was perched behind the desk in the entry and wished her good-bye and, again, good luck.

The snow had thickened while she was eating. A good half-knuckle's worth had stuck to the flagging, and most people had abandoned the street for dryness and warmth. But the streetlamps here were more closely spaced than those near the Blue Swan, so Miranda stepped out unafraid.

After a time she began to have the uneasy feeling that she was being observed. She turned to look behind her but

saw only a dark sexless shape looking into a shop window
some distance away. *Silliness*, she told herself, and went
on. The Railway Inn wasn't far, now: just a few short
blocks lay between her and safety. The hour wasn't that
late. No reason to let her imagination make specters out of
the snow. . . . But the sensation of eyes on her back would
not go away.

Reaching a darker place between streetlamps, Miranda
glanced over her shoulder and saw no one behind her; just
the line of her footprints coming into view under the last of
the lamps she had passed and fading into shadow beyond.
At the next corner, she noticed that the buildings beside her
were part of one of Bierdsey's triangular blocks; the angle
of the cross-lane was sharp. That lane, too, was well lit.
Miranda changed direction to walk along it, very nearly
in the same direction from which she had come. At the
next crossing she turned again and jogged back to the street
she had originally taken. There in the snow were her own
footprints, overlaid by those of a stranger—spaced far apart
from walking quickly.

She jogged to the sharp point of the triangle where she
had first left her way. Yes, the second set of footprints
turned there, also, still widely spaced. Would anyone, in
this damp snow, walk two long sides of a block when he
could take one short one?

Only if he didn't know where he was going. As if, for
example, he were following someone.

Scared, Miranda broke into a run.

THE BLUE SWAN

1

By the time she reached the little park on the other side of
the railroad tracks from the inn, Miranda's side ached as
if she'd been stabbed, but she didn't dare slow down. She
still heard running steps behind her, somewhat masked by
the snow underfoot and her own gasps for breath.

A train whistle sounded not very far away.

She could gain a few seconds by crossing the tracks
ahead of the train, forcing the person chasing her to use the
footbridge. Still running, Miranda angled toward the bridge
in case she had misjudged the distance of the whistle and
glanced down the tracks. A headlight bored through the
falling snow, at least ten seconds away—

Try it, she thought with a double leap over the first set of
tracks before she could change her mind. Her foot slipped
as she landed. She staggered. Pain coursed up her right leg.
A glare of light caught her. The train's bell sounded, too
close. She leaped the next set of tracks and vaulted onto
the platform, her cloak lifted by the wind of passage as she
rolled aside and the train roared into the station.

A near thing, Miranda! She scrambled to her feet—
ignoring the shouts of a trainman and the hot pain of a

twisted ankle—and ran past the station, across the lane, and into the inn where she stopped, winded, just inside the door. Her left knee hurt.

"Mrs. Glivven!" The landlord rose from behind his desk with eyes wide. "What's happened? Are you all right?"

"Yes," she panted, beginning to shake in reaction to her narrow escape. "Yes, I think so."

"My dear woman, you look like a ghost! What happened to you?" He came around the desk and took her by the elbow. Miranda felt herself begin to sag against him and willed herself erect.

"I almost got hit by a train."

The landlord stared at her, for once speechless.

Still panting, she told him, "Someone was chasing me."

"You really should not go walking by yourself at night," the man admonished her. "You've torn your trousers, did you know?"

"No." Miranda looked down. What luck, to be wearing her plain blue pair, instead of the embroidered ones!

"Helsa?" the landlord called. "Helsa, come here a moment."

Oh, no, Miranda thought, in no mood to be fussed over. Helsa came bustling out of the office as the landlord opened the door of the inn and looked out.

"Why, lamb, what's wrong? Look at you!"

Miranda's heart had begun to slow down, her chest to heave less deeply. She managed a chattering smile for the landlord's wife.

"No one there," the landlord reported.

"Maybe I lost him." Miranda unfastened her cloak. Even in the warm inn, the air that seeped into her clothing when she swung the cloak off seemed cold. She was sweating. A curious customer looked out of the ale room.

"Please," she said. "I think I'd just like to go up to my room and catch my breath. Maybe I could arrange for a hot bath?"

"Oh, why, of course you can, lamb." Helsa's tone became businesslike. "That will be a quarter luker. Shall I put it on the bill?"

"Yes, please."

"Fifteen minutes, then."

Miranda climbed the stairs. The pain in her right ankle was easing: no great damage done. She leaned the door shut and was greeted by the cat rubbing its head against her boots.

"What a day, cat!" She remembered the chunk of roast beef she had wrapped in the envelope of Bikthen's letter and had tucked into her purse. Ripping the sides of the envelope open to make a plate, she set the beef on the floor. "I don't know what I've got myself into, but it's not pleasant."

The cat, already crouched over the beef, stopped sniffing at it and looked up at her.

"People chasing me—I've torn my pants—" She plunked herself down on the edge of the bed and examined the damage. Mendable, just. "Skinned my knee—on the platform, I guess—and I nearly got hit by a train—"

The cat mewed once and jumped up beside her. It stepped onto her lap with its almost inaudible purr. Touched, Miranda picked it up and hugged it.

"My own fault for trying to be clever," she told it. "But it was terrifying." She squeezed her eyes shut, seeing again the gleam of light along the rails, hearing the onrush of the huge steam engine. A sob broke from her throat. "I could have been killed! What would Hathden and Steth have done then?" The cat put one soft five-toed paw on her cheek. Rocking her whole body, Miranda fought for calm.

"I have got to be sensible, cat," she whispered. "It's the only way I'll ever find him."

Over the next few minutes Miranda stopped shaking, only to jump when somebody tapped on the door. "Mrs. Glivven?" called a woman's voice. "Your bath is ready."

She'd forgotten all about the bath. Miranda opened the door and was handed two huge fluffy white towels, a loofah, a thin bar of soap, and a small flagon of vinegar in case she wanted to wash her hair and rinse the soap

away. The bathroom the maid led her to was as large
as the room she had slept in for the past three nights.
Thanking the maid and closing the door, Miranda pushed
the bolt home and viewed the room with pleasure. Dark
green tiles lined the walls and the floor, and the tub itself,
while narrow, was deep and filled with steaming water. On
a shelf above the tub stood a line of tiny bottles: four kinds
of scented oils. She chose apple blossom and tipped a few
drops into the bath, undressed, and eased herself into the
hot water.

What luxury! For the first time since boarding the train
at Gwynn-on-the-Main, Miranda began to feel almost normal. A woman who usually showered, she'd forgotten how
healing to the spirit a long hot bath could be. Just to lie back
in the warmth, feeling her taut muscles loosen, made life
seem more bearable. Even the sting of the water against her
skinned knee wasn't unpleasant.

She returned to her room with her damp hair wrapped up
in a towel. As she was combing the tangles out, she heard
a soft knock on the door. "Who's there?" she called.

"It's me, lamb. I've brought you some hot tea."

Miranda opened the door. The landlord's wife hustled
herself in, carrying a tray with a pot and two cups. *Oh,
dear!* Miranda resigned herself to at least a half-hour's
ill-concealed questioning. The cat scurried under the bed.
Miranda was tempted to join it.

From the chat with Helsa, the landlord's wife, Miranda
received the surprising encouragement to go back to the
Blue Swan and question that inn's landlord about visitors Alexi might have had while staying there. "Such a
long time, lamb. We seldom have guests for more than
four or five days, though of course we know many of
them from more than one visit. And I'm sure he must
converse with his guests—it's only good business, and
most innkeepers are naturally friendly souls. As is Jem
Rodde, from what I know of him. So he might know
why your husband decided to move, lamb, now mightn't
he?"

The snow had stopped before dawn, after dropping an ankle-deep layer over the town. The grime that repulsed Miranda on her daily hikes was covered; under a blue sky each cornice and railing bore a stripe of purest white. Miranda wondered whether Alexi could see the snow, wherever he was, and how he would describe the sight, if only he could write to her. That idle thought brought a wave of despair. But at least her ankle seemed recovered from her adventure of the evening before: the walk to the Blue Swan awakened only the dullest of pains.

"Why?" The landlord at the Blue Swan eyed her. "You want to know *why* he left?"

He'd taken twenty minutes to present himself after she'd inquired at the desk and a young maid, scarcely older than her own Steth, had been sent to hunt him up. Miranda had been almost ready to give up when the man had finally stalked down the creaking staircase and ushered her into the deserted ale room with a jerk of his head. The room had been dark; he'd flicked on some lights and set two chairs at a table.

"If you have any idea," Miranda said.

"Oh, I've got an idea, all right. Maybe if you hear it you'll have the sense to go home and forget about that bastard you married."

She felt her jaw start to sag, not just at the man's words, but at his rancor.

He scowled at her. "He ran off with my wife, that's what."

Not so. Miranda knew for a fact—or did she? She'd never really asked whether Alexi had stayed at the Red Door Inn by himself. But wouldn't one of the Fastels have told her if he'd had a companion?

Maybe not, whispered the imp.

"What makes you say that, Mr. Rodde?" she asked.

"Oh, she was taken with him, I can tell you that!" The landlord pressed his lips together and gave her an angry glance. "Him and his yellow hair! From two days after he came, it was 'Mr. Glivven this,' 'Mr. Glivven that,' and every other minute, 'Why can't you be more like Mr. Glivven?' " he mimicked in falsetto.

Miranda made a helpless gesture. The landlord's belly strained his tunic, his burgeoning flesh clearly furrowed by the unseen waistband of his trousers. His body odor was sour and his breath stank of stale beer; his dark beard hadn't been shaved in three or four days nor his hair washed in far longer. It was all Miranda could do not to wrinkle her nose. She, too, might have been moved to compare her husband unfavorably to a well-groomed stranger in Mrs. Rodde's place—but that didn't mean she'd desert him.

"So one day she's just *gone,* not a word to anyone, and by midnight I'm frantic. Two days later he's up and out with not an hour's warning—one minute sitting over there in the dining room eating his breakfast and reading a newspaper. Five minutes later, whoops, off he goes, and thank you very kindly. What does it look like to you?"

Miranda gazed at him a moment. "It looks to me as if your wife left for some reason of her own, and two days later my husband had some other, quite independent, reason to move on. Don't forget, Mr. Rodde, I've known Alexi almost all my life. I can't help but know him far better than you do. He's no sneak. If they'd gone off together, he'd have told you."

"You were in here the other night." Rodde waved to include the whole room. As her eyes followed the sweep of his hand, Miranda noticed that the young maid who'd earlier been sent to find him was standing just outside the open door, all ears. Apparently Rodde didn't see her, or didn't care. "You think a man who can handle a crowd like that can't put a scare into somebody?"

"In that case, he'd have left a letter." Miranda shrugged. "Did you report your wife missing to the Guard?"

"The Guard! Hah! 'She's a grown woman, Mr. Rodde, and where she goes is her business, not ours.' " He stared at her with a hangdog expression Miranda understood all too well.

"Yes, that does seem to be their attitude," she agreed.

"Not like it was a few years ago," Rodde added sullenly. "Then, you could no more have kept them away than flies from honey." He glared at her from under his brows. "I want my wife back."

The coincidence of dates occurred to Miranda. Was Mrs. Rodde the woman whose body had been found in the river a month after she'd gone missing? *Should I tell him?*

The imp stirred. *But what if Alexi killed her? He certainly wouldn't have left a letter confessing that!* But why would her mild-tempered Alexi kill anyone, let alone a woman who couldn't have been more than a flattering annoyance?

"And I want Alexi back," she said to Rodde. "Can't you help me?" She spread her hands in a plea. "For instance, could you tell me whether he had many visitors while he was here?"

The Blue Swan's landlord stared off into space. After a moment he said, "None that come to mind." Looking back at her, he added, "But I don't butt into my customers' private affairs. Not a good idea, as a general rule."

Remembering the brawl reported in the newspaper, Miranda decided he was probably right.

"Missus? Missus!"

Miranda turned to look back. The young maid from the Blue Swan ran after her, waving both hands.

"Missus," the girl said breathlessly, reaching Miranda. "I've something to tell you."

"Where's your cloak, child?" Miranda demanded. "You'll freeze! Go back to the inn."

"No, no. Mr. Rodde would have my hide, if he knew I'd left without asking leave, even for one minute." The girl rubbed her arms to warm herself. "But I've got to tell you—the day she went away, my mistress found somebody in your husband's room who didn't ought to be there."

"Are you sure?" Miranda asked.

"Yes'm. I was cleaning across the hall, where the other man had moved out, and I heard her say, 'Who are you? What are you doing here?' and I couldn't hear an answer,

but she said, 'What's that you've got? A hair?' So it's my
mind, missus, that they've both been magicked—her *and*
Mr. Glivven!"

"Nonsense," Miranda said. "There's no such thing as
magic."

The girl tucked her bare hands under her arms and hopped
from foot to foot in the snow. "Now you sound like my
father!"

"Have you ever known anyone to be magicked?" Miranda
persisted. "No? Or ever seen anything changed by a spell?"
The girl shook her head. "Or anything made to work by
a spell when it shouldn't? No? Or anything stopped from
happening when it should?"

"Never," the girl admitted.

"Or known anyone whose word you can trust who would
swear that they had?"

"No, I guess not."

"Of course not. That's because your father's right. Use
the brain you were born with, girl! Don't let people try to
get the best of you by scaring you with *magic*."

"But he did take the hair, I think," the maid protested.

"And much good it did him. I've found out where my
husband went after he left the Blue Swan, and he was
perfectly healthy then."

"Oh." The maid's shoulders sagged. "Well, I thought I
should tell you."

"Thank you," Miranda said more gently. "I'm glad you
did."

The maid started away. After a couple of steps she turned
back. "Oh, and missus? She said—my mistress did—'Don't
I know your face, sir?' but I didn't hear more than that.
And she was quiet all the rest of the morning, frowning and
thinking, and in the afternoon she went out. And she never
came back." The maid's expression took on a stubborn
set. "So don't you think *she's* been magicked? To keep
somebody's secret?"

Miranda gazed at the shivering girl. Older than she'd first
guessed but still not over Hathden's age. "No, I don't," she
insisted. *I think she's dead.* "Did you see that man?"

"No, missus. I didn't want him to catch me peeping—not a man who knows magic!"

Miranda sighed. Frustrated again. "Run back to the inn, now, before you catch cold," she told the maid. "No, wait." Remembering city custom, she fumbled in her purse for a quarter luker coin and pressed it into the girl's hand.

"Thank you, missus, but you don't need to." The maid tried to hand the coin back.

"Keep it," Miranda said. She watched the girl run back to the Blue Swan and turn down the alley beside it, to slip into a rear door and avoid her irascible master, no doubt. Miranda walked on slowly, feeling a little numbed. If the dead woman really was the landlord's wife, as seemed quite possible, what did that mean for Alexi?

2

Miranda had intended to go to the library after talking to the landlord at the Blue Swan, in order to read more of Bierdsey's old news—a chore even more urgent now—but while passing the City House, she changed her mind.

Climbing the wide steps past a man scooping the snow away, she went straight back through the rotunda and marched in the door marked "Municipal Guard." Two men, strangers, sat at the two desks inside. One looked up. "Yes, missus?"

Now that she was here, for all her resolve Miranda wasn't quite sure what to say. "I was here a few days ago," she told the guard who had spoken. "Asking about my husband, who's been missing since the end of September—"

"If a man willingly—" the guard began.

"Yes, yes, they told me that before," Miranda interrupted. "But since then I've discovered where he'd been staying and that he left a letter to me unfinished when he went wherever he went. Why would he do that unless he meant to come back?"

The guard sighed. "What's the name?"

"Alexi Glivven," she said firmly. "He's the lightkeeper at Gwynnhead. He has *always* had a reputation for reliability. And this time I am not leaving until I get some promise of action from you."

The two guards exchanged glances. Miranda took three steps into the room and sat on the nearest desk.

"Unless the person is underage," the second guard began.

"I've heard the whole speech, thank you, in a number of versions," Miranda said crisply. "No need to repeat it."

"Missus," the first man tried again.

"Glivven," Miranda interjected.

"You're interfering with the work of the Guard," he said a little louder. "Now, if you don't want an unpleasant-ness—"

"I see no reason why you can't work, just because I'm waiting." She met the guard's eyes with more spunk than she felt. "If you don't think you can help me, perhaps your superior could." Again, the guards exchanged glances.

"Have it as you like it, missus," one said.

Miranda sat with folded arms for several minutes while the two guards pretended to ignore her. Eventually a door on the far side of the room opened. A man with some sort of emblem on the sleeve of his tunic started into the room, a sheaf of papers in one hand.

"Missus," started the guard whose desk she was sitting on, a shade nervously.

"Mrs. *Glivven*," Miranda said. "That's three times I've told you my name. You can call me by it."

The man with the emblem on his uniform glanced at her. "What seems to be the problem here?"

"My husband disappeared two months ago under very sus-picious circumstances," Miranda said. "I've already been put off once, and now I've decided to stay right here until I have a promise that the Guard will make a search for him."

"Mrs., er, Glivven, did I hear you say?" the man said. "Allow me to explain. Adults are not prohibited from trav-eling as they please. So it is not the policy of—"

"I've heard all about 'not the policy of,' " she said. "Do you people ever listen? I said, *suspicious* circumstances."

The officer—Miranda decided that must be what the emblem meant—shrugged and laid the papers down on the other desk. "Attend to these," he said to the guard, and to Miranda, "All right. Come into my office and I'll hear your story. But I can't promise any more than that."

For all the grandeur of the facade of the City House, this man's dingy office was barely large enough for a small desk, two chairs, and some cupboards. Miranda sidled into it and seated herself on the chair he pointed at.

"Now," he said, clasping his hands on his desk. "What are these circumstances you think are so suspicious?"

His indulgent tone only quickened her determination to get some kind of result from this visit. "First, on the day he vani—on the day he disappeared, my husband had started to write me a letter. He'd gotten as far as the greeting when he was interrupted by a visitor to the inn where he was staying."

"What inn was that?"

"The Red Door Inn."

"A very quiet place. I'd be very surprised to hear of any, er, criminal actions there. Not like some others."

"So I've learned," she said. "But my husband *left* the inn with this visitor and never came back."

The guard shrugged.

"He was reported missing, and apparently your standard excuse for not bothering to do anything was given to the landlord."

"I've tried to explai—"

"Before my husband signed into the Red Door, he'd been staying at the Blue Swan." *That* got a different reaction. "The landlord there tells me his wife is also missing. Oh, don't you smile"—the man hastily rounded his mouth—"Because what happened to *her* is that she came upon someone searching my husband's room for stray hairs. She was sufficiently unwise to remark that his face was familiar to her. That afternoon she went out and never came back. The young maid at the Blue Swan told me all this. In her opinion, both my husband and the landlord's wife have been magicked."

The guard cleared his throat. "Now, Mrs. Glivven. You know, and I know, that the practice of magic, that is, chanting spells in the Elder Speech, is against the law, and for some very good reasons. But the fact of the matter is that these spells just don't work. The evidence some people are pleased to take as proof invariably turns out to have some perfectly ordinary explanation as soon as one examines it closely. Do you understand what I'm saying? There is no such thing as magic. It's only because so many people believe—"

"I agree with you completely," Miranda broke in. "Magic as people think of it simply does not exist and never has." The man nodded.

"But the maid at the Blue Swan believes that someone was looking for hairs from my husband's head in order to gain magical power over him—which in and of itself constitutes treason—and when the landlord's wife remarked that she felt she knew the person's face, she sealed her fate. That far, I think the girl's right."

"What do you think happened to the landlord's wife?" the guard asked warily.

"I've been reading newspapers, trying to find some clue to my husband's whereabouts," Miranda explained. "Yesterday I read about the body of a woman cast up by the river on October thirteenth or fourteenth. The story said the body had been in the river for about a month. The landlady disappeared on the afternoon of the seventeenth of September. Close enough."

The guard nodded slowly. "Yes . . . That, we'll look into. The wife of the landlord of the Blue Swan, you said?"

"Yes."

"And how does this bear on your husband's disappearance?"

Miranda took a long breath for courage. "Magical practice is treason. The penalty for treason is death. Don't you think if someone tried to cast a spell on my husband and it didn't work, that the person might then . . . do something?"

A long silence. Miranda waited.

"It's possible."

"And besides that, last night someone was following me."

The officer shrugged. "This is a large town, Mrs. Glivven. Not a North Coast village." He eyed her dubiously. "Women out on the street in some neighborhoods will be followed. Fact of life."

"Here's another fact of life," Miranda said vigorously. "My husband may be only a lightkeeper to you, but he was doing some kind of secret work at the personal request of His Grace the Governor. You might think about that, too!"

The man gave her an odd glance. "Oh yes," he muttered. "The lightkeeper."

"I just don't understand your attitude," Miranda protested. "In Gwynnhead, if a man doing a dangerous job left an unfinished letter and never came back to his lodgings, it wouldn't take his wife coming along two months later to persuade the Guard to look for him. They'd do it right away, and try to stop them!"

"That's Clunn Province," the officer said, "and Gwynnhead's a tiny village. This is Bierdsey Province. Bierdsey itself is a large town where people sometimes *come* to get lost, so it's our policy—"

"I don't care about your imbecile policy," Miranda said, "and Alexi didn't come here to get lost. Will you see a little sense, and help me look for him?"

He gave a resigned sigh. "Where are you staying, Mrs. Glivven?"

"At the Railway Inn."

"I'll check with my superiors and get back to you," he said.

"Thank you. And your name is?"

A look of mild alarm crossed the guard's round face, quickly smothered. "I'm Captain Lafass," he told her.

"Thank you, Captain Lafass." Miranda stood up. "I'll be waiting to hear from you."

Rather proud of herself for having routed a captain of the Guard, Miranda descended the steps of the City House, avoiding a small flock of pigeons squabbling over discarded bread. The library was only a couple of blocks away. She took a shortcut across the park and went in by the main door. She had intended to head straight for the newspapers, but her steps slowed as she started down the long corridor.

What if someone did try to cast a spell on Alexi? What exactly did that mean?

Like anybody else, Miranda had a few vague ideas about what magic involved. For some spells, one needed a few strands of hair or fingernail parings—the source of the ancient custom of throwing these things into the fire; a custom no longer much followed, even by the credulous, since the advent of central heating. That was about all she knew.

She turned on her heel and headed for the marble staircase inside the entrance, so intent on her goal that she collided with a man just coming in.

"Beg your pardon," she muttered and dashed up the stairs. At the top, she glanced along the rows of books. Thousands of them, tens of thousands! Where would the ones on magic be? Maybe not even on a shelf, maybe locked away where the name of someone asking for them could be taken, perhaps reported to the Governor, and a watch put on that person . . . In Gwynnhead, she'd had no interest at all in magic, and so had no idea where such books might be shelved. But if they were on the shelf at all, probably they were with the psychology books.

She was relieved to find that the spines of the books were marked with the same letter codes as were used in Gwynnhead. Drifting along the ranks of shelves, glancing at the codes from time to time, Miranda first found history, then sociology, and then, grouped in the middle of a next-to-the-bottom shelf, a dozen or so books on magical practice.

No one was about. She sat cross-legged on the floor and pulled the first book from the shelf to leaf through it. A series of studies of the psychology of people arrested for the practice of magic over the last fifty years. All written from a skeptical point of view, as was the next book and the one after that . . . But here, also asserting that magic was pure superstition, was a slim historical study that described some of the customs, although of course it gave no exact spells.

A strand of hair, it seemed, "bound" the victim to the person who cast the spell, making him compliant to the magician's will. Counterspells could be said if one had the "power" oneself. How one would know enough to say them, Miranda couldn't figure out. But then, a lot of these concepts seemed a little wobbly around the edges.

Magicians in the old days constantly tried to steal power from one another, according to this author. A favorite method was to gain control of a cherished possession, through which a connection to the other magician—different in some unspecified way from the one established by a hair—could be made and the victim's power drained for the use of the victor for as long as the less fortunate magician lived. Wars of spell-casting were described, apparently waged to little or no effect. Miranda easily saw what Captain Lafass had meant by "perfectly ordinary explanations."

All very confusing. Miranda put the book back on the shelf and went down, shaking her head, to read newspapers.

The man she'd bumped into had retaliated by taking her usual seat—Miranda recalled seeing him at a table in the corner the previous afternoon. She went to the newspaper racks and carried the *Bierdsey Record* for the nineteenth of September to the seat the man had occupied yesterday.

Somewhere in this newspaper she should find a clue. Alexi had sat at his breakfast reading this newspaper, and something he read had made him change his mind about staying any longer at the Blue Swan. But what?

Nothing Miranda could recognize. She read every word: the title at the top of the first page; stories about a new building planned for an intersection she didn't know, the provincial prefect's official meanderings, the closing of an inn on the Andrevver road; a Lieutenant Lafass's promotion to captain of the Municipal Guard—here she paused, squinting at the tiny print, not sure what to wonder—all the

way through to the last line of the last advertisement for a
lost dog. At closing time she let herself through the small
door and walked slowly away from the building, mulling
over all she had learned and making no more sense of it
than before.

The cat! It hadn't been fed since that small piece of beef
last night. The poor thing would be so hungry—

From the next street vendor she bought a hot kidney pie,
the kind the yellow cat had polished off to the last crumb
two days ago, and headed for the Railway Inn.

"Letter come for you, lamb." Miranda stopped her blind
charge past the desk and looked over. Captain Lafass,
already? "Did you find anything out from the man at the
Blue Swan?"

"Not really." Miranda approached the desk and took the
envelope Helsa extended. Not mailed; hand-delivered. Not
from the captain, it was a plain envelope. "Who brought
it?" she asked.

"Just a regular messenger." Miranda tucked the envelope
into her cloak. "Aren't you going to open it?"

"When I get a moment to sit down," she said.

"But no news from the Goose," the landlord's wife said
with a grimace of disappointment. "Well, that's too bad.
What did you do the rest of the day?"

"Read newspapers in the library."

"Oh, what a good idea! Find anything, lamb?"

Miranda smiled ruefully. "No."

She went up to the room and opened the letter. Two lines
had been written on the single sheet of cheap paper: *It is not
necessary to run in front of trains. Please don't do it again.*
An upright script with an air of disguise about it. Whose
could it be?

3

The cat wasn't the only one who was hungry, but buying
the kidney pie had left Miranda with less than a luker in

cash. Tomorrow, first thing, she really must get to a bank. Meanwhile, she could eat at the inn and have the cost added to her bill. A bill that made her mind shy away from doing the multiplication required to estimate what it might be.

She went downstairs. A man was standing in front of the landlord's desk. The landlord's wife reached out to clasp his hand. The man looked familiar, but Miranda couldn't place him.

"Here she is now," Helsa said. She sounded distressed. "Come here, lamb, you've got company."

"Mr. Rodde," Miranda said blankly, as the man at the desk turned to look at her. He had washed his hair, shaved, and changed his clothes. Fat around the middle he still was, but he'd made himself as presentable as possible in the hours since she'd left his inn.

"I want to talk to you, Mrs. Glivven," he said. "My own establishment is a little boisterous for a lady like you, and I surely wouldn't want you walking back through those streets after dark, so I've come to invite you to share a supper here."

Miranda glanced toward the dining hall. The Railway Inn's landlord stood in the doorway with his mouth hanging open.

"Go ahead, lamb," his wife told her. "I think you'll be glad you did in the long run."

"Very well." Miranda found a small smile for Rodde. "Thank you. I accept." She let him guide her to the dining hall door.

"Give us a place with a little privacy, Lavran," Rodde said.

The landlord led them across the quiet room to a corner where few people were sitting. "Haven't seen you in quite a while, Jem," he remarked on their way.

"Nup."

"Just got a longing for a good dinner, eh?"

"Yup." Rodde fended off each pleasantry until the landlord had held the chair for Miranda, then gave him a dismissive glance not even a statue could ignore. Miranda watched her landlord retreat. He looked as if he had to restrain himself from breaking into a run to ask his wife what was going on.

What *was* going on? She glanced at Rodde.

"They've found my wife," he blurted. A waiter approached. "Just give us the special," Rodde said, and waved him away. "And an ale," he called after the waiter. He glanced at Miranda and called, "Make that two."

"I don't—"

"You may want it." Rodde sounded grim. "If you don't, I will."

So she had been right about the woman in the river. Miranda clasped her hands in her lap. "I take it she's dead," she said.

Rodde gazed at her a moment and nodded sharply once. "You knew, didn't you?"

"I guessed."

"How?"

"The maid who fetched you this morning ran out after me when I'd left," Miranda said. "She told me Mrs. Rodde had confronted someone she found searching Alexi's room for a loose hair."

She'd surprised him. He sat with eyes narrowed for several seconds, as if calculating.

"She said your wife had remarked to the man that he looked familiar," Miranda told him. "Not the wisest thing she could have said. I'd read a story in the *Bierdsey Record* about a woman's body cast from the river. The timing seemed right."

Leaning toward her, Rodde pounded his chest with stiffened fingers. "Why didn't you come back and tell *me?*"

"It was just a guess." Miranda opened her hands to him. "I didn't want to upset you if I'd guessed wrong—you can see that, can't you? So when I went to the Guard to demand that they help me search for Alexi, I told them about it."

"And you actually got them to do something?" Rodde raised his eyebrows. "Never underestimate a determined woman." He sighed, staring at the table. "Not that I wouldn't rather still be waiting . . . and hoping."

The waiter returned with two large mugs of ale and two bowls of lamb stew on a tray. Rodde watched him serve them, while Miranda watched Rodde. Surely the man wasn't buying her supper just because her questions had sent the Guard to tell him what had happened to his wife!

When the waiter was out of earshot, Rodde turned to her. "Did you get them to help you?" he asked.

"I got a captain to say he'd check with his superiors and let me know," Miranda told him. "But that's all."

"Good luck!" Rodde drank off a third of his ale. He set the mug down and looked at her. "I didn't know about what my girl told you this morning when I came here," he said. "It was in my mind that your Alexi might have killed my wife."

She stared at him. "And you offered me supper?"

"I had plans for revenge."

Miranda started to rise. "No, no. Sit down," Rodde said. "I won't hurt you, I promise. I'm not sure I ever could have, really. That's not saying I wouldn't like to lock my hands around the throat of the man who did kill her, but right now I just want to know what you think happened."

She reseated herself and watched him swallow more ale. He'd be drunk in no time, at this rate. "I think your wife made a serious mistake when she told the person she caught searching Alexi's room that he looked familiar," she said. "Especially since she'd commented that he was holding a hair."

Rodde winced. "Zara never did know when to hold her tongue."

"The maid said your wife seemed deep in thought the rest of the morning," Miranda continued. "And she went out that afternoon without, as you told me, saying anything to anyone. I think she remembered who the man was—or at least, how to find out for certain—and decided to make sure she was right."

Miranda recalled a passage from one of Alexi's letters: *I'm always happy when I think of you safe in Gwynnhead. People here do silly and dangerous things, and sometimes they turn out to have stabbed themselves with their own knives.* Had Alexi known—or surmised—what had happened to the landlord's wife? Was *that* why he'd moved? Miranda reminded herself to check to see exactly which of the letters he'd said that in.

"Magic's treason," Rodde grunted. "Isn't that what they're always telling us?"

"Exactly."

"Then what about your husband?"

Miranda picked up her fork, although her appetite was gone. "What do you think Alexi did when whoever it was tried to use his hair to cast a spell?"

Rodde started on his stew. "So we're both alone," he said after a few minutes.

Miranda glanced sharply at him, but he was looking at his dish and his face was too sad for him to have meant anything more than what he'd said. "Possibly," she demurred. "I don't know whether Alexi was present when the spell was recited, see? If he wasn't, he wouldn't know about it, so he'd be no threat. At least, not that way. The person would only have to find some real way to control him, then. So possibly Alexi's just locked up somewhere."

"You hope," Rodde said.

"Of course I hope. There's no other way to live."

The landlord of the Blue Swan set down his fork and drained the last of his ale. Miranda grasped the handle of her own mug as he reached for it. "You're drinking too fast," she told him. "You'll never get home on your own feet, and it's too cold to sleep in an alley."

"Does it matter?"

She couldn't think of anything to say to that.

"We didn't have two sons, like you and your mister," Rodde said. "Just one little girl who took the cough and died. Five years old, she was. Almost killed me."

Miranda recalled Helsa's sympathetic handclasp. "You've got friends, haven't you?" she asked.

Rodde was trying to catch the waiter's eye. He shrugged. "Zara always swore the girl was magicked," he said. "Always swore she'd see every magician she found put to death. Never did find one."

Miranda said nothing.

"Because there aren't any, of course, but try to tell Zara there's no such thing as magic!" Rodde had twisted his napkin into a cord. He looked at the cloth and dropped it into his lap. "Don't you think I'd have seen it at work sometime in my life, after all these years running a place they call the Bruised Goose? And have I? No. But once that woman's mind was made up, up it was made." He glanced at her. "That's why, when she took to your husband . . ."

Miranda gathered her courage. "But did he take to her?"

Rodde slowly shook his head. "I never thought so until the morning he left."

Thank you, Miranda thought. So much for the imp. "What did the Guard do?" she asked. "Today, I mean."

Rodde shrugged. "Two of them came around to the Swan—late morning, it was—and said they'd had a body out of the river last month, did I think it might be my wife? Knocked the breath out of me, I'll tell you. So I asked, what did she look like, this woman in the river? And could I have a look?"

Miranda shuddered.

"Wasn't much left I'd know of her, they told me, save her red hair. Like a flame, that hair used to be." Rodde gazed forlornly at the tabletop. "Used to joke about warming my hands . . . I wasn't let to see her, but they showed me her wedding ring, and that I knew well."

"Best remember her living," Miranda said.

"Good advice," Rodde told her, looking up. "Living and young and happy and in love with me. Remember that advice, woman. You may need it."

THE FIFTH DAY

1

Much later, Miranda lay hugging herself in her bed as it slowly grew warmer. She was nowhere near sleep. The wind roared through the alley outside her window, setting something metallic to banging irregularly in the distance. A cold insistent draft seeped around the rattling window sash. *My fifth night here,* she thought. And what had she learned?

Very little. Alexi left home on the fourth of August, took the two-day train trip to Bierdsey, signed the register at the Blue Swan on the sixth, stayed there until the nineteenth of September—two days after the landlord's wife had disappeared—then moved to the Red Door Inn, from which he vanished eight days later.

Hold on.

Miranda stared at the dim ceiling, scarcely breathing. *A night's missing!* Alexi would have stayed in Clunn the night of the fourth and come straight to Bierdsey the next day. Where had he stayed on the night of the fifth?

Not at the Railway Inn. With four days of reminding, the proprietor or his inquisitive wife would surely have remembered a handsome North Coaster. Unless, of course, they had some reason for concealing that night . . . but for almost two months afterward, Lexi had been perfectly all right. So, even if there was something—*But what on earth could it be?*—something her new friends Lavran and Helsa wanted to hide, they couldn't expect her to have any reason to go ferreting it out.

She'd ask to see the records the next time the extra clerk was at the desk and see what happened.

Alexi had been investigating something. No, some*one*: that much, Miranda thought she knew. He must have been getting close to his quarry. Why else would anyone be desperate enough to try to cast a spell on him? *But did Lexi even know the man had been in his room?* Miranda frowned. No way of telling.

Poor Zara Rodde! All she'd done was catch a man looking for a loose hair to hang onto while he spouted his Elder Speech nonsense, in her own home, where she felt safe enough to accost him. And he'd killed her. *One hair!* That a woman's life had ended because of one of her long-loved Alexi's bright hairs made Miranda shudder.

The river ran close beside the Blue Swan. Had whoever it was just waited for the landlord's wife to leave the building and then attacked her? He was someone who would not be missed from his usual affairs for several hours, if so. Because he certainly hadn't planned to be caught, had he?

Before leaving Miranda, Rodde had told her he planned to question the staff of the Swan, to see if any of them could tell him anything, and would tell her whatever he learned. So there was another possible lode of information not yet mined. And the young maid could be asked whether she'd said anything to Alexi about the stranger. Miranda sighed. *Assuming Rodde is what he seems to be*, she cautioned herself. Suspicion was not one of her usual habits of mind, but it seemed she'd need to encourage it.

Miranda turned onto her side, careful not to roll onto the cat sleeping beside her, and listened to the wind whistling at the loose edges of her window while she considered what she should do the next day.

Most urgent of all: a trip to a bank.

•   •   •

For once, fortune smiled.

When Miranda went downstairs the next morning she saw that the reserve clerk was at the desk. Surprised—usually the landlord manned the desk in the morning—she was wondering how to approach the man when he called out to her.

"Letter for you, Mrs. Glivven." He held out an envelope laden with too many stamps. The postmark was Gwynn-on-the-Main, the handwriting Hathden's. Miranda felt her heart lift.

But this was her chance. "Excuse me," she said: the clerk's attention was on sorting the rest of the mail. "Could you do me one small favor?"

He raised his eyebrows and nodded.

"Could I see the guest register for the fifth of August? Please?"

"I don't think your husband ever stayed with us, if that's what you're looking for," he said, but promptly got down from his stool and went into the office. He returned in a moment with a large, shabby clothbound book and handed it to her.

"I just want to see if there's any name I recognize," Miranda told him. No point in saying she could envision the landlord as a liar to his employee's face.

"Ah, good idea." The clerk returned to sorting mail.

But Miranda saw no name she knew in the list for the fifth of August—Alexi's or any other. She handed the register back to the clerk with a smile and thanks. He grinned and took it away to the office without putting his hand out first, thank fate; she had so little in coin that the largest tip she could have given would have been an insult.

Seated in the crowded dining room, Miranda opened the letter from Hathden while waiting for her breakfast to arrive. Enclosed were three more letters of credit for two hundred lukers each—more than had been left in her account, she was quite sure. *I talked to Mr. Meazie at the bank*, Hathden's note explained. *And we agreed that you'd probably need a lot more money if you're to stay in*

*Bierdsey any length of time. This is a loan against Father's
next salary check, but don't worry about paying for it. Mr.
Meazie isn't charging anything extra, as his part of helping
us find out what happened to Father.*

Miranda pictured Hathden talking to the banker with his
most earnest expression: all he had to do was round those
gray eyes and wrinkle his brow, and he could win anyone
over, even her. *Bless you, Hathden*, she thought, scanning
the rest of the letter. How serious he was! Andreu had been
told about the cat's getting onto the train and was relieved
to learn that it was not lost; she was not to worry about that.
The beacon would be lit every night; she was not to worry
about that. Steth was keeping up with his schoolwork very
well; she was not to worry about that. The cats were in
good health; she was not to worry about them. He and Steth
were in good health; she was not to worry about them. The
kitchen was being cleaned thoroughly every evening; she
was not to worry about coming home to a greasy mess.

All in all, she preferred Alexi's letters.

When her omelet arrived, Miranda folded Hathden's note
into her purse and picked up her fork. After the light supper
of the night before, she was starving.

"Pardon me, mistress?" The waiter stood at the other
side of her table, looking diffident. "Do you mind if I seat
someone with you? We've no empty tables left."

"No, not at all," she said, continuing to eat, but now
aware of a background noise of chatter and the chink of
cutlery against china. Selfish of her not to have noticed
before and made the offer. The waiter returned shortly with
a plump elderly man in his wake.

"Good morning, mistress," the man said. "I do thank you
for putting up with me."

"No trouble."

"Kind of you, nevertheless." He sat down and folded a
newspaper in quarters, the better to read it while it lay on
the table beside his plate. *I'll have to buy my own copy as
soon as I get some cash*, Miranda thought. The cat—and
therefore she—would be in a lamentable position if she
didn't.

"Tch," the man said. "What is the matter with Shells!"

"Morten Shells?" Miranda said, since some comment seemed expected of her.

"Who else? It's my mind the man's brain has been addled these past two or three years," her companion continued. "For all he's only fifty-seven years old." He tapped the newspaper angrily. "Did you read the terms of this farm agreement?"

"No," Miranda said. "I didn't."

"Disgraceful!"

"I'm afraid I'm not very conversant with Bierdsey provincial politics," she said.

"No, mistress, I suppose you wouldn't be, a North Coaster like you. I must say, you people are fortunate to have that man at Clunn, the prefect, what's his name?"

"Landers Bikthen?"

"That's right, Bikthen. Now *he* seems to have his skull screwed down tight. But Morten Shells?" He shook his own gleaming head. "You just wait until the farmers read about this. They'll be marching on the Province House in droves, how much do you wager?"

A rhetorical question, Miranda decided. She turned her mug right side up and poured some tea into it from the pot that had just appeared at her elbow. "Would you care for tea?" she asked, as the elderly man extended his mug without a word.

"Thanks." He slurped and set the mug down with a bang. "Can you imagine! Shells has agreed to let Lengues Province export summer produce to the Bierdsey markets, in direct competition with our own local farmers."

"Has he," she murmured.

"And without drawing any benefit for Bierdsey Province in return! Do you have any notion of the importance of perishable vegetables to Bierdsey's economy?" She didn't, of course.

"I do believe the man's gone senile," her companion rushed on without waiting for any answer. "The Governor would do well to retire him with honors and appoint someone else in his place."

A response was required for politeness. "Do you think so?" Miranda said.

"Oh, absolutely. That senior assistant of his, Welkin, seems quite sound."

"Does he," Miranda said, now mildly interested.

The man tapped the newspaper again. "Says here, Welkin's on record as opposing the trade agreement."

"Good for him," she remarked, without having the faintest idea whether opposing the agreement was reasonable or not.

Her tablemate beamed. "Now that man of yours, what's his name, Bikthen, is in town to negotiate a renewal of our last agreement with Clunn," he continued. "What do you wager he goes home with first prize, too? Good man, Bikthen."

"You think so?" Miranda asked absently, more concerned to discover whether the pot held more tea.

"Oh, yes, absolutely! The way Shells is going, Bikthen will probably go home with the Province House in his purse!"

"Rather a tight fit, I should think."

The man stared at her a moment. "I'm boring you, am I?" he deduced, chuckling. "Be glad you're not my wife, mistress! Poor woman has to put up with me expounding upon the news every day. Except when I'm here in Bierdsey, of course."

A man at the next table, leaning over to be heard, interrupted. "Actually, I don't think Morten Shells is doing a bad job at all," he said somewhat truculently. "There's a great deal to be said for competition. Keeps people on their toes."

"Ah, but underselling?" Miranda's tablemate turned away to take on this challenge. Relieved, she broke open a biscuit and buttered it. After biting into it, she looked around the dining room at the other breakfasters. A small child not far away stared at her and whispered to his mother, touching his hair. Yes, she was the only blond in the room: a sense of being alone, far from home, washed over her. She swallowed her bite of biscuit and sipped at her tea. The child's mother whispered back, frowning, and the child stopped staring at Miranda for all of five seconds.

"Now, this lady's from Clunn," the bald man was saying. "Ask her what she thinks!"

"I haven't really been following what you've been saying," Miranda objected, to no avail. Both men were only too willing to instruct her in the finer aspects of Bierdsey politics. If they concurred on any single point, she couldn't tell what it was. Certainly not the agricultural trade agreement!

"Now, don't you think that in eighteen years as prefect, Morten Shells has learned what's good for the province and what isn't?" the man at the next table demanded.

"Oh, five years ago, he knew something, all right," the bald man agreed. "But over the past three or four, whatever he knew then has gone clean out of his head, *phweet*, departed."

If the Governor were to put his seal to any pact that carried the prospect of causing such division, no matter who had negotiated it or how long he'd been Prefect of Bierdsey, then he was a far less adroit administrator than was generally believed. Miranda hoped the two men wouldn't come to blows. They, and four others, were still arguing when she asked the waiter to put her breakfast on her bill and escaped.

Getting directions from the desk clerk, Miranda set out to find the nearest bank. The day was clear and very cold. The wind had abated somewhat since the night before, but still gusted around corners to make her eyes water. Wisps of snow laden with grit and bits of trash swirled along the cobbled streets. She wondered what the weather was in Gwynnhead, and wished she could have been standing on her doorstep to wave good-bye to her sons as they started off to school. *I really must write to Evelyn*, she thought again. Better still would be to sit in Evelyn's warm kitchen, or her own, and have her friend's clear common sense help her sort things out.

The bank cashed one of her letters of credit without any of the difficulties Miranda had half expected. She went back into the frozen sunshine feeling replenished. As she descended the steps, she noticed the discreet signboard of a small inn across the street. So that was the famous Sun.

With its streetside plantings of neatly sheared evergreens and a glossy black, brass-trimmed front door, the Sun looked a little opulent for Alexi's blood. But since she was so near, she might as well check to see if he'd stayed there on the fifth of August. She went in to find herself clearly in the wrong world. Instead of the usual tall counter placed where someone could keep an eye on all who entered, the registration desk was in an alcove to one side. Satiny wood paneling, with a fine glowing grain that reminded Miranda of fur, served to draw the attention of the prospective guest. Everywhere, except where marble tile provided a waterproof surface just inside the door, thick, dark green carpeting covered the floor and flowed up the steps of a stately curved staircase. The woodwork was painted white, its carvings picked out in gold. In the center of the entrance hall ceiling a light fixture, brightened with dozens of hanging crystals, seemed to represent a miniature sun.

"Perhaps you can help me," she said to the man quietly reading a book behind the desk. No scuffed board hung with keys here! And the guest register was bound in leather.

He set the book aside. "Yes, mistress?"

"I am trying to find someone who may have stayed here last summer." Her confidence in dealing with strangers had increased greatly over the past five days, a alteration of which Miranda was barely aware. She was surprised by the clerk's respectful manner. "I would like to see your registration records for the night of August fifth, if I may."

"Certainly, mistress." The Sun, while ornate, was not large; the clerk merely flipped back through the book that was spread on the desk and turned it to face her. "May I ask whom you seek?"

"A North Coaster named Alexi Glivven."

"The name is not familiar, mistress."

No, but midway down the page devoted to the sixth of August Miranda saw a name that was familiar: Landers Bikthen had signed in that evening. "I see." Miranda smiled formally at the clerk. "Well, it was far from certain. Thank you."

"No trouble, mistress." He had been holding a finger in the book to mark the current registrations, and now he slid the pages back into place. Near the top of the left-hand page she saw the same boldly written name: three days ago, Bikthen had again signed the guest book of the Sun. *So it could have been him in the station.*

"I see Prefect Bikthen's signature," Miranda said. "Is he still with you, by any chance?"

"Oh, yes."

"Perhaps I'll ask him for help."

"He's not in at the moment, mistress, but you can leave a message for him, if you like."

"I'll think about it," Miranda said. First she wanted to look at a newspaper—without some opinionated man's treating her like an apprentice politician—and find out exactly why Bikthen was here. She left the clerk frowning, as if he wondered whether he might have said the wrong thing.

She stopped on the flagging just outside and looked back. Something about the man who had entered the inn as she left seemed familiar . . . but he wasn't Bikthen.

On the chance that Captain Lafass had heard from his superior officer and left her a message, Miranda returned to the Railway Inn. But no, no messages.

She had bought a newspaper from the vendor who sought shelter from the wind in the train station entrance, and slowly climbed the stairs reading the front page. She could understand why the terms of the farm agreement might prove to be a bone of contention. The elderly man who had complained so vehemently over breakfast had a good point; whoever had written the report seemed to take his side. Letting herself into her room, Miranda shut the door, dropped her cloak on the bed, and turned to the commentary on the second page.

The newspaper's editor was not happy with the pact, either; while he wasn't as daring about criticizing the provincial prefect as her breakfast companion had been, he seemed to be making much the same point. *Interesting.*

Miranda turned the page. Given what had become of Zara Rodde, she could scarcely stop checking for the news she did not want to read: that of a blond man found dead. As she glanced over a middle column, the name of Landers Bikthen caught her eye. The Prefect of Clunn Province was in Bierdsey for an official visit, as the gentleman who had shared her breakfast table had stated. The purpose of the visit was to renew the cooperative management of train and telegraph lines, apparently considered routine, and to resolve a dispute involving the jurisdiction over certain unspecified classes of criminals.

"Ah," Miranda exclaimed aloud, finding the detail she wanted: Bikthen was scheduled for three days of conferences with Shells, who was expected to return to Bierdsey this morning. So Welkin was here, too? . . . Not until tomorrow, she discovered, returning to the story about the agricultural agreement. Welkin had stayed behind to tie up loose ends, protesting to the interviewer that he felt the agreement to be deficient in some crucial respects. That bold statement was reported without comment.

So. Tomorrow both Bikthen and Welkin would, in theory, be available should she need their help. Exactly how a North Coast lightkeeper's wife in "unsophisticated" dress would gain access to either of them, Miranda wasn't at all certain. A poor omen that Bikthen had not told her he was coming to Bierdsey during their conversation in Clunn. Surely the trip had been planned long in advance?

"Here you are, cat," she said finally, and put the folded newspaper down on the floor.

2

Inaction proved intolerable.

Miranda decided to walk again to the Blue Swan and see what progress Rodde might have made in questioning his employees. To her great annoyance, as she got ready to go out she discovered that at some point in her morning's walk she'd lost her gloves.

Had she taken them off while at the Sun? She didn't think so. Maybe to buy the newspaper? But the vendor, when she crossed the lane to ask, didn't recall seeing them. She went back to her inn to ask at the desk whether anyone had turned them in, but the reserve clerk hadn't seen them, either.

She had probably left them at the bank. *Wouldn't you know*? she thought. Exactly the opposite direction from the Blue Swan, and a fairly long walk. The gloves were old and rather worn; if they weren't at the bank the next time she went in that direction, she'd just buy new ones. Meanwhile she rolled her hands in the edges of her cloak and crossed her arms for warmth as she usually did anyway.

The wind was still gusty. Sunlight glinted cheerfully on the bare branches of the trees in the center of the high street, and the snow cupped in the ivy leaves growing beneath them had not yet been stained with the grime Miranda saw everywhere in Bierdsey. As she walked, she imagined writing to Alexi, wherever he was, to tell him how the town had changed with the season. Blue floss-flower had provided a margin to the ivy circles when Alexi had seen them—perhaps not on this street; he had also mentioned a similar planting of white petunias. Curious, she examined the edge of the next ivy bed she came to. Neither petunias nor floss-flower, she decided, but what the border had been, she wasn't sure. Not of a plant she knew well enough to recognize once it had been reduced to tattered black leaves and a few broken dun-colored stems.

Miranda had seen two steaming horses pulling a wagon laden with barrels down the alley beside the Blue Swan. *Beer,* she'd thought, *being delivered.* So she was surprised to find Rodde himself at the desk when she pushed open the door. He looked up with a wry little smile.

"Anxious, Mrs. Glivven?"

Miranda shrugged.

The landlord sighed. "I'd be, myself, in your place. But I don't have much to tell you, I'm sorry to say."

"I guess I haven't given you much time," Miranda said.

"Oh, time enough. This isn't the Province House, after all. Come into the dining room and have some hot tea—

you're pale with cold, do you know?"

And a bit shivery, Miranda noticed. She followed Rodde into the sunny room, empty of customers in midmorning. He pointed at a chair and went into the kitchen. Miranda watched him go with a touch of the amusement she'd normally feel: while she couldn't begin to imagine Rodde's ever calling anyone "lamb," in his own way he seemed to have as much inclination to fuss as did Helsa.

He was back several minutes later with the pot of tea and a mug, which he filled and pushed across the table to her.

"Well?" she said.

"Couldn't do much last night," he reported. "Walked into a small riot in the ale room and had to put a stop to that first, so I didn't have much of a chance." He shot a glance at her. "Comes of leaving the kid on his own. No clout, you see?"

She felt she should murmur an apology, but he waved it away.

"No luck with the night staff, anyway."

"I think the man was here in the morning?" Miranda suggested delicately.

"Right. And one person did see him." She sat forward. "Oh, don't get your hopes up. My clerk was in the ale room tapping a fresh keg when the man came in," Rodde told her. "Bastard peered around the edge of the door—it's got a bit of a squeak in one hinge when the weather's hot; that's what made my clerk leave the keg and come out to see—and when the dog's-son saw no one at the desk he slipped up the stairs quick as you please. How he got out, I don't know. Sneaked down the back stairs and out through the kitchen, maybe." He jerked his head toward the front door. "My clerk was out there waiting for him, but he didn't show."

"Did your clerk say what he looked like?"

"Not really. Nothing much about him that stood out, he tells me. Dressed like a tradesman, except that his boots looked like the best quality and what my clerk saw of the bastard's hands looked very fine."

"Fine?" Miranda echoed. "Well-shaped, you mean?"

"No, fine." Rodde shrugged. "Your hands, for instance, have a beautiful shape, and you use them gracefully, but they're not *fine*. Anyone can tell you haven't hired a maid to do nothing but pamper your hands."

"I wouldn't, even if I could," Miranda exclaimed.

"No." Rodde shook his head slowly. "It's a different way of thinking, that. But I'll bet this man had it."

It gave Miranda an odd sensation to realize that while she'd been talking to Rodde, he'd categorized her hands. She felt almost as if he had invaded her in some way. She set down her mug and folded her hands in her lap so he couldn't look at them. "I've never even thought to observe hands," she said. Rodde's were large-jointed and muscular, with scarred knuckles and fine black hairs on the backs, and the nails were trimmed extra short.

"You should," he advised her. "I train everyone who works for me to look at hands first. Sometimes they'll tell you more than faces." He sighed. "But not this time."

"Too bad," Miranda murmured. *Another blind turn.* "There's something I wondered about last night, after you left," she added. Rodde blinked, as if she'd wakened him. "Did you think to ask that young maid whether she'd told Alexi that someone had been in his room?"

"No, I didn't." Rodde stood up and went to the kitchen door. "Kerran!" he bawled. "C'm'ere!"

Waiting, Rodde said something to someone in the next room about the beer delivery. Miranda heard footsteps thumping down a staircase. The girl came to the kitchen door, which Rodde held open. "Mrs. Glivven wants to ask you a question."

"Yes, missus?" the girl asked breathlessly.

"I just wondered whether you ever mentioned to Mr. Glivven that someone had been in his room looking for a strand of his hair," Miranda said.

"Oh, no, missus." The maid glanced at Rodde. "I wouldn't ever do that, no."

Even the Blue Swan had some appearances to keep up, Miranda reflected. "Do you think Mrs. Rodde might have?"

"She couldn't," the girl said. "She went out before he came back that day, missus, and that was the last we ever saw of her."

"I see." Miranda sighed. "Well, thank you, Kerran."

"You were wondering if he moved out because of that?" Rodde asked. She nodded.

"Beg pardon, missus, but it wouldn't have done any good," the maid said. "Not once the stranger had that bit of his hair."

"Why not?"

"Because when he said the right spell, he could make the hair point to its proper head, now, couldn't he?"

"Kerran." Rodde blew an exasperated breath up his face. "That's nonsense."

"That's what people say," the maid insisted. "Isn't it?"

"Who fills up your silly head with this junk? If anything like that had a chance in ten million of working, don't you think I'd have found a magician to put a spell on every hair I could comb out of Zara's brush?" Rodde asked angrily. "Law or no law? Get on with your work, girl, and don't go uttering lunacy."

At a loss what to do next, Miranda walked back to the Railway Inn. "Ah, there you are, lamb!" the landlord's wife exclaimed as she entered. "Got a pair of gloves for you." She brought Miranda's gloves out from a shelf beneath the desk. "You've missed them on a day like this, I imagine."

"How did you know they're mine?" Miranda took the gloves. Hers, yes. Ordinary, carefully mended brown leather with a knit wool lining worn through at the fingertips; nothing set them apart from thousands of others.

Helsa looked at her as if she'd left her brain behind instead of her gloves. "Why, the man who brought them told me they were yours, of course, lamb."

"Oh. I must have left them at the bank," Miranda said. "How kind of them to send them to me."

"Oh, it wasn't a messenger brought them, lamb, just someone walked in off the street. I suppose you must have dropped them nearby."

"But how would he know my name?"

Helsa sucked in her upper lip, frowning. "Do you know, I never even wondered that! The morning train from Andrevver had just come in, and it was a rather busy time."

Chosen for that? Miranda wondered. "What did he look like?"

The landlord's wife shrugged. "A very ordinary man," she said. The echo of Steth Fastel's words made Miranda's scalp prickle.

"But what did he look like?" she demanded.

"Oh, a little taller than average. Dark hair."

"Dark eyes?" Miranda asked.

"Why, no, not particularly. Light brown, I'd say, or hazel, or just possibly gray. Nothing striking about them, or him."

"How very odd." She remembered Rodde's advice. "You didn't happen to notice his hands, did you?"

"No, lamb, I didn't. He was probably wearing gloves himself, don't you think?"

"Yes, I suppose so."

Shaken, Miranda went on up the stairs. *Somebody who knows my name is following me everywhere I go,* she thought. Somebody ordinary, like the man who had asked for Alexi at the Red Door Inn. Or the man who had looked for one of Alexi's hairs at the Blue Swan a few days before that. *Waiting to see what I find before deciding what to do about me.*

But how had he even known she was here, and so fast? Miranda could think of only one explanation: at least one of the helpful people she had met in the past few days was not to be trusted. Who?

"But he told me not to run in front of trains," she said to the cat, which looked up at the puzzled sound of her voice.

Why? And why return her gloves?

3

Lunchtime came and went with no word from the Guard, so Miranda decided to walk to the City House and confront

Captain Lafass once more. The skin over the blister she had developed that first day trudging from inn to inn had hardened. Now it began to hurt once more.

It's the little things that make this so difficult, she thought. Favoring her left foot, she climbed the wide steps. She crossed the sunlit rotunda and pushed open the door to the Municipal Guard office. Different men sat at the desks once again.

"Yes, missus?" asked one.

"I would like to see Captain Lafass, if I may," she said.

"Captain Lafass?" The guard glanced at his companion. "He's been transferred, missus."

"Transferred! But I talked to him just yesterday."

The man shrugged.

"Well, hasn't someone taken his place?" Miranda asked.

Both guards glanced toward the door of what had been Captain Lafass's office. One nodded.

"May I speak to his replacement, then, please?"

"Regarding what, missus?"

"A suspicious disappearance."

"Of a child, missus?" The man eyed her dubiously.

"Of my husband."

"Guard policy—"

"Spare me the lecture on Guard policy!" Miranda glanced at the shabby green walls of the room. Those walls and the damnable policy seemed to be the only stable aspects of this entire organization. "I've heard it all before, thank you, and I don't need to hear it again," she added, sitting down on the nearest desk hoping to get the same result as yesterday.

"Missus, you'll have to move," said the guard at the desk.

"Fine. There's an extra chair in the captain's office. I'll sit on that." She stood up.

"Just a moment." The other guard got up to tap on the door of the inner room. At a word from the other side, he put his head in and said something. "Go ahead," he said turning back to Miranda, sounding surprised. He held the door for her.

"Good morning," Miranda said to the new man behind the desk in the cramped little office. "May I ask with whom I'm speaking?"

"Captain Kovan," the man said, half-standing to extend his hand. "And you are?"

"Miranda Glivven."

Kovan sat down. "Please have a seat, Mrs. Glivven," he said. "Now, how may I help you?"

Miranda started again on her story, while her heart settled into her belly. *Useless.* Would this man offer to check with his superiors, too, and would she come back tomorrow to find he'd also been transferred? *No, too ridiculous*, she told herself. Her luck couldn't be that bad!

"This is my first day here, missus," Kovan said, when she'd finished.

"I know. I talked to your predecessor yesterday morning."

"I see. What did he tell you?"

"That he'd check with his superior and tell me whether the Guard can help me search."

"Ah." His face was blank, but Miranda, glancing at his hands, saw them tighten. "I'm just here temporarily, I'm afraid," he said.

Afraid, yes, Miranda thought. *What's going on?*

"Who is your superior, then?" she asked. "I'll go to him myself."

"The Guard reports directly to the Provincial Prefect, missus," Kovan told her. "He's a very busy man, however, so I doubt he can find any time for you."

"He has assistants, doesn't he?"

"Er . . . I don't think you'll have much luck there. It's a matter of budget, you see. We've been prohibited, as a matter of economy, from looking for people who voluntarily disappear. I don't think you'll get any of the bureaucrats to agree to, er, exceptions that might be used as, er, precedent for expenditures that, er—"

"I see." Miranda tore her gaze from Captain Kovan's very well-kept hands and met his light brown eyes. She felt a chill travel slowly down her spine. "Thank you,

Captain." She got up and left his office, moving through the outer room in a fog of bewilderment. Somehow she crossed the rotunda and was at the outer door when one of the lower-ranking guards caught up with her.

"You're the lightkeeper's wife, aren't you?" he asked in an undertone.

"Yes. What—?"

"Shh!" he warned. "Be careful, missus, whatever it is you're doing. The captain, our real captain, said he'd be back. We don't know *him*." He jerked his head toward the office she had just left. "And he doesn't know the Guard."

"But—"

"It's all to do with you, missus," the man whispered. "So be cautious always, yes?"

"Thank you," Miranda managed to say. "I will." He clapped her shoulder and sped back across the rotunda. Two or three people about their own business there watched him go.

She slipped through the tall bronze door and dashed down the outer steps. *Now what?*

Crossing the frozen park, Miranda went into the Central Library. At the door she paused to look back. No one else was visible on any of the paths through the park. Once inside, she went straight to the newspapers, took down the first of the *Bierdsey Record*s that came to hand, noted the address of their editorial offices, and put the paper back.

The library had a more constant staff than the Guard. She stopped at the desk and asked her officious acquaintance how to get to the newspaper office.

"You think they may have some information about your husband they didn't publish?" he asked. "That's a good idea, mistress."

She hadn't thought of it, but she nodded.

"Good luck to you, then. I'll just draw you a little map." He had already begun sketching a small maze. Miranda took it with a smile and thanks and left through the main door.

The newspaper building proved to be a good half-hour walk from the library, near the river, well upstream from the Blue Swan. Miranda detoured twice, peering back around the corners of buildings to try to spot anyone following her, but either no one was or he was very good at it. She saw nothing that struck her as suspicious.

She arrived chilled and limping. Now, here was a building with no pretensions: dingy utilitarian red brick with BIERDSEY RECORD chiseled into the stone lintel over a plain wooden door one step up from the cobbles. A thumping sound coming from inside seemed almost to make the ground quake under her feet. Miranda pushed down the latch and entered.

Inside was a large, high-ceilinged room lanced with dusty sunbeams spilling through narrow windows. She put her hands over her ears. The thump had become a complex rhythmic clank issuing from a huge steam-driven machine that spewed piles of printed paper onto a table. At least three tiers of scaffolding, reached by flimsy-looking steps, surrounded the machine. A dozen men tended the machine; most feeding sheets of paper to the spinning cylinders. The room smelled of heated metal and oil mixed with dust and steam and ink, strong enough that Miranda almost gagged. At the base of the machine other men gathered the sheets of paper from the table where they landed and fed them in thin sheaves into a second machine, from which they emerged folded into the familiar newspaper shape. No one noticed Miranda.

So that's a printing press, she thought, fascinated. After a few minutes she went over to a young man and tapped his elbow to get his attention. Startled, he gaped at her for a moment, then turned and shouted a name.

" 'Scuse me, missus," he shouted at Miranda, pushing past her. She hastily backed up to let him continue gathering the paper without missing his turn.

"Here, what are you doing on the printing floor?" a voice demanded. Miranda felt herself seized by the arm and swung to face the fearsome glare of a red-faced old man.

"I was looking for the editor," she shouted.

"Well, you won't find him here. Go to the office and get out of our way!"

"Where's the office?" The man waved at a set of steps going up just inside the door she had entered. Miranda saw that part of the building had been divided into normal-sized stories, and that the upper story had windows that looked down onto the large room she was in. Beyond the windows she saw ordinary ceiling lights and someone moving about.

She went up the stairs and opened the door at the top. At the noise she let in, a young man sitting at a desk looked up. "Yes?" he bawled.

Miranda shut the door. The noise was immediately reduced to the muffled thump she had heard from outside the building. "I want to see the editor," she said. "I have a story he may find interesting."

"Society editor's not based here," the man said. "You'll have to go—"

"News, not somebody's party," Miranda interrupted.

"Oh." He got up. "Just a moment."

The editor of the *Bierdsey Record* proved to have an office somewhat larger than that of the Municipal Guard captain, but it was choked with papers piled on every possible surface. He cleared some from a chair and invited Miranda to sit.

"Now," he said. "What's the story?"

He listened with ink-stained hands clasped under his chin and narrowed eyes. "Very polished recitation," he commented.

"I've told it often in the past five days."

"You're not making all this up? Your husband came here on business, disappeared in the middle of writing you a letter, and the Guard refused to have anything to do with searching for him?"

"That's right. It's policy, they say, not to look for adults who seem to have disappeared willingly. But it's not the policy of the Guard in Clunn Province. The prefect there, Landers Bikthen, was told that the Guard had mounted a search and could find no trace of my husband. But I did, easily."

The editor's eyebrows shot upward. "Landers Bikthen got himself involved?"

I'll never make him understand about the cat, Miranda thought. "Alexi was working for the Governor," was all she told him.

"Doing what?"

"I don't know. It's a secret."

The editor drew back. "His usual job?" he asked, in a doubtful tone of voice.

"No, he just does these things from time to time. The last one was four years ago and only took a few days. But this time he was gone two months, and then his letters stopped coming—"

The man made a shushing gesture. "What is his usual job, then?"

"He's lightkeeper at Gwynnhead."

"A lightkeeper!" Now she was frankly stared at. "I'm sorry, Mrs. Glivven, that's a story I just can't touch."

"Why not?"

"Well, you see how it looks, don't you? Secret jobs for the Governor carried out in Bierdsey Province by a resident of Clunn Province? Mix that up with the death of the wife of the landlord of an inn with a highly unsavory reputation? And just when your own prefect is in town for some sticky negotiations? No, I'd have to get approval from Morten Shells for a story like that, if not the Governor himself, and the prefect's a very busy man just now."

They sat looking at each other in silence. Miranda shook her head. "No, I don't understand," she said.

"Mrs. Glivven, don't you think the Guard might have had a good reason for refusing to look into your husband's departure?"

"Disappearance," she said sharply.

"Whatever you want to call it. When the prefect's office institutes a policy change for the Guard, don't you think they might have a good reason? Bierdsey isn't Gwynnhead, you know."

"There's such a thing as an exception."

The editor leaned back in his chair. "Well, I'm sorry. I'm not going to disturb the prefect over your husband. Let's leave it at that."

"When the negotiations with Clunn are over, perhaps?"

"No. The answer is no." He got up and went to the door, but Miranda kept her seat.

"Tell me something," she said. "This morning you published a report of some trade negotiations with Lengues."

"Yes," the editor said warily.

"Someone in the dining hall at my inn complained bitterly about the terms agreed upon, so I read the story *and* your comment on the second page." She gazed at him with her chin raised in challenge. "It seemed to me that you didn't approve, either."

"Well." The editor propped himself against the closed door. "The terms weren't very favorable, we all have to admit that."

"Is this common? I mean, that your provincial prefect drives such a poor bargain?"

"Ah—" He took a deep breath and let it out. "Let's just say, he's done better in the past."

"Someone described him to me as a self-important man who wouldn't want to be bothered with, mmm, small matters."

"Self-important?" The editor cleared his throat. "Oh, I wouldn't say that, and I've known Morten Shells a long time." He frowned, a puzzled-looking frown. "Losing interest, maybe, over the past few years. But he's had the sense to promote Jon Welkin to senior assistant, and that makes up for a multitude of evils. Why do you ask?"

"Pure curiosity. You have to agree, it's strange."

"Far stranger things have happened, Mrs. Glivven."

Miranda shrugged. While being rebuffed, she'd thought of another plan. "Tell me, how do I go about placing an advertisement in the paper? One of those little ones on the back page?"

"Saying?"

"Just asking whether anyone has seen my husband since he disappeared."

"That doesn't sound very helpful to me." The man went back to his desk and sat down. "What if someone did happen to see him a day, two days, after? How would anyone remember exactly when that was, after all this time?"

"He disappeared the night of the meteor. So I'd just ask if anyone had seen him since then."

"The night of the meteor, eh? September twenty-seventh." The man tented his fingers. "Let me propose a compromise, Mrs. Glivven. I'll put that advertisement in, free of charge; I'll even compose it myself for you and give it a boldface first line, but I won't print one more word about this business."

"Very well," Miranda said. She would *not* thank him.

"Now run along," the editor told her. "I've got a newspaper to put together."

Not until she got back to the print floor did it occur to Miranda that if they were printing the paper, it must already be put together. But it was clear that climbing back up those stairs would do her no good at all. She left the noisy, stinking printing plant with relief and resigned herself to the long cold walk back to the Railway Inn.

JON WELHIN

1

The walk back from her unsatisfying exchange with the *Bierdsey Record* editor chilled Miranda with more than winter cold. In the hard light of the blustery day she had reviewed everything she had done since coming to Bierdsey. What more could she do?

Only one possibility looked open: asking for Jon Welkin's help, despite the advice of her own provincial prefect to avoid contact with the government. After all, she had traced Alexi for two months further than the Guard had—not that the Guard had done anything. And if the trail went on from there, how was she—one lone woman—to cast about for further scent? She needed some hounds, and Welkin was the man who had hold of their leashes.

Weary and discouraged, Miranda pressed open the door of the Railway Inn. What a pleasure to be out of the wind and cold! Still shivering, she stopped at the desk to arrange for another hot bath and for a maid to sponge and press her best tunic and pants and do some personal laundry.

"Will you be dining with us tonight, Mrs. Glivven?" the landlord asked.

"Yes, I believe so."

"Good. Then I'll have a table saved for you. You'll like tonight's special better than last night's, I think. I noticed you scarcely ate anything."

"The lamb stew was delicious," she told him. "Last night's company and conversation weren't very good for my appetite, that's all."

The landlord cocked an eyebrow, but Miranda ignored it. *I'm turning positively loquacious,* she thought, distressed. *Can I really be that lonely?* She excused herself and took the meat pie she had bought across the lane to her room and set it down for the cat. She cleaned up what the cat had done with this morning's newspaper and put down a new one. As she straightened up from her task, she heard a tap on her door.

Jorja, the housekeeper, had been sent to collect her laundry. Miranda had remained quietly friendly since the trouble over the cat, and during the past couple of days the woman had seemed to soften toward her somewhat. *There's one thing I've left undone,* Miranda thought.

"Jorja," she began tentatively. "Do you mind if I ask you a question?"

Jorja finished counting Miranda's underwear and said, "What's that, missus?"

"When did you notice that my cat has extra toes?"

The maid tucked the underwear between the folded pants and tunic and picked the pile up before saying, "While I was cleaning the room, missus, as the landlord told you."

"Really? During the dinner hour?" The woman glanced away. "I'm not angry that you were in the room then," Miranda added quickly. "I'm just curious. Somebody's been following me ever since I got to Bierdsey, I think, and it scares me, because I don't know what he wants."

"Truly?" Jorja asked.

"Truly."

Jorja ran a finger over the embroidered cuff of Miranda's tunic. "Yes, that would be upsetting," she said, nodding. "You a woman all alone."

"So you can see why I've wondered whether someone might have suggested that you look closely at the cat, that's all."

Jorja took a deep breath. "He just caught me up on the stairs and gave me a three luker bill and said, 'Take a good look at the cat in Mrs. Glivven's room, and do what you have to,' " she said rapidly. "I thought, *that pretty creature*? For I'd only spied it running under the bed as I came to do the room before that. I didn't even know what the man meant until I looked at its feet, and then I just ran downstairs to Helsa." Now the woman met her eyes. "I might know the man again if I saw him, missus, but I can't tell you what he looks like so's you'd know him in the street."

"Why not?"

The housekeeper shrugged. "He was so ordinary."

Ordinary. Who would have thought that such an unassuming word could gain such power? "Tall? Short?"

"Ordinary."

"Well," Miranda sighed. "Thank you."

"I'm sorry I caused you such trouble, missus." Jorja hugged the laundry and looked down. "But when I saw the cat's feet, that scared me."

"Yes, I can see why it might."

A second maid came at that moment to tell Miranda her bath had been prepared and to give her the towels and other things she might need. Jorja hurried away with her shoulders drawn in as if she were ashamed of something.

After dinner, Miranda stopped at the desk, where Helsa was now on duty, to see whether Captain Kovan of the well-kept hands had improved his masquerade by leaving a message. He had not. The train from Clunn had come in when she was eating, bringing a rush of customers, but that had passed and Helsa was now in the mood to relax.

"Come have a cup of tea with me, lamb," Helsa suggested, shoving the stack of messages back onto the shelf. "I can watch the desk from the office."

Ensconced in one of the sturdy chairs, Helsa sitting opposite with the heavy brown teapot between them on the square oak table, Miranda again had the sense that this room was a home. Reminded of Evelyn's kitchen, she lifted the cup of lemony tea to her lips with a mixture of pleasure and homesickness.

"You've been five days with us, lamb," the landlord's wife remarked. "Six nights, tonight."

"That's true." It occurred to her that Helsa might be asking a question. "I've got the money to cover the stay, don't worry. My son sent me more than I could possibly need."

"Oh, I hadn't even thought of that," Helsa replied, sounding flustered. "It's just—lamb, do you think you've really done anything here in Bierdsey?" she asked, her muddy brown eyes wide with concern. "Anything useful?"

"I've learned where Alexi stayed." Miranda slowly rotated her mug between her hands, hearing its faint *skritch* against the table. She picked it up and sipped. "And I've got most of his belongings back, except what he had with him when he left the inn. I know exactly when he disappeared, and that he left with someone he seemed acquainted with."

"But that's not much, really, is it?" Helsa pointed out.

Miranda sighed. "And I know that someone searched his room at the Blue Swan for a hair to cast a spell with."

"Much luck with that!" The landlord's wife sniffed. "If the hair-pointer worked, we'd have no trouble collecting our due, now, would we? Oh, gracious, what we innkeepers wouldn't give to have the power to cast that spell, lamb! Not that we'd break the law, of course," she added quickly. "But it's not every day a wife comes back weeks later to pay her husband's lodging."

"It's the intent that counts," Miranda said, and thought instantly of Bikthen, sitting in her room at Cluṇn with his crystal glinting on its fine gold chain.

"Yes, I suppose so," Helsa admitted, sucking at her lip. If she thought what Miranda tried so hard not to, that this might mean that Alexi had met Zara Rodde's fate, she kept the idea to herself. "What I meant to ask you, though, lamb, is whether there's really any use staying longer? I hate to see you letting so much money just slip away, when I'm sure you and your boys can use every luker."

"Tomorrow I'm going to go ask the prefect for help," Miranda said.

"Morten Shells? Much luck to you."

"He's got a responsibility, hasn't he?" Miranda asked. "To see that his province is safe to visit? Or live in."

"Yes, well, you see . . ." The landlord's wife took a deep breath. "Don't you get Lavran started on this, lamb, or you'll have cobwebs growing over your ears before he lets the subject go, but the past two or three years haven't been good for Bierdsey Province. Something's gone so wrong with our prefect that even we common people can see something's not right. Lavran believes, and I do, too, that it's his assistants who are running the province. To cover something up, you see?" She bit her lip for a moment. "A stroke, maybe. Or some other sickness. Not that the assistants aren't capable men, all of them. But they have no real power, or shouldn't."

"Well, but I imagine that's partly true everywhere," Miranda said. "No one man could even begin to attend to everything that must come to a prefect's office."

"Yes . . . yes. To some extent, that's so," Helsa agreed. "But they've a firm hand at the top, you see? Here, that firm hand's gone loose. And when the hand does tighten, like as not it squeezes something out of shape." Breaking off, she frowned. "I'm not making much sense, am I?"

"I've heard other people say the same kind of thing," Miranda told her.

"Have you! Things *are* bad."

"Even in the newspaper this morning." Miranda gestured at a paper lying open on top of one of the cupboards. "As I read it, the editor didn't think very much of the new agricultural agreement."

"No," Helsa sighed. "That's one of the squeezes. But I'll also say, for the most part our prefect's the best in the country. Things as bad as that pact he just made with Lengues are unusual, fortunately. And we can always hope there'll be enough public outcry that the Governor will refuse to set his seal to it and send them back to negotiate again. Oh, look, there's someone at the desk. Excuse me, lamb."

Relieved to have a moment's silence, Miranda finished her tea and poured herself some more. Helsa came back and sat down. "But it couldn't hurt to try him," she said, as if no one had interrupted.

"Or one of his assistants," Miranda said. "I'll have to go to the Province House, won't I? Where is it?"

"Way out at the edge of town," Helsa told her. "Way out. You'll have to take a train, lamb. Three or four go every morning—I've got a schedule out by the desk. It's not too expensive, I don't think." She stopped to gaze at Miranda. "I suppose you'll never forgive yourself if you don't do it," she added. "I know I'd be the same if it were Lavran. But do just *think* about when the time to give up and go home might come, lamb. You can't stay here the rest of your life."

2

Miranda caught the third train to the Province House the next morning, wanting to give Welkin a chance to arrive well before her. Only two cars long, the train joggled slowly along the track, giving Miranda plenty of time for second thoughts.

Miserable, despite the brave words she had at last written to Evelyn the evening before, she stared out the window as the train left the station and almost immediately plunged into a tunnel. Stone walls trundled past her, lit only by the shadowy yellow light of the train. The wheels groaned against the rails. After several minutes the walls grew lighter, bluer, and suddenly vanished. Miranda jerked her face away from the sunlight that poured through the window.

Nothing about the close-set houses next to the tracks lightened her mood, however. Somebody's frost-stiffened laundry waved awkwardly from a sagging rope, gathering soot from the smokestacks of every passing train. For some reason it reminded Miranda of the woman pulling beets in Gwynn-on-the-Main. How hopeful she had been, sitting beside Andreu with the golden cat on her lap! Was she a fool to even have come, as Helsa had implied last night?

As for making a fool of herself—What if Bikthen hadn't notified Welkin, as he'd told her? The very morning Bikthen claimed to have notified him, Welkin had left Bierdsey to go to Lengues. How could any notice have reached him?

The dip of a wire into sight as her window went past it reminded Miranda of the telegraph. Yes, of course. Bikthen could have telegraphed. A fault she'd always had, that she tended to forget the existence of things she never used herself. The idea distressed her. What else was she forgetting about that might have led her to Alexi?

The houses fell away in the distance to be replaced by larger ones farther from the tracks, barely glimpsed through thick evergreen plantings. *Here is where the truly wealthy must live*, Miranda thought. Officials, like Shells or Welkin, and merchants with far-flung profitable enterprises, the sort of people she had only heard about and had never known as real people at all.

The distance was far too long to have walked in this cold, even wearing winter clothing. The train made the journey in only half an hour. Miranda got off onto the open platform. A sign pointed to the Province House, but it was scarcely necessary.

She and Alexi had once gone to Clunn—*my goodness, before Hathden was born*—and seen all the sights together, including the Province House there. But Clunn was neither as large nor as rich a province as Bierdsey. Clunn's center of government reflected these facts, although at her first sight of it, Miranda had been overwhelmed. She wondered what she would have thought if the first Province House she had ever seen had been this one. Set on a low bluff above the river, built of a pale creamy-yellow stone, its ornately carved, almost lacy façade made the City House and the Central Library look like the meanest of hovels.

That's an exaggeration, Miranda chided herself. Still,

both the library and the City House were smaller and simpler. Neither enjoyed anything like the wide avenue bordered with topiary that led up the low rise from the station to the Province House, or the long flowerbeds, now covered in straw, surely ablaze with color in summer. . . . She could almost hear the low hush of water climbing the sky or falling in sheets from the many fountains—dry in this season. All of this extravagant ornament had been planned to lead the eye to that distant building set like a jewel on a broad expanse of close-cropped lawn. With the green grass of summer, the effect must be stunning.

She started up the long approach, soon lagging behind the people who had gotten off the train with her. Someone in a horse-drawn gig swept past, such a rarity that Miranda stopped dead and stared. Some high official, no doubt— perhaps Morten Shells himself—too rushed to have time for a ten-minute walk up the smoothly flagged avenue. *A pity,* she thought. But to those who saw it every day, even this splendor must eventually grow familiar. She wondered whether Alexi had ever come here: he couldn't have written to her about something like this, something so instantly recognizable, not when he wasn't supposed to be writing at all.

The tall carved doorway was flanked by guards. Here the purple and blue uniforms Miranda had seen all her life looked almost out of place, as did the red noses of the two young men wearing them. Inside, patches of brilliant color stained the white marble of the floor: colored glass filled small windows and dyed the sunlight streaming through. Magnificent.

Why did I come? she asked herself, standing awed in the middle of the entrance hall. She was conscious of wearing trousers embroidered with flowers in the style of several years past, an unsophisticated tunic, and a plain blue cloak sewn up at home using her worn-out one as a pattern: a naive middle-aged woman two days' train journey from anyone who knew or loved her. Miranda closed her eyes a moment for strength, and began to ask passersby for directions to the prefect's office. Someone pointed out a signboard attached to one wall. She went over to consult it.

"A map would help," she muttered aloud, finding the offices listed by names, not numbers, and no clues to their locations.

"What are you looking for?" asked a man standing beside her, hands in his pockets as he stared at the board.

"The Blue Room."

"Jon Welkin?" He turned and pointed. "You see the hall that goes straight back? Take that and turn left when it comes to an end. Go until you see more of these colored windows, and turn left again. There should be a sign on the door."

Miranda smiled at the man—a pleasant-looking man a little taller than average, with brown eyes and brown hair prematurely flecked with gray—and thanked him.

"If there's no sign, there should be plenty of people about," her informant continued cheerfully. "But I should warn you, he's always very busy, and likely even busier than usual today. You may have some trouble getting in to see him if you don't have an appointment."

As she had feared. "Thanks," Miranda said again, and headed for the hall the man had pointed out. What a long walk, *inside* the building! She had a momentary vision of the gig that had passed her on the avenue, the horse in its blinders trotting down the hall ahead of her, and had to suppress a titter. Nerves.

At least the directions had been correct. Welkin's name was on the door at the end of the small hall they brought her to. Miranda didn't know whether or not to knock. Surely one didn't just walk into the office? But to knock, and interrupt the senior assistant to a provincial prefect at his work? Surely one didn't do that, either?

A man came through the door and held it open for her, so she went in. Ah. A reception area. Of course.

The man at the table across the room was so well dressed that Miranda had to remind herself he was nothing more than a desk clerk. He was slitting the envelopes of a stack of mail with the aid of a long slender knife, not reading the letters, but although he flicked a glance at Miranda as she walked into the room, he ignored her.

No one else was waiting. After a moment Miranda said, "Excuse me."

He looked up and grudgingly said, "May I help you?"

"Yes," she said, crossing the blue carpet. "I would like to see Mr. Welkin for a few minutes, if I may."

Her clothing was slowly assessed from the floor up. Her pale hair earned her a slightly raised brow. Miranda steadily returned the man's gaze. "Is he expecting you?"

"No."

"Mr. Welkin is an extremely busy man, mistress. I much doubt he can make time to see you, if you have no appointment."

"If I wait, could I talk to him when he has a moment or two?"

"Not very likely, mistress."

"I see." Miranda made a conscious effort to gather her nerve. "On my way to Bierdsey I talked to the Prefect of Clunn Province," she said. "He suggested that if I required any help while I am here, I should come to Mr. Welkin."

The man reassessed her clothing, got the same result as before, and said, "Oh, yes?"

"My name is Miranda Glivven. Landers Bikthen said he had notified Mr. Welkin that I might need his assistance."

Now she was given a smile that looked pushed into the face of a dead man. "However, Mr. Welkin is a busy man, as I told you, mistress. His schedule is far too tight to disrupt."

"Yes." Miranda sighed. "Well," she said, hoping she sounded sufficiently ingenuous, "I suppose I'll have to stop at the Sun later on, when Landers is done negotiating for the day, and tell him I couldn't get any help. He might have another suggestion."

The man sat absolutely still for six or seven seconds. "Have a seat, Miss Glivven," he told her. "I'll inform Mr. Welkin that you're here and let him decide."

"Thank you." She returned the dead-man smile, swung her cloak off her shoulders, and claimed one of the velvet chairs that stood in front of a row of long windows at the other side of the room. The receptionist opened a door and slipped through it. Several minutes later he slipped back out, shot a poisonous glance at Miranda, and went to his desk. Behind him, the door stood open.

A man came to it, said pleasantly, "Come in, Mrs. Glivven," and beckoned to her. "I'm Jon Welkin."

Breathless, she went into the inner office, a large elaborate room with tall windows looking out on the river. She had expected—she didn't know what she had expected. Someone whose face she would have to tilt her head back to see, broadly built, a handsome man with the brow of a genius. Jon Welkin was no more than a fingerbreadth taller than she was herself, quite average in build, neither handsome nor unattractive. Brown hair, as was common in Bierdsey, warm greenish-brown eyes; a beautifully sculpted—it was the only word that came to mind—moustache, easily the most elegant of the scant half-dozen she had seen since coming south. He had a friendly air. She was sure it stood him in good stead in his job.

"Now." Welkin gestured at a chair as he circled his desk to sit down. "I'm sorry to say I can't give you more than ten minutes, fifteen at the outside—one of my problems is that I'm always scheduled to do four men's work and can only do one and a quarter. But I did get Landers's telegram just before I left for Lengues last week, and I've been wondering ever since how—and what on earth—you were doing. So, to soothe my own curiosity and as a favor to my good friend Landers Bikthen, I'm glad to make room for you." He set his elbows on his desk, laced his fingers together, and leaned his chin on them. "Tell me the problem. Landers wasn't at all specific."

Miranda had perched on the edge of the chair he'd offered. "My husband was in Bierdsey last summer," she began. "He had received a letter from His Grace the Governor, asking him to do something secret. I don't know what it was."

"No idea?" Welkin inquired.

"Some kind of investigation, I think, though he never said. He's gone away at the Governor's request before, but never for more than a few days," Miranda explained. "This time, he's been gone almost four months, and his letters stopped coming at the end of September. You can see why I'm worried."

"Oh, he wrote to you," Welkin said. "Then it can't have been all that secret a project."

"Well . . . he wasn't supposed to," Miranda admitted, feeling herself flush. "But he had left me with the impression that he'd be back in a week or two—as he always had been before—so when he discovered that it would be much longer, he wrote so I wouldn't worry. He never did say where he was, but the letters were postmarked Bierdsey. So, when I decided to look for him, that's where I started."

Welkin nodded gravely. Recalling Rodde's advice, Miranda looked at his hands. Fine, yes; she saw what Rodde meant by the term now: like Bikthen, Welkin had never done work that left scars or calluses or developed any muscle. His skin looked softer than her own, and his nails were perfectly shaped. The hands were rather small for a man.

"So I came to Bierdsey, but first"—she sighed, not wanting to go into the whole unpleasant history of the cat—"when I was passing through Clunn I encountered Prefect Bikthen, who is also concerned about Alexi, and told him what I was planning. He encouraged me to go ahead with my search, since the Guard hadn't been able to find any sign of him, and Prefect Bikthen thought I—" She shrugged. "He thought people might be more willing to help me than to talk to the Guard."

"Ah. The Guard had mounted a search for your husband, then?"

"That's what Prefect Bikthen was told. But they don't remember it. At least, no one at the Municipal Guard office in the Bierdsey City House knows anything about it. All they'll tell me is that it's settled policy that the Guard does not trace the movements of adults traveling of their own free will, whether their silence worries their spouses or not."

"Quite true. An economy we were forced to make some years ago. But if the job your husband was doing was secret, it may well be that the Guard's search was, too," Welkin pointed out.

"So secret they never even asked anybody where he could be?"

Welkin blinked. "I'm sure they'd have gone to all the inns on some pretext—"

"But they didn't!" Miranda leaned forward, not even aware that she was interrupting the senior assistant to a provincial prefect more powerful even than her own. "Because *I* went to the inns, and *I* asked, and no one had been there before me."

Welkin smiled. "But did you find any trace of your husband?"

"Oh, yes." Miranda sat straight and lifted her chin. "I found where he'd stayed from the day after he arrived; I found out when he had moved from there, I found the place he moved to—where he'd gone away leaving a letter to me half-written and never come back; and I recovered his belongings."

The senior assistant's mouth parted slightly. Miranda became conscious of her vigor and tried to control it. "There's more," she added. "First, I found evidence of treason." Welkin leaned back in his chair, attentive. "Someone searched my husband's room at the first inn he stayed in looking for hair to cast a spell, if you can believe it," Miranda continued. "The landlord's wife caught him and he killed her. Or at least," she backstepped, seeing Welkin blink, "she went out that afternoon and never came home, and now she's been found dead."

Welkin sat for a moment rubbing the middle finger of his right hand, as if toying with an invisible ring. "Extraordinary."

"Not as extraordinary as the Guard," Miranda said. "I went back, day before yesterday, and talked to a Captain Lafass."

"Ah, yes, Lafass. A good officer."

"He listened to my whole story and told me he'd check with his superiors, for permission to investigate, I suppose, and let me know what was decided. But yesterday I got impatient and went to see him—and he'd been transferred! Then, when I was leaving the City House, one of the guards caught up with me and told me that his replacement, a Captain Kovan, wasn't even a member of the Guard and that there was some plot afoot to do with me!"

"Really, Mrs. Glivven." Welkin folded his arms, frowning. "That scarcely sounds credible."

She spread her hands. "It happened."

He stared at her a moment longer. "Well, let's leave that aside for now. Where had your husband been staying?"

"First at the Blue Swan, then at the Red Door Inn."

"He wrote and told you this?"

"No, no. He never mentioned names in his letters. I told you, he wasn't supposed to be writing them. But he described the front door of the Blue Swan—his letters are always full of little word-pictures, and this was one of them. The landlord's wife at the Railway Inn recognized the description. So I went to the Blue Swan to see whether he'd stayed there, and sure enough, he had. But he'd moved away—"

"Before or after the woman was killed?" Welkin broke in.

"After, two days after."

Slowly and thoughtfully stroking the same finger, Welkin asked, "So he must have told them at the Blue Swan where he was going?"

"No, I found the other inn quite by accident. Alexi had described an iron railing in one of his letters. It had amused him because each of its curlicues had a sparrow sitting in it." Welkin smiled briefly. "And he'd mentioned a keg sawn in half and planted with geraniums in the same letter. I took a shortcut down an alley and I saw the railing and two half-barrels with dirt caked inside them. Alexi had said the geraniums stood on each side of the door of an inn. There was an inn quite close, so I went in and asked whether he'd stayed there. The woman behind the desk remembered him right away."

"Extraordinary," Welkin murmured again. "And that's where you found his belongings?"

"And ransomed them, I suppose you could say, yes."

"Your husband moved from the Blue Swan because someone there told him about the search of his room, I take it," Welkin said.

"No. Whatever his reason, that wasn't it—I asked. He was out when the man was discovered, and the landlady was gone before he came back. But one of the staff overheard her conversation with the stranger and told me about it. She didn't tell Alexi because, well, it doesn't reflect well on the establishment to have strangers make free use of the guests' rooms."

"Not that the Blue Swan has much of a reputation to uphold," Welkin remarked. He sat for several seconds pushing his lips out and sucking them in, doing strange things to his moustache, then got up and went to the door.

"Jem, find me half an hour tomorrow to talk to Mrs. Glivven, will you?" he asked the man outside. Returning, but not sitting down, he said to Miranda, "If your husband described two spots in the town of Bierdsey well enough to lead you to him, maybe there are clues in his other descriptions, too. I grew up in Bierdsey and I know the town quite well. Bring the letters to me tomorrow and we'll look at them together. Meanwhile, I'll see what I can find out about the Guard's investigation, and that other strange business. Kovan, you said?" She nodded. "Will that help?"

"Oh, yes, thank you," Miranda exclaimed. "Thank you very much. I know you're very busy—"

"Hush, Mrs. Glivven. You've captured my imagination, and I must say that after this past week I consider myself owed some diversion by the province." He followed her out the door. "Jem, have you found that half hour yet?"

"Before office hours or after," the receptionist sniffed. "I simply don't see any other way."

"Not before," Welkin said. "She's got to take the train. Mrs. Glivven, could you be here around, let's see . . ." He leaned over the desk and examined an appointment book. "Six? Jem will give you a pass, so you can be admitted after hours." He put out his hand, which Miranda took in a bit of a daze, smiled, and went back into his office.

"Never," muttered the man at the desk. He handed her a slip of cardboard—the pass—and glared at her. "I never."

Miranda presented him with her most triumphant smile, wished him good day, and walked sedately to the door. By a great effort of will she did not skip through the long, august corridors of the Province House.

3

Miranda loitered in the Province House for the next hour, not only to explore its public splendors, but also to keep warm until the next train was scheduled to leave. Guards stood about here and there, especially near windows like those in Welkin's office. The windows were actually doors opening onto the lawn, Miranda noticed. *What an interesting idea*, she thought. Doors in Gwynnhead were uncompromising divisions of indoors from outdoors; who would think of admitting a storm to his sitting room? Here, where spring came sooner and winter later, the attitude of builders must be different. Walking up to one of these doors, Miranda found the glass was doubled in the frame: not so impractical after all.

"Please do not attempt to open the door, missus," warned a nearby guard. "They are not to be used." She flashed him a startled glance and went on down this corridor. In a hearing room paneled in the same silky-looking wood used at the Sun, three bored men listened to arguments from a fourth, while several others sat about in assorted stages of attention. Miranda wondered why the door had been left open. People wandered in and out for no apparent reasons. One man glanced at his watch, reminding her of the train. She looked at her own and decided to leave.

Her timing was good: she stood on the bare platform not more than five minutes before the engine huffed to a stop beside her. A few other people had also been waiting. When she got on the train and surrendered the return half of her ticket, she saw that one of her fellow passengers was the man who had given her directions to Welkin's office.

"Hello," he said, with the same friendly smile. "You look happy. Success?"

"Some," Miranda told him. "Mr. Welkin talked to me for ten minutes."

"Very good. I hope he could help you?"

Miranda nodded but said nothing, not wanting to continue a conversation with a stranger, however friendly, unless needed. She took a seat well down the car from the man and looked out the window. Seated on the same side of the train as before, she got a different view and discovered that the tracks followed the edge of the river before curving toward the center of Bierdsey and entering the tunnel. Watching a steamboat churn downstream, she thought of the sea, the rocks of Gwynnhead, and the beacon, and felt herself go hollow with loneliness.

"Got some help, cat," she said with satisfaction. It raised its head and looked at her. She lifted her cloak onto the hook on the back of the door, saying, "Remember Jon Welkin? The man Landers Bikthen said to go to? I went."

The cat gazed at her as if waiting for her to say more, although probably it was just wondering why she hadn't produced the meat pie she *surely* had remembered to bring. But she hadn't, so she went on, "Luckily, he's a man who likes a mystery," and sat down beside the cat to scratch its head. "He's going to put the Guard on Alexi's trail for certain, this time."

The cat pulled its head away from her hand and tried to climb into her lap. "Oh, don't! You'll get fur all over my clean trousers," Miranda said, pushing it away. She had not yet finished writing her letter to Evelyn. "I ought to tell her about Jon Welkin," she told the cat, and knelt to pull her suitcase out from under the bed. She tilted the lid back.

On her knees, staring down at the neatly packed clothing, Miranda felt anger begin to rise. Someone had searched through her things, going to the trouble of refolding all her clothing, but not quite the way she ever folded anything.

Miranda took everything out and laid it on the bed. Nothing seemed to be missing. She checked Alexi's case, too, and found it had also been searched. She wasn't quite as sure about his things, but she didn't think anything was missing there, either.

"He didn't find anything, but he's told me something," she said to the cat. "There's something in Bierdsey for me to find. Oh, cat!" she added shakily. "I hope it's Alexi!"

Wiping her tears, Miranda pushed the suitcases back under the bed and sat down. She should complain to the landlord that someone had gone through her belongings while she was out.

Stop and think this through, Miranda, she told herself. The natural thing to do would be to complain. But someone had gone to great trouble to try to make it look as if nothing had been disturbed. What if it had been the landlord himself, or his wife, who had made the search? Would it be better to let them think they'd gotten away with it or to warn them that she wasn't as stupid as they thought?

And if it had been someone else, what point would there be in complaining?

Maybe, if she just hinted? Miranda decided to go down to the desk to see whether she had any messages.

The landlord's wife handed her two envelopes: one had come through the mail with Evelyn's handwriting on it; the other had been brought by a runner, and the return address printed in the lower right corner was that of the Sun. That handwriting she recognized, too.

"What happened at the Province House, lamb?" Helsa asked, as Miranda thanked her for the letters. "Did you get in to see Morton Shells?"

"No, but I saw his senior assistant."

Helsa made a disgusted face. "That's too bad."

"I thought it better than I should have hoped, myself," Miranda said.

"Oh, well, I suppose he's good at his job," Helsa replied,

"but to me he'll always be plain Jon Welkin."

"Do you know him?" Miranda asked, surprised.

"Know him! Everybody in Bierdsey knows Jon Welkin, lamb, or should, and me better than most. Not that he'd admit he knows *me* since he's gotten so high in the world! Why," Helsa added indignantly, "he scarcely shows his face in town anymore! But that can't change the fact that he worked as a runner for Lavran and me for two years while he was casting about for some way to join the prefect's staff. Now, Jon's quite good at whatever he chooses to do, I'll grant you that," Helsa rattled on. "But it's made him too full of himself, lamb, and that's a fact. Just look at those elegant clothes of his! But you mustn't pay him any mind. I suppose he just looked at you with a long nose and sent you away."

"No, not at all," Miranda protested, astonished. "He was quite friendly and interested. He's even offered to look at Alexi's letters and see whether the little word-pictures might give us any more clues."

"Has he?" Helsa smiled tightly. "Be careful, lamb. You're a fine-looking woman, blond hair or not, and not yet all that far past your youth. Jon always did have an eye for the females, and I don't suppose fifteen years in the prefect's office has changed that!"

Miranda gaped at her. "No, really, I think it's the puzzle that's intrigued him," she said. "So many strange things—"

"You just be careful. He's a charmer, lamb. Please do believe me."

Miranda stared down at Evelyn's neat familiar script, mentally reviewing her talk with Welkin. No, not a hint of interest in her as a woman. Still—

"I'll be careful," she said. She lifted the letters in her hand. "These were all? No one asked for me earlier?"

"Not while I was here, lamb."

Anyone near the desk that morning could have heard Helsa telling her the train schedule, could have watched— from the station itself, if not from the inn's dining hall— her buy her ticket, and once she was on the train could have gone to her room sure that she couldn't be back for an hour at the least. No point in worrying Helsa, if that was what had happened. Miranda thanked her again for the letters and went back up the stairs.

Evelyn's letter would be cheerful and full of good advice. She set it aside and opened the other. "Dear Miranda," Bikthen had written. "I'm told you were asking for me yesterday. I do hope it wasn't an emergency. If you need more money, let me know, or if you need help with the Guard or other government offices, don't hesitate to call on Jon Welkin. Good luck to you, my dear. Landers."

An offer of more money was all but guaranteed to keep her away from him, as the Prefect of Clunn Province must surely know. Miranda sighed and opened Evelyn's letter. It sounded much like Hathden's, with assurances that the boys were being fed well-balanced meals substituting for the discussion of her bank balance. Finished reading, Miranda sat with the letter in her lap, gazing forlornly at the rug. How far away her own world seemed!

PROVINCE HOUSE

1

Miranda finished her letter to Evelyn without mentioning the help offered by Welkin, after all. She said only that she still had some hope, if not of finding Alexi, at least of finding out what had happened to him. *I'd rather discover that Alexi's dead than have him a mystery forever,* she wrote. Looking at that sentence, she crumpled up the page and rewrote it, leaving that out. In her heart, senseless as it sounded for someone who valued certainty as much as she did, Miranda knew she would rather have Alexi's fate remain a mystery than know him to be dead.

She wrote a shorter, more hopeful note to Hathden and Steth, sealed the envelopes, and went down to the front desk for stamps. The reserve clerk was on duty: no messages from Captain Kovan of the Guard, or from anyone else, had arrived. Miranda went out to drop the letters into the post and buy a newspaper and supper for the cat.

By now it was very late in the afternoon, altogether the wrong time of day to run her errands. The working day had just ended in Bierdsey; the railroad station was crowded with people boarding trains headed in one or the other direction. Miranda waited for several people to buy newspapers before her turn came, and inside the station she was forced to join a long line at the food vendor's stall, feeling impatient. But she had left herself little choice, so she pushed the hood of her cloak back, shook her head to free her flattened hair, and stuffed her gloves into a pocket.

Unfolding the newspaper, Miranda turned it over to see what sort of advertisement the editor had written for her.

None.

"I don't believe it," she muttered, reading again about every last lost dog or purse and all of the household goods for sale. But she'd been right the first time: the editor had gotten rid of her with a promise he hadn't kept. In Gwynnhead, no one would dream of doing such a thing . . . But it fit with the way others had treated her in Bierdsey, didn't it? Starting with the Guard. *What is Welkin planning to do?* she wondered, thinking of Helsa's mistrust. Would she take the train out to the Province House tomorrow afternoon, only to find his office locked and deserted?

Depressed by the idea, she moved ahead as the line shortened by one and turned the paper over to read the front page. Morten Shells was quoted as defending the farm pact; a spokesman for some agricultural organization was quoted as denouncing it and calling for a protest from local farmers. What a hornet's nest the man seemed to have uncovered! Thank fate she lived in Clunn Province, where the prefect still had his skull screwed down tight.

"Missus?" a man said by her ear. "It's Glivven, isn't it? Mrs. Glivven?"

He was a tall young man whose rugged face and blue eyes seemed familiar. After a moment, the purple and blue cloak placed him for her. This was the guard who had walked with her back to the inn the night of her ill-advised first trip to the Blue Swan. "Yes, it is." Miranda smiled. "Hello, and thank you again for walking with me the other night."

"Oh, I was glad to." He frowned anxiously. "Could I talk to you, missus? When you've bought what you're waiting to buy?"

"Of course," Miranda said. "Unless you want to talk now?"

"No, no. It's too complicated for a busy place like this. If you'd join me for a cup of tea, maybe, across the lane? That is, if you're going back to your inn?"

Now intensely curious, Miranda nodded. The guard jerked his chin forward. She saw that a space had opened in the line ahead of her and closed it up. "Is something wrong?" she asked.

"Wrong, yes, but I don't know what it is. I thought maybe you could help me figure it out."

When her turn came, Miranda bought a meat pie. She crossed the lane holding the paper sack and her newspaper, with the young guard beside her.

"Just a pot of tea, Lavran," he said to the landlord when they got to the dining hall. "Is that possible, at this hour?"

"Surely." Her host swept his gaze over Miranda with a *What next*? expression. "Would you want the back room?"

"Oh, good idea."

Calling to a waiter to take his place at the doorway, the landlord led them to a small room off the noisy, bustling kitchen. "Tea in a minute or two, Ethan," he said to the guard, and hurried away, leaving the door open.

In Gwynnhead the room would be called a snug: a tiny sitting room with one narrow window looking out on the darkening alley, the white curtain pulled casually aside. The walls had been papered in a thin cream and silver stripe, an affordable luxury where there was so little wall. Two comfortable chairs, each with a lamp beside it, a low shelf stuffed with books, and a single small table were all the furniture.

The guard turned on one of the lamps and sat down. "It's their private sitting room, really," he said to Miranda, undoing the clasp of his cloak and letting it fall back. "I suppose Lavran doesn't want a uniform in his dining hall. Not at the dinner hour."

Miranda took the other chair. One of the kitchen help came in with a pot of tea and two mugs. "Want a tea cake, Ethan?" he asked.

"No, thanks. What about you, Mrs. Glivven?"

"That's kind of you, but no," she said. The man went out, shutting the door behind him.

Ethan put his hands on his knees and regarded her with a sober expression. "I may as well come straight out with it," he said. "Something very funny is going on in the Guard. It's because of you—or because of a lightkeeper's wife, and you're the only one I know of."

"How strange." Miranda picked up the teapot, filled the mugs, and offered one to the guard.

"I was surprised to see you still here," he said, taking the cup with a nod of thanks. "I'd have thought you'd have given up and gone home by now—that was almost a week ago I rescued you, wasn't it?" Miranda nodded.

"Have you found some sign of your husband, then?"

Miranda told him what she'd been doing, and about Zara Rodde.

"Is that who that was!" he said. "I didn't know about the red hair, or I'd have poked Jem to come forward. Do you know how she was killed?"

"No."

"Nor do I. Someone must have looked." He sat still, clearly deep in thought. "Maybe when they hauled her out of the river she was too far gone for anyone to tell."

What a thought! "You said you hoped I might help you figure something out?" Miranda reminded the guard.

He nodded. "I was on day duty today," he said. "Have been since two days after I saw you. Lots more chance to gossip when you're on days, and gossip never hurts—not on my job. I hear you went back to the Guard office the day before yesterday, isn't that right? And talked to Captain Lafass?"

"Yes," Miranda agreed. "I went back yesterday, too, but Captain Lafass was gone."

"He's back with us now." Ethan swallowed tea. "The story I heard was that somebody came to the office yesterday morning and announced that Captain Lafass had been transferred and he was taking over, but Captain Lafass hadn't said a word about it to anyone the day before, and that's not like our captain. This man's name was Kofal, Koman, something like that."

"Kovan," Miranda supplied.

"Was that it? Anyway, just before I saw you in the station I was talking with one of my pals. Happens he drew office duty today. The new man was there most of the day making a mess of things, my friend said, but a couple of hours ago Captain Lafass came back with new orders, and he told this—Kovan, you said?—that he could handle whatever came to the Guard, including the lightkeeper's wife. Well, at that my pal started to listen, 'cause I'd told him about you, see?"

Normal curiosity, she supposed.

"He didn't understand it all," the guard went on. "Not everything comes through that wall, and besides, they were talking about something he doesn't know anything about. But he did hear Captain Lafass tell Kovan that he was three times a fool for trying to take things into his own hands when all he had to do was wait a few days and the lightkeeper's wife would be no problem. That sounded ominous to my friend. It does to me, too."

"Maybe he just meant I'd soon give up and go home, as you yourself expected," Miranda said.

"Maybe." The guard frowned. "But as far as I can see, this is just a case of somebody not being where he's expected to be—your husband, I mean—and we hear about a couple dozen of those every year. So why should this Kovan even think of taking over from the captain, when he doesn't even know the job? That is, your husband's been gone—how long did you say?"

"Four months, all together, but I had letters from him up until almost two months ago."

"So why should it matter now? That is, I see why it matters to you, and I hope my wife would do the same as you have in your place, but why does it matter to the Guard? Or to someone over the Guard, that you've come looking for him?"

Miranda thought of Kovan's soft handshake and wondered. She could scarcely confide in a foot patrol that

Alexi had been doing secret work for the Governor—apparently without the knowledge of the Prefect of Bierdsey Province—although that was the only reason anyone should care that came to mind. Could the prefect's office have searched without the knowledge of the Guard, including Captain Lafass? How?

"I'm sorry to disappoint you, but I don't have the faintest idea what could be going on," she said.

"Well." The guard drained his mug. "I'd have come looking for you here anyway, if I hadn't seen you in the station. Just to tell you something's not right."

"I know something's not right." Miranda sighed heavily. "And not just that the Guard has refused to help me. Someone's been following me. Not when I saw you, I think, and maybe not the day after, but certainly since that next night."

"Guards?"

She shook her head. "Not in uniform. I got a nasty letdown from the editor of the *Bierdsey Record*, too, and someone searched my room while I was gone, and . . . other peculiar things have happened."

"You've got to be careful." Ethan's eyes narrowed. "See, if it was the Guard following you, I don't think you'd know. The men who draw that duty are very good at it. They know how to keep out of sight."

"But they can't avoid leaving footprints in the snow," Miranda said. "And I did see those."

"Did you complain to Captain Lafass about being followed?"

"I did. He didn't seem to think it remarkable."

"Strange." The young guard fell silent.

"It's kind of you to tell me all this." Miranda glanced out the window at the dully lit stone wall opposite. "I don't quite see why you have, though."

"Because the Guard's been interfered with, and none of us likes that. And it's all because of you, but I'd talked to you, see, so I knew you weren't the *cause*, if you take my meaning. Just the excuse. And mostly because when I left you the other night, you thanked me."

"Well, but you'd earned my thanks," Miranda protested.

"Oh, Mrs. Glivven! Hardly anybody ever thanks a guard for doing his duty, let alone offers to shake his hand." He shrugged lightly, smiling at her. "It sounds such a small thing, but it's not, not really. Now I'd best go catch the late train, or my wife will start to worry, if she hasn't already."

Miranda thanked the guard, and also thanked the landlord for the use of his sitting room, and went upstairs. The cat greeted her, twining around her ankles: "Feed me," the eternal refrain of the domesticated feline, dropped only for "I want to be on the other side of this door." *As it well might,* Miranda thought, *cooped up in this tiny room for almost a week when it's accustomed to roaming as it pleases.*

"Here you are, cat," she said, unwrapping the meat pie she had bought in the railroad station. She set it down on the paper sack it had come in. "I just talked to the nicest young guard," she said, watching the cat settle itself at its supper. "Can you believe there's something strange going on in the Public Guard, because of me?"

The cat glanced up at her as if to say it could well believe just about anything of humans.

"Actually, I suppose, it must have to do with Alexi," she mused aloud. "Because they talk about me as 'the lightkeeper's wife.' Otherwise, they'd give me a name, wouldn't they? Or call me something like 'that blond woman'?" She thought of Kovan's well-kept hands. Was he someone from the prefect's staff acting, or overreacting, in his absence? But what would the Prefect of Bierdsey care if a lightkeeper's wife came looking for her missing husband? Even if Shells had murdered Alexi with his own bare hands, he'd had two months to cover it up so deeply no housewife from a tiny North Coast village could hope to dig anything up, even given help from his senior assistant.

Unless Welkin was *pretending* to help her, just to throw her off the track? That seemed, as he had said about the Guard, scarcely credible. All anyone needed to do was let her bumble around by herself until she got tired, or ran out of money, and went home.

"I don't know why they're following me, either, cat," she said. "Unless there's some place I might go that would tell me something about them? As if I'd care about anything but finding Alexi!"

After a quick supper in the dining hall, Miranda decided to read through all of Alexi's letters to refresh her memory.

"I really can't have Welkin reading this," she muttered, when she got to the one Helsa had read with such a knowing smile. "Not if he really is that much of a rake."

It was one of the later letters. *Ah, Miranda!* Alexi had written. *How much I long to be home, you can't imagine. To lie in our bed with you, with the wind whispering around our tower and the beacon pulsing beyond the shutters, and feel your sleek skin against mine—it's the strangest feeling, but the skin of my chest and belly actually aches at the thought of pressing against yours* . . . He had devoted the rest of the page, and part of the next, to his plans for bedding her when he got home. *When I think of caressing the curve of your waist, of the softness and warmth of your breasts* . . . She wouldn't have wanted her sons to get hold of the letter, let alone some strange man with a reputation for indiscriminate seduction. The only Bierdsey scene described in it that could possibly interest Welkin was a house, a large house of elaborate design with a courtyard and narrow pointed windows. Five-petaled flowers set in the arch of each window had caught Alexi's eye. She could keep an eye out for such a house—*had* kept an eye out for such a house—as well without Welkin's help as with. She tucked the letter into the pocket of her suitcase and retied the rest in their bundle.

Tomorrow she would relax, until it was time to go to the Province House. Probably the men who were following her would welcome the chance to rest their feet.

Unless, of course, she was imagining it all. Miranda supposed that was possible: the whole idea just a series of unconnected incidents she had tied together in her mind,

the only one really to do with her, the man who had paid
Jorja to look at the cat.

"That makes more sense, doesn't it?" she asked the cat.

The cat shifted its feet beneath it with a clear air of, "How
do you expect *me* to know?"

I have *been away from home too long*, Miranda thought.
Putting words in the mouth of a dumb beast!

"Not as dumb as you, Miranda," she murmured. She'd
forgotten the note about running in front of the train and
the promptly returned gloves.

2

The train to the Province House the next afternoon was
packed with farmers who had come in from the countryside
to mount a demonstration, every seat taken and the aisles
jammed with large men shifting about as the train jolted
along. Miranda sat close to a window, listening to their
angry talk—thankful that she herself had no hope of ever
becoming a provincial prefect.

"That was a near miss we had five years ago," a man
in the seat ahead of her said loudly, turning to talk over
the back of the seat to the one sitting at her right. "If the
assembled prefects had chosen Shells as Governor when old
Perknis died, where do you think we'd be now?"

"You were disappointed enough at the time," her seat
companion shot back. "Seems to me I saw a letter of yours
in the newspaper, didn't I?"

"Well, but at that time Shells hadn't yet gone crazy," the
man ahead of her defended himself. "Rising young administrator was what we thought him—You, too, if I recall."

"Times change," her seatmate said.

"Times will change a lot more than we like," said a third
voice, "if this pact goes through. *I* think we're wasting our
time here. We should go straight to the Governor."

"That's a long way," said the man ahead of her. "Expensive, and a lot of time taken, when we're looking at a big
cut in our income."

"Be thankful this didn't come at harvest time," the man beside her put in.

Miranda blew a quiet sigh between tightened lips and looked out the window. Yesterday's landscape had not changed in the slightest, although a gray sky promised to fill the snow-free patches on south-facing slopes, and the bare branches of the trees seemed to chatter with cold in the twilight. How spiteful the wind was here, compared to the wind at Gwynnhead!

"I said, where are you from, mistress?" the man beside her asked a few minutes later. Miranda looked at him. Yes, he was speaking to her; the discussion around her had languished while she had been occupied with her own thoughts.

"The North Coast," she said.

"Ah, I thought so. What brings you to Bierdsey?"

"My husband had some business here," she said, and left it at that. The farmer went on trying to be sociable while Miranda tried to stay courteous. After several minutes the conversation failed, probably as much to his relief as hers.

When she left the train at the Province House station, part of as large a crowd as could be jammed into two railroad cars, she stopped to stare. One of the men who emerged from the second car was the same man who had directed her to Welkin's office yesterday and inquired about her success on the return trip. Yet he was talking animatedly with someone wearing brown overalls under a padded jacket no town-dweller would ever have put on his back, and was wearing such a jacket himself.

The two seemed to know each other. But to Miranda's eye, one of those jackets looked altogether too new. She started toward the friendly, *ordinary*, stranger, but somehow he got lost in the crowd jostling along the avenue. A little frightened at being among so many antagonized large men, she dropped back and in the dusk he got away.

She reached the top of the low hill a few minutes after the farmers had marched into the Province House, still so early that she did not need the cardboard pass Welkin's secretary had given her. With almost an hour before her appointment, Miranda could think of nothing to do.

The shouting of the farmers echoed in the corridors. Out of a vague contagion of interest, Miranda walked slowly toward the noise. Where she would have turned left at the end of the first long corridor to go to Welkin's office, the sound of angry voices came from her right, so she turned in that direction and walked on. Not much farther, she encountered the back fringe of the crowd choking the passage.

Miranda hugged the wall. Toward the front of the press someone with a deep voice was calling for attention. Gradually the farmers quieted. She slid forward along the wall to see who could have had this miraculous effect upon them.

Her jaw sagged. Wasn't that Kovan?

She couldn't quite be sure. The dark hair was the same color, caught back with a golden clip instead of the simple headband of the Guard, but dark hair was almost universal in Bierdsey. She was too far away to see the color of the man's eyes. Certainly his clothing was far more distinguished than the uniform of a captain of the Guard: a tunic of deep red, the color of wine, with a glint of silky embroidery on the yoke and the wide, banded sleeves of new fashion. But the light shone on the top of his head, leaving his face shadowed eerily. She couldn't be sure.

"Who's that?" she whispered to a man near her.

"An underassistant," he muttered back.

"What's his name?"

"Navnok, Navoke, something like that. Never heard of him, that's how under an assistant he is!" He glanced at Miranda, then turned to shout, "Where's the prefect? We want to talk to Morten Shells!" A rumble of agreement arose nearby.

Miranda could feel a shift of mood begin in the crowd. *Oh, dear*, now *what have I started*? she wondered, sliding backward along the wall. More loud voices joined the man she'd talked to, some shouting curses at the prefect. The farmers pressed forward, leaving her behind. Thankful, she headed back to the entrance hall. Surely there must be a bench where she could wait.

Just after she turned toward the entrance, she heard someone running along the hall she had just left. Looking over her shoulder, she saw Welkin headed for the mob. Miranda stared at the carved stone wall opposite the end of the corridor in which she stood, irresolute. She heard Welkin's voice raised, a soothing sound, although she could not quite make out the words because of the echoes. Shouted questions got soft answers. The angry grumble she feared she had started began to calm.

Some minutes later, two farmers came past her. "If we can believe him," one was saying. "I'm not making my mind up yet, I'll tell you that." Others followed, straggling toward the door in twos, threes, and fours. She saw the man who had sat next to her on the train, who raised a hand in greeting as he passed, then the man who had turned around in the seat ahead of her.

But I haven't seen the one with the new jacket, she thought. Where was he? Looking toward the end of the corridor, she saw Welkin walk quickly toward his office, with the underassistant beside him shaking his head and making a pleading gesture with both hands. She backtracked, looking at each face as she passed, but when she got to the place where the man in burgundy had addressed the crowd, only half a dozen farmers remained talking to one another. The ordinary-looking man with the new jacket was not among them.

Strange.

Considering the disruption to his schedule caused by the farmers, Miranda half-expected Welkin to refuse to see her. Province House seemed to have no benches, so she had slipped into the back of one of the hearing rooms, only to be evicted when her watch told her she still had fifteen minutes to waste. She decided to brave the eye of Welkin's guard dog and sit in the reception room until six o'clock.

The guard dog was not at his desk, however, although the outer office door stood open. The room was empty. Miranda went in and perched on one of the chairs near the windows. Dusk had deepened while she had been watching the farmers. Black night now pressed against the glass, giving her the creepy feeling that someone was watching her.

About ten minutes before the hour, the inner office door opened and Welkin looked out. "Ah, Mrs. Glivven, you're here," he said, sounding pleased. "I'd hoped you would be. Have you been waiting very long?"

"Not at all," Miranda said.

"We had a small disruption a while ago," Welkin said. "Causing one of my appointments to be canceled, so I've got time for you now. I hope you didn't get caught in that mob of farmers? Unhappy men."

"Not really." Miranda smiled as Welkin took her cloak from her and dropped it over a chair. "I traveled out from Bierdsey with them, but they were quieter then."

"Just working themselves up, I imagine, eh?" Welkin sounded almost amused. "They've nothing to fear, really. I'm sure the Governor won't approve that ridiculous agreement Shells managed to negotiate."

"What's the matter with your prefect?" Miranda asked bluntly. "Does he know how much talk there is?"

Welkin frowned. "I don't think he recognizes how much of a threat to his position the talk has become," he said slowly. "A pity, because he really is a competent man most of the time. It's just that once in a while he does something so—" He broke off and shrugged. "I shouldn't be talking like this. But it's a painful puzzle, and has been for several years now." Welkin shook his head. "When I first knew him, he was brilliant."

"I heard someone speculate that he might have had a small stroke," Miranda said.

Welkin's eyebrows flicked upward. "An interesting idea. I suppose that would explain his behavior, yes. I wonder." He paused, his face a mask. After a moment he said briskly, "Well, but that's not what you came for. Did you bring your husband's letters, all of them?"

"Yes." *Not much of a lie*, she told herself, going to her cloak and taking the bundle out of the inner pocket. She'd only left the one behind.

"Ah, done up in ribbon," Welkin commented, reaching for the bundle. He tugged at the bow and fanned out the folded papers on his desk. "Are they in order?"

"More or less."

"They're looking a bit worn, Mrs. Glivven," he said with a smile, opening the first. "You can't have been married long."

"Eighteen years."

"Really? A lucky man, your husband, to have such a faithful wife." He was scanning the letter as he spoke. This one, Miranda recalled, contained a small vignette of a boat on the river, a sailor shouting to someone on the shore. "They say people grow to be alike when they've been married that long," Welkin continued. "Would you say that's true?"

Miranda stopped to reflect. "I've seen that happen, yes," she said. "But Alexi and I started out two birds of a nest, so I don't know that we've come to resemble each other any more than we did at first. Possible, I suppose."

Welkin gave her a sharp glance. "What's he like?" he asked. "If I know something about him, it might help to figure out where he could have gone."

"He's quiet," Miranda said. "Or do you mean what he looks like?"

"That, too."

"Half a head taller than you, somewhat thin, blond hair a little lighter than mine, gray eyes. Very North Coast."

"He should stand out in Bierdsey, then." Welkin folded the first letter and opened a second. This was the one that described the door of the Blue Swan so well Helsa had known it right away. "Ah, yes, and a gift for words," Welkin said. "But if you didn't know he was in Bierdsey, you wouldn't know the door belonged to the Bruised Goose. I'm sure others in the province have the same kind of carving."

She'd never thought about that.

"Well, go on," he prompted. "Is he timid, for instance?"

"Oh, no," Miranda said. "Far bolder than anyone ever suspects on first meeting him, because he's so quiet and courteous."

"Yes," Welkin drawled, a preoccupied sounding agreement. "They say lightkeepers have strong personalities."

Miranda remembered the young guard, Ethan, asking whether it was true that lightkeepers were—what? He hadn't said. "Is that what they say?" she asked.

Welkin glanced up at her. "One needs to be strong to live in a light tower, doesn't one? So exposed to the wind, and the sea so close."

"It's only a way to live, that's all," Miranda said. "Let's see. Alexi's not as talkative as me, and he's more forgiving." Welkin flashed her another glance. "I—it's hard, you know, to describe him. I know him in Gwynnhead, and he might be different in Bierdsey. I know I am."

Welkin pulled open a drawer and brought out a piece of paper. "I'm going to list the places I recognize," he said, uncapping a pen and writing something on the page. "The clock at Dames' Alley, for example. Have you been to the market since you arrived, Mrs. Glivven?"

"No, I haven't."

"Much more comfortable and colorful in summer, of course," Welkin said. "Your husband seems to have enjoyed it . . . Ah, here's the Firkin Lane pier. Seamen are always drawn to boats, it seems."

Miranda sat twisting her wedding ring, while Welkin read the letters. Once he looked up, saying, "I suppose he didn't put names in because he wasn't supposed to be writing to you. But he's so good at detail, no one who knows Bierdsey would ever doubt where he'd been." A little later, he glanced at her hand and remarked, "That's a handsome ring, Mrs. Glivven. I don't think I've seen one quite like it before."

She held out her hand for him to see it better. "Alexi designed it. The ivy symbolizes faithful love."

Welkin chuckled. "Must be a charm. One of the few that works."

"A charm! Hardly," Miranda said.

"But you must cherish it all the more for your husband's having made the design."

"Oh, yes." Miranda began to feel uncomfortable discussing the ring. She folded her hands in her lap, and Welkin, with a small formal smile, went back to Alexi's letters.

Within half an hour, Welkin had extracted a list of nine recognizable places, and a further seven with question marks beside them, one of those the Red Door Inn.

"Did you find out anything about the Guard?" Miranda asked, folding the list after she'd glanced at it.

"That's very strange," Welkin said. "Apparently an order to search for your husband was given, but somewhere between Morten Shells and the underassistant in charge of the Guard's day-to-day business it got lost. I strongly suspect that that underassistant was the man who tried to take Captain Lafass's place. He's got his neck to save."

"Kovan?"

"The man's name is Navocque. If you turn the sounds around, you get Kovan. Can you describe the man you saw?"

Miranda shrugged. "Brown hair and light brown eyes. He was rather ordinary, really, except for his hands. Those were quite well kept."

Welkin nodded. "That could be Navocque, all right. In any case, Captain Lafass is back in command as of yesterday afternoon, and the search should go forward. Let me know if you have any further trouble with the Guard."

And what about their trouble with the lightkeeper's wife? Miranda wondered. But she couldn't ask: she'd have to say where she got her information, and that would get that nice young guard, with his worrying wife, and his gossipy friend into trouble. "Thank you," she said.

"I'd go home and let them get on with their job, if I were you," Welkin advised. "Give them that list, and they can send a man around to ask after your husband."

Miranda had her doubts. But Welkin was already standing, smiling, and offering her his hand, urging her not to miss the next train to Bierdsey. "Yes," she agreed. "I've got to get back to the inn and feed my cat. It'll be starving."

"A cat? You're traveling with a cat?" Welkin exclaimed.

"Yes."

"How . . . bizarre. Isn't that a bit, er, inconvenient?"

"A bit." Miranda smiled. "It's nice to have a friend along, though," she added.

"Yes, I suppose so," Welkin agreed. "Good luck with it." She allowed him to lift her cloak onto her shoulders and said good-bye.

On the train, Miranda thought too late of other things to say about Alexi: that compared to her he was not only quieter but more indirect; that though he was no more intelligent than she, he was cleverer.

Thinking this, Miranda had a sudden insight. The scarlet geraniums, "reflecting the splendor of the door," in Alexi's phrase, had been blooming freely beside a public street when he wrote of them, not deadened by frost and dumped onto a compost heap somewhere, the dirt-encrusted barrels they'd been growing in stacked in an alley.

He couldn't have realized how long it would be before I decided to come, she thought with a sense of having failed him. *Oh, Alexi!*

And if another inn had painted its door red and placed geraniums in tubs beside it—on the road to Andrevver, say, or somewhere in Clunn? Then the railing with the sparrows perching in it was provided for confirmation that she had found the right place.

He'd written to her so that she wouldn't worry. But having decided to write, feeling threatened but still not wanting her to worry, he had put into the letters the means of finding him. Described the not really all *that* memorable door of his inn. Then described the one he moved to—*why?* What about that list of places Welkin had just given her? Were *all* of them clues? Were *some* of them clues and the rest just there as disguises? Or as confirmations? How was she to tell one from the other?

And all those words of love in the letter that described the house. Sincerely meant, without the slightest doubt, but

Miranda knew her Lexi just as well as he knew her: he didn't want her sharing the description of that house with anyone. What better way to make sure she kept it to herself than to pair it with something she'd want private?

Yes, Miranda thought. She'd give the list to the Guard. But she'd also look at all those places herself. She found a fountain pen in her purse and copied Welkin's list onto the blank space at the end of one of Alexi's letters, folded it up, and stuffed it back into her cloak.

She arrived at the Railway Inn to find the landlord stiffly indignant and Captain Lafass standing at the desk.

"Mrs. Glivven," both said at once as she entered. The landlord continued, "More trouble about your cat, Mrs. Glivven. It seems someone who's been staying here reported it to the Public Guard."

"Oh, dear." Miranda glanced at the captain. "I suppose you're here to arrest me?" The man who had walked through the door immediately behind her stopped to watch the encounter.

"I'm here to investigate," Captain Lafass said.

"I told him about your paper from the Prefect of Clunn," the landlord said. "I went up to your room and looked for it, but I couldn't find it."

"No," Miranda said. "After that other time, I've got it with me." She threw the wings of her cloak back and opened her purse. The letter of conduct was looking even shabbier around the edges than Alexi's letters. Miranda pulled it out and handed it to Lafass, who asked, "Does the cat have five toes?"

"It was born that way," Miranda said easily. "A complaint was made when I stopped in Clunn to wait for the Bierdsey train. Prefect Bikthen examined the cat, tested it, and found it to be a normal animal." At this, the nosy bystander—familiar-looking, Miranda noticed; probably another guest who'd been here awhile—went on up the stairs, to be replaced by a man who came out of the ale room and paused to find out why a captain of the Guard should be in the entrance hall of the Railway Inn.

"Yes," Lafass said, reading. "So I see. Do you recall how he performed the test?"

"Not really," Miranda told him. "He tested me, too, with a crystal and hypnosis, at the same time."

"Oh, he did use the crystal?"

Miranda nodded. "Fortunately, the man has a sense of humor. Apparently while being tested, I questioned his intelligence and sanity so vigorously, one of the guards with him nearly fainted."

Lafass smiled at that and handed the paper back. "May I see the cat for myself?"

"Surely."

"If you don't mind, I'll come up with you," Lavran said. The man who had been in the ale room was blocking the foot of the stairs and seemed not about to give up his vantage point. "If you'll excuse me?"

"Pardon?"

"Excuse me," the landlord repeated with heavy politeness. "You are standing in the way."

"Oh, sorry." The man moved slowly away from the stairs, still staring at the group inquisitively.

For the second time, her host led the way up to Miranda's room to look at the golden cat, Miranda and Lafass behind him.

The door of her room stood open. The cat was gone.

3

"No, Mrs. Glivven," the landlord said worriedly. "I'm quite sure I closed it, not ten minutes ago. I distinctly remember taking my key from the lock."

Lafass, examining the latch, agreed. "See these scratches?" he said. "The lock's been forced. That's the trouble with spring latches—anyone with a pocketknife can pop one open. You ought to have dead bolts."

"Our guests prefer doors that lock automatically," the landlord protested.

"But my cat!" Miranda said.

"Now, Mrs. Glivven," Lavran said. "Don't be upset. If the cat got out of your room, it's got to be somewhere in the inn, now, doesn't it? It could scarcely get outside by itself. We'll find the cat."

Miranda, recalling that this particular cat had managed to board a train unnoticed, was not that certain. Besides, "What if someone took it?" she pointed out.

Captain Lafass gazed speculatively at the landlord. "That would be quite a coincidence, wouldn't it? Coming just when the Guard took an interest?" He turned to Miranda. "Where were you coming from, just now?"

"The railroad station," she told him. "I'd been talking with Assistant Prefect Welkin and took the train from the Province House."

Lafass pulled a watch from his tunic pocket and looked at it. He nodded. "You're a healthy-looking woman, Mrs. Glivven, but I don't think you'd have had time to assess the situation, go 'round the block and in the kitchen door—"

"That's always locked from outside," the landlord put in.

"—gain admittance," Lafass went on, with a bow to Lavran, "release the cat, come back around the block and walk in the front door. At least, not without being quite out of breath."

"But who would want my cat?" Miranda clasped her hands and bowed her face to them. She was beginning to feel a surprisingly painful loss.

Lafass sent a messenger to the Guard office, requesting help. While they waited for the men to come, Miranda gave the captain the list Welkin had made and explained what it was, but before she could get any promise of action, three uniformed men had arrived and were searching the inn from top to bottom, knocking on doors and questioning guests. The landlord was white-lipped with fury. "Never before," he declared. "Never before, in all the years I've had this inn—"

But they found no cat, and no one had seen it. The Guard went away. Captain Lafass expressed regrets. The landlord could not bring himself to speak to her. Miranda retired to her room and sat on the bed, disconsolate.

A few minutes later, she heard a knock. Dragging herself to the door, she opened it. No one was there.

Prrrt, said something at her feet. Frozen with joy and amazement, Miranda watched the yellow cat slide past her ankles and jump onto the bed.

"There's an open skylight," Helsa reported later that evening. "If it wasn't one of the searchers left it open— and I will complain to them, lamb, do believe me—then maybe your cat got out and wandered about on the roof for a time."

"We could look for footprints," her husband said doubtfully.

His wife glanced the length of his broad body. "Not you, Lavran," she said. "Nor me, neither; I'm too stiff to climb up there."

"I'll look," Miranda volunteered. Again they climbed the stairs, this time to the third floor. In a storage room Helsa pointed out the open skylight. Miranda took a lamp on a long cord and stood on an upended wooden box to look out. Yes, many little five-toed footprints in the snow on the roof, just like the ones she had seen on her doorstep what seemed half her life ago. No large boot prints, as she had expected. A few white flakes were drifting out of the sky, the promise of the gray afternoon about to be fulfilled.

"That's where it was," she said, climbing down and closing the skylight after her.

"But it had to have help!" Helsa complained. "How did it get there? We don't leave skylights open. We'd have a room full of snow by morning."

The latch of the room bore scratches like the ones on her own, Miranda noted. So someone had taken the cat from her room and put it through the skylight. Maybe even closed the skylight and relocked the door. And when the Guard had gone, that someone had retrieved the cat, knocked so she would open her door, and retreated unseen.

"We won't tell Captain Lafass about this," the landlord stated.

"But Lavran, we really should, shouldn't we, dear?" his wife protested. "It's such a peculiar thing for anyone to do."

"I do not want the Guard tromping about in my inn asking questions of my guests twice in a single day. It's insulting and it's bad for business." The landlord gazed at Miranda. "Have you made a friend among the guests, perhaps, Mrs. Glivven?"

She shook her head. "Not that I know of."

"Or the staff? But no," he answered himself, "anyone on the staff could have used a key. The extras all hang on that board in the back hall. Well," he sighed. "We'll just leave it that the cat came back, and thanks to whomever." They started down the stairs, Miranda stopping at her room and Lavran and Helsa going on down to the first floor.

Miranda had to admit she was grateful. But she also had to admit that she would be much happier if she knew why the cat had been moved. "I *do* know who did it," she told the cat. "That man who came in right behind me—I noticed that he looked familiar, but I was taken up with the captain at the time and didn't think much about it." *Where had she seen him before?*

Giving up the effort to recall, Miranda opened her suitcase to get out her nightdress. It had been searched again— by the same hands as before? By the landlord, who had *told* her he'd looked for her letter of conduct? Or by the unknown skylight-opener?

No way to tell. Miranda bolted her door and went to bed. She was almost asleep when she remembered where she had seen the man who had puzzled her that evening: in the Central Library, reading the same newspaper for hours at a time.

ROSTT

1

Before going down to breakfast the next morning, Miranda read over her copy of Welkin's list. Sixteen places Alexi had described, with Welkin's firm or tentative identifications. She'd find out where each was and go look. Maybe, as at the Blue Swan and the Red Door Inn, she'd find someone who remembered Alexi—and, most important, anyone who had been with him.

At the dining hall entrance she paused. The room, as usual at this hour, was rather crowded.

"There'll be a short wait, Mrs. Glivven," the waiter said. "Unless you'd be willing to share a table."

Miranda had been scanning the room. In a far corner she glimpsed a face that looked familiar, before a newspaper was quickly raised. Now the face, from the eyes up, reappeared momentarily, then was hidden again. "That gentleman over in the corner," she said to the waiter. "Is he expecting anyone? Seat me with him."

"I'll have to ask his permission first, of course," the waiter told her, and started across the dining hall.

Now I'll get somewhere, she told herself grimly. The waiter stopped at the table. The newspaper was lowered slightly. After a moment the waiter started back and nodded to her. Miranda met him in the middle of the room and followed him to the table while giving her order. She sat down. Her new breakfast companion kept right on reading.

"You'll have to put it down sometime," she said quietly. "Unless you don't mind cold fried eggs."

The paper stayed up.

"Who are you, may I ask?" she continued. "The Guard doesn't seem to know about you." Still no sign that she had been heard. "I could make an official complaint, I suppose—"

"Oh, don't do that." The man lowered the newspaper. Just as she'd thought, the same man who had been so helpful at the Province House the day before yesterday; the same one who had worn the new farmer's jacket yesterday afternoon.

"I hope the jacket didn't cost much." Miranda smiled sweetly. "It wasn't that good a disguise."

Her breakfast companion rolled his eyes toward the ceiling. The waiter came back with her pancakes and tea.

"But I would like to know how you knew I'd be on that train," Miranda went on after the meal had been set.

"You're an anxious woman," the man said. "And I'd had a glance at Welkin's appointment book after you saw him. Six o'clock, Miranda Glivven. I didn't think you'd take the five-fifteen train. That left the four-thirty, and I knew about the demonstration from the newspaper."

She hadn't really expected an answer, but having one, saw no reason she shouldn't have more. "Why are you following me?"

"Because that is what I've been paid to do."

"By whom?"

Her tablemate raised his eyebrows. "A man with a deep purse, I can tell you that."

"What's he paying you to do, besides follow me?"

"Keep you out of trouble."

Miranda cut a rolled pancake with the side of her fork. Blueberry jam oozed out. "That's kind of him, whoever he is, but I think it's a waste of money."

He shrugged.

"I suppose you're the one who sent the note about not running in front of trains."

"No."

She continued to eat. Her companion laid aside his folded newspaper and started on his cooling eggs. "And the gloves?" she inquired.

"That was me."

"Thank you. And hiding the cat from the Guard, last night?"

"Two of the others."

"*Two* of the others! How many of you are there?"

"Four. That I know of."

"Did they search my room, too, a couple of days ago?"

"Don't know."

And wouldn't say if you did. "You can tell your employer, from me, that if he didn't have people trying so hard to keep me out of trouble, I wouldn't be tempted to run in front of trains."

"I'll pass it on."

"I am grateful about the cat. I suppose Captain Lafass would have taken it away to have it tested, or just destroyed."

"We're supposed to make sure the cat's all right, too."

Miranda gazed at him for several seconds. *Landers Bikthen.* Nobody else would care about the cat. What had the man gotten her into, that his conscience bothered him this much? Because it had to be Bikthen, didn't it? He was the only wealthy man she knew, other than Welkin, whom she'd only met two days ago. Unless it *was* the Guard? But then, why rescue the cat? "Keep that paper with you," her companion said. "The one you showed Lafass."

But I'd have left it in the room if Jorja hadn't complained, Miranda thought. She gazed at her companion with narrowed eyes; he seemed interested in his plate. "Were you the one who paid Jorja to look at the cat?" she asked.

"Don't know any Jorja." He turned the newspaper over.

But he wasn't surprised. One of the others, then. "And what about Alexi?"

"He's your problem."

"Hmm." Miranda tilted the teapot over her mug. Watching the pale brown stream, she asked, "When's your employer going home?"

The man across the table cleared his throat. "What makes you think he's not at home?"

Miranda knew that tone of voice, and the far-too-innocent expression that went with it: Hathden and Steth had trained her well. "A lucky guess."

"Far as I know, he is at home." The man drained his mug. "Nice talking to you, Mrs. Glivven. You're not planning to go out to the Province House again today, are you?"

"No."

He smiled: the friendly stranger again. "It would be nice to have my ticket in advance. Got a nasty bruise on one shin running for the train the other day."

"I'll try to move more slowly today," she told him. "You'll be glad to know I'm planning to travel on foot."

"A great relief." He got up, smiled at her, and walked quickly out of the room.

I suppose I'll never see him again, Miranda thought. Not the best idea to confront him, maybe. Now she'd have to figure out who his replacement was.

With Helsa's intrigued assistance, Miranda mapped out the most efficient route connecting her sixteen sites. She set forth filled with hope, which dwindled with each failure to find anybody who remembered Alexi from the late summer. Other than a woman in a shop near Dames' Alley who thought she *might* recall selling him an orange, she found no one. No guards had been asking for him at any of the spots she visited.

Hungry, she decided to return to the Railway Inn for lunch, and to check to see whether anyone had left her a message. A train was nearing the station when she crossed the footbridge.

"Yes, lamb, there's a letter for you," Helsa informed her cheerfully. "Came by messenger just after you left. Looks promising." She held out an envelope: thick, creamy paper addressed to her in black ink, not a hand Miranda knew.

"Thanks," she said, tearing the envelope open.

"That's wealthy paper, that is, lamb," Helsa was saying. "Nobody common sent you that!"

A different hand had written the message inside. Miranda recognized Welkin's tidy script and read eagerly,

> I've found someone who may know something about what happened to your husband, but since I'm not nearly as familiar with the case as you are, I would like you with me when I go to question him. Take the one o'clock train to Rostt. It's the same train as stops at the Province House. I'll join you on the train if at all possible, but take this letter with you to serve as introduction if I'm prevented from getting away.

"The one o'clock train to Province House!" Miranda wailed, glancing at the clock behind Helsa. "Oh, no! I'll never make it."

"It's about your husband, lamb?"

"Yes, but—"

"Go, go, go! You can buy your ticket on the train!"

Miranda flung herself back through the door and across the lane. The train was still at the platform. She rounded the end of the station and saw the sign for Province House on the side of a car. Stretching her stride, she made a dash.

The trainman saw her coming. He let the steps drop back into place and held out a hand. She grabbed it and swung aboard the slowly moving train. "*Phew*," she said. "Thanks."

"Left it a bit late, missus," he commented.

"Only just got word of an appointment," Miranda panted. "Important. I hope I can buy a ticket from you?"

"Province House?" the man asked.

"No—" She still held the letter in her left hand, not even folded; she glanced at it and said, "Rostt."

"Return?"

"Yes."

"Wait here a minute, until I get us secured," the trainman told her. He came back five minutes later, when the train was moving through the tunnel, and handed her a ticket stamped *Rostt.* "A luker each way, missus," he said. "That's two."

Miranda found coin to pay him and swayed down the aisle to drop into a seat. Hardly anyone else was on the train. She couldn't believe her luck. What if she hadn't decided to go back to the inn? A growl from her stomach reminded her of why she had gone. "Hush, you," she murmured. *I'm going to find Alexi,* her heart sang. *I know it, I know it, I know it!*

The train seemed to dawdle unconscionably, and as it slowed for the Province House station, Miranda pulled out her watch and looked at it. Half an hour, just as scheduled. She'd chosen the wrong side of the car to see who might be on the platform, and as the train began moving again waited anxiously to see whether Welkin would appear.

"Ah, there you are," he said from behind her. He slipped his cloak off and leaned across her to hang it on one of the hooks beside the window, smiling. "I was afraid I might have sent my letter too late to catch you this morning."

"I did just make it," Miranda told him.

"I'm glad you did," he said, sliding into the seat beside her. "I have great hope of this."

She was surprised at how plainly Welkin was dressed. The first day she had seen him, he had been wearing an elaborately seamed tunic of dark green wool over green trousers with a heavy gold purse-chain encircling his waist; the second day, dark blue with smocking on the yoke and the wide sleeves Bierdsey fashion favored, worn over gray trousers. Today he had chosen something Jem Rodde might easily find in his closet: under a plain blue wool cloak not all that different from her own, Welkin's tunic was unadorned brown wool, his trousers the same.

He saw her glancing at his dress and grinned. "No fancy appointments today—Prefect Bikthen's gone home to Clunn, the advisors aren't in session, nobody's scheduled a hearing. Why dress up? Just puts more wear on the clothes."

"Yes, I suppose so," Miranda agreed. She liked to dress up, but not every day. She was wearing her mended blue trousers, a fact she only now recalled.

"Did you find your cat well?" he asked. "Yesterday you seemed a bit worried about it."

"You know, that's the strangest thing," Miranda said. "When I got back to the inn, there was Captain Lafass of the Guard. Someone at the inn had complained of the cat."

Welkin blinked at her. "And called a captain of the Guard?"

"It's that the beast has extra toes," Miranda sighed. The trainman came by for Welkin's ticket. They were riding through the same sort of neighborhood she had seen just the other side of Province House: large homes screened with evergreens. A desultory snow was falling.

The trainman moved on. "Extra toes," Welkin said musingly. He had a faint aura of satisfaction about him. "So I suppose the captain wanted to see the beast for himself?"

"Yes, though I showed him the letter of conduct Prefect Bikthen gave me when I passed through Clunn. And then—"

"Wait, wait. You're going too fast for me, Mrs. Glivven." Welkin gave her a perplexed sort of smile. "What letter of conduct is that?"

Miranda sighed and told him about the old woman at Clunn, the test, the letter.

"Ah, I see. But you showed Captain Lafass the cat, and he too was satisfied?"

"No, that's what I'm trying to say. When we got up to my room, the cat was gone."

"Gone!" Welkin echoed. "So you've lost your friend? How trying for you!"

He is *a charmer,* Miranda thought. "No, not really. After Lafass left, somebody returned it."

Welkin gazed at her sideways, a stare that had something of calculation in it. "The cat is healthy, then," he said.

"Yes."

The man looked almost relieved.

The train began to slow. Miranda, recalling the list of destinations on her ticket, figured herself one stop short of Rostt.

"Let's get off here," Welkin said suddenly, getting up. "I'd like to stop at home for some papers I don't have with me."

"Won't this person be waiting for us at Rostt?" Miranda objected.

"Yes, but I'm sure he'll wait a few minutes longer," Welkin assured her. "It won't take more than a minute or two to fetch the papers out of my study, and then we can take my gig to Rostt. The road's a lot shorter than the track. We might even beat the train." He had his cloak on and was holding hers, waiting for her to present her shoulders.

She murmured her thanks and preceded him along the car. The iron wheels shrieked against the track as always; the brakes puffed air. They stopped with a jolt.

"I didn't telegraph for anyone to meet us," Welkin said apologetically as they descended the train steps. "But it's less than five minutes' walk."

"I'm used to walking." Miranda gathered her cloak around her and followed Welkin across a desolate platform and onto a wide lane through the evergreens. "So many spruce trees," she remarked. "All along the track."

"They're a sound barrier," Welkin explained. "So one can live conveniently close to the railroad without having to listen to trains rumbling past at all hours."

"Ah," Miranda acknowledged. The uses of wealth!

On the other side of the band of spruces, the lane went on, now parallel to the track, to press back into the barrier a little farther along. Miranda was happy to see they were heading toward Rostt—at least they wouldn't lose time backtracking.

"That's the house," Welkin said, nodding toward a steep gray slate roof visible through more spruces and some bare-branched trees Miranda thought must be lindens. "And there's the drive. Not far at all."

Miranda glanced at him. Had she detected a faint edge to his voice? As if he were nervous. *What am I walking into?* she wondered. Whatever it was, she would have to brave it: she couldn't let cowardice jeopardize her chances of finding Alexi.

The house had a multitude of narrow windows, she saw as they came to the end of the drive. Narrow windows with arched tops, somewhat pointed, a five-petaled floral shape inset in each arch. Exactly what Alexi had described in the letter she had tucked into her suitcase pocket.

Welkin's house.

He was walking to the side, around the end of one wing. "We'll go straight into my study from the court-yard," he said. "It's fastest. Unless you want to wait out-side?"

Did he *want* her to wait outside? *What is he hiding?* Miranda wondered. "No," she said. "I'll come in."

Enclosed by this wing of the house, the body of the house, another wing, and a high wall was what looked to be a fairly large courtyard. Welkin pushed open a tall, very new-looking wooden door and led her in. She thought she knew precisely what she would see.

But the courtyard did not match Alexi's description: the stone-bordered windows were shaped the same, but the stone here was blackened, with a glassy sheen; where Alexi had said an ancient oak grew to shade the court stood a charred stump only half again as tall as a man. All the wooden window sashes were new, or freshly painted. What had once been lawn was now tumbled ground, the snow sifting gently into a huge glassy scar.

"What happened here?" Miranda exclaimed.

"Lightning struck the tree, late last summer." Welkin started across the courtyard, talking over his shoulder. "A freakish incident, and just my ill luck to suffer it. It was a miracle no one was hurt."

"It looks it." Miranda couldn't tear her gaze from the tree stump.

"The tree must have been three hundred years old," Welkin went on. "A lovely, huge old white oak. I won't see another like it here in my lifetime. A pity, but we're on a bit of a hill here. I suppose if I'd had the sense of a nanny goat I'd have fitted the tree with a lightning rod. Never occurred to me."

"Were you here?" she asked.

"No, thank fate, and I'd given the servants a day out. No one was home." He'd reached a door, which he pulled open. "A lot of expensive repair," he went on. "And it will be a full year before that court's presentable again. You saw the crater?" He was climbing steps inside. Miranda followed, glad to leave the courtyard. Imagine, that lightning could begin to melt granite walls, in one brief instant! But maybe the strike had been repeated. That sometimes happened to her own tower—*well*-grounded, thank you!

At the top of the stairs, Welkin crossed a landing and opened another door. "Here we are," he said. "I'll just be a minute or two."

The hallway had been cool, but in Welkin's study a fire had been built some time ago, making a good bed of coals. With the central heating, the room was almost too warm.

"Books!" Miranda said, walking over to a bank of shelves as Welkin hung her cloak on a cloaktree. *Imagine owning all these books!* Hundreds of them, on shelves that completely lined the walls, shelves broken only by the door, the fireplace and its hood, and the narrow windows with the—the "roses," Alexi had called them—set in the pointed arches. Filled with colored glass, Miranda saw now that light came toward her through them, yellow centers and pink petals, like the wild roses that grew among the dunes on the mainland east of Gwynnhead.

"You enjoy reading, Mrs. Glivven?" Welkin asked pleasantly. He had gone to a large table that seemed to serve as a desk, and now he sat down behind it, casually moving aside a large round crystal paperweight with a spiral of white inside it, and opened a drawer. Miranda glanced at the books near her. Philosophy and theory of government, mostly, with a heavy salting of history and foreign policy.

"Yes, I do," she said, moving to scan the next section of shelves. More history; a few biographies of famous statesmen. After a moment it struck her that she did not hear Welkin moving, or any rustle of papers. She turned.

He was still sitting at the desk with his fingers interlaced and his chin resting on them, watching her.

"What about those papers?" she asked. "Won't the person you want to talk to be wondering where we are?"

"I'm sure it won't be a problem."

"Are you?" Miranda walked to the desk, too agitated to hold still. "Please, Mr. Welkin—"

"Sit down, Mrs. Glivven."

A quiet command; one that held no option of disobedience. Miranda sank onto a nearby chair.

"You should have gone home and let me handle all this," Welkin said. "That's what the simple housewife you pretend to be would have done. But you didn't. Did you?"

"Gone home?" Miranda repeated, confused. "No! You said you could help me find Alexi! That's why I came with you—"

"Did you really think you had fooled me?"

Miranda stared. Now Welkin lifted his head and clasped his hands on the desk. On the middle finger of his right hand he was wearing a broad band of gold set with a cabochon sapphire. The band was chased with a design of twining ivy. She had drawn the pattern for those leaves herself, and seen the ring nearly every day for eighteen years.

"That's his ring!" She shot to her feet and tugged at Welkin's hand. "You've got his ring!"

Welkin jerked his hand away. "And you know what that means, don't you?" He stood up. "I've got your husband's power, Mrs. Glivven, for all his life, and in just a little while I'll have yours, too."

"Power?" Miranda's jaw dropped. "What are you talking about?"

"Two birds in a nest, you said. If you have half the power to do magic your husband did, nothing on earth will stop me from becoming Governor."

"What?"

"A few more calculated blunders by Shells, poor fellow, and I'll be chosen Prefect of Bierdsey. And I will be a good one, Mrs. Glivven, that I promise. But the country needs me even more than this province does. I'm a hard worker,

a sensible man, intelligent and knowledgeable enough to
deal with other heads of state—"

Miranda shook the meaningless words away. "Give me
Alexi's ring," she demanded.

"You must see that it's for the good of all of us," Welkin
said reasonably. "I had to take severe measures when Shells
wasn't chosen Governor: that meant far too long a delay.
Your husband was trying to stop me. That I could not
permit."

"Give me my husband's ring."

"What kind of idiot do you think I am?" Welkin laughed
incredulously. "Give you his ring? After what I went through
to get it?" He gestured toward the courtyard windows. "You
saw what he did out there."

"It's chased to my design," Miranda said, sure that if
she could just explain how important it was to her, Welkin
would hand the ring over. "The gem was my grandfather's.
My father gave it to me just before he died, for Alexi."

"Exactly." Welkin began to gesture slowly with his right
hand, murmuring phrases in the Elder Speech. None of the
poems she'd learned by rote in school, none of the old tales
of wise ancient women or voyaging heroes.

"What are you saying?" she demanded. "I can't understand the Elder Speech. Tell me what you've done with
Alexi."

He muttered louder. She caught the word *vexelen:* change,
repeated in a commanding tone. Suddenly she understood.
"Are you trying to work magic on me?" She gasped, still
not able to believe a modern, intelligent man could credit
such nonsense. "You silly man!"

Welkin frowned. His chant shifted, became faster and
more rhythmic, while Miranda shook her head at him, her
mouth stretched in such astonishment she almost forgot
the ring.

"Vexelen, Mirant, zau akomt, vexelen!"

Miranda said scornfully, "Next you'll be wanting a hair
of my head." Welkin continued chanting, louder and faster.
She combed her fingers through her hair until a loose strand
caught between them and held it out between finger and

thumb. "Here, does this please you?"

"Why isn't it working?" Welkin sounded as disbelieving as she was herself.

"Because magic is nonsense, that's why," Miranda snapped, tossing the hair on the fire. She crossed the room and reached for her cloak. "You've stolen Alexi's ring. If you won't return it, we'll see what the Guard has to say. You aren't above the law, just because you're senior assistant to the Prefect of Bierdsey."

. Welkin rushed across the room. He grabbed the back of her tunic and yanked. She staggered backward. Before she could catch her balance, he was on her, hands at her throat.

Rage swept down her spine. She heaved herself sideways with all of her strength, only to roll both of them over. Welkin's fingers still gripped her neck. His lips were drawn back over his teeth.

I will not be killed by hands that wear Alexi's ring, Miranda thought. She got her elbows between Welkin's arms, forced them apart, jabbed a knee into his belly, and levered herself away. Scrambling to her feet, she dashed for the door.

"Abskleesen!" Welkin said sharply.

Miranda tugged at the door. Locked.

"Locked," she whispered, turning to face Welkin. Panting slightly, he stood a couple of yards from her.

"Not locked, Mrs. Glivven," he said softly. "Under a spell. As long as I will that door shut, no power on earth can open it. Not even yours."

She filled her lungs and screamed.

Welkin chuckled. "Do you think I'd bring you to the house if it weren't empty? Do you think any passerby could hear you through these walls? Come, come, Mrs. Glivven!"

He'd attacked out of panic, Miranda saw. Now he was back in control, more dangerous than ever: he had a bungled job to finish. She darted to the windows. Stuck shut. A long drop, anyway. Backed against a bookcase, she said, "I'll get out somehow," trying to sound calm and by some miracle succeeding. "And then we'll see what the prefect thinks of his senior assistant engaging in magical practice."

"That," he told her smugly, "is precisely what Zara Rodde said, not ten seconds before I used the letter opener." Miranda thought of the windows in Welkin's Province House office, windows that were also doors, windows that opened all but directly above the river where Zara Rodde had drifted, rotting, for almost a month. She felt a chill begin in her stomach. Welkin walked unconcernedly to the fireplace and picked up the poker. "Now, Miranda."

Her eyes were drawn to the poker's sharp point, meant to prick at a falling log and bent upward for leverage. She edged away, looking for a weapon of her own. Welkin ducked the books she snatched from the shelves and threw at him. Moving sideways, her gaze locked with his, she tripped over a chair. Shoving it at him, she dodged around the desk.

The paperweight! Miranda grabbed for it. The crystal sphere was hot to her touch. She held on and flung it at Welkin. With a cry, he tried to catch it and missed. It shattered against the hearth. A wisp of white smoke came out. A thick, musky, floral odor filled the air.

"That was unwise," Welkin remarked. "But now that you've loosed it, let's see what it can do." He started to chant, "*Vexelen, Mirant, zau akomt, vexelen, vexelen.*" Even so, he must have realized that his chant couldn't work; he began to stalk her with the poker raised. Heart in her mouth, Miranda decided to stand her ground.

The poker slashed down. Miranda sidestepped. The steel rang against the desktop. Welkin winced and recovered. He circled the desk, seconds ticking away between his steps. She tried to keep the heavy wood between them, tried to see the small movement that would herald his attack.

Suddenly she had a better idea. The fragments of the crystal sphere were rounded: treacherous footing. If he hit and missed, standing on those? Miranda began to circle the room just out of Welkin's reach, drawing him after her. When his feet were almost among the shards she stopped. He stepped forward. The poker whistled toward her.

Dancing back, she crowed as he slipped and fell.

"I'll get you," he said, still unruffled. "We have all afternoon." He rocked back onto his knees and stood.

Miranda wrenched at the door, but the knob seemed to slither out of her grasp. She glanced to see where the bolt had been thrown, saw none, barely pivoted away from the descending poker. Welkin dropped it and caught her by one arm.

That he had touched her again filled her with fury. She set her heels and tried to pull away, but he dragged her off her feet and rolled onto her. Miranda hugged her head to protect her neck. Welkin pried at her arms. One hand reached her throat. He shifted his weight onto it. Again, she twisted sideways and managed to displace him. The poker was within her reach. She grabbed it and pulled away, but now he had her left arm in both hands and she could buy no room to swing.

A few stitches popped in the armhole seam of her tunic, ridiculously loud. She struggled onto one knee. The image of the letter opener sliding into Zara Rodde's throat, or her heart, filled her mind. *Ah, but the poker is sharp!*

With all her weight behind the thrust she stabbed beneath Welkin's ribs. A look of bewilderment crossed his face. His grip loosened. Miranda pushed harder, going for the heart without having to think. The poker sank deep into his body.

"You," he gasped. "You just don't believe. That's why. You really don't believe."

She pulled the poker out. A red stain spread quickly over his chest. He tried twice to get up and fell back. "Extraordinary," he whispered. A bubble of blood came out of his nose.

"I'm sorry," Miranda breathed. "I'm sorry."

He looked toward her and nodded slightly. His lips formed a word, with no sound behind it. The bubble of blood collapsed into his moustache. There wasn't another.

Crouched out of reach, Miranda watched the man's face slowly empty in death. After a time, the door clicked and sighed open.

She got up. *Alexi's ring.* Welkin's fist was clenched, but his hand was far smaller than Alexi's, the ring far too big. She worked the circle of gold over his knuckles and out of his palm, shuddering at the touch of the dead flesh. "I'm sorry," she whispered again, and steeled herself for one more touch, to close the blank eyes.

2

How Miranda got out to the courtyard, she wasn't quite sure. Cold wind on her face brought her out of a sort of daze. She'd left her cloak in that room.

The dark windows of the house looked down on her. No one home, Welkin had said. Where were his servants? Had anyone been waiting at Rostt?

No. *He brought me here to kill me,* she thought, astounded. *What threat was I to him?* Shivering, Miranda went reluctantly back to that room and took her cloak from the stand just inside the door. *Don't look, don't look,* she ordered herself, but she did look: Welkin had not moved.

What was that he had said about Alexi's power? *Think, Miranda!* Something about having his power, for all his life? Hadn't he *said,* "For all his life?" Power because of the ring?

The cherished possession! Yes. Miranda tried to recall exactly what the book she had skimmed in the Central Library had said about cherished possessions . . . they could transfer power. Wasn't that it? And Welkin had believed that because he had Alexi's ring, he had Alexi's power. His remark about how she must cherish her own ring, so casually made while reading Alexi's letters, took on a chilling significance.

But if Alexi had to be alive for the power to be usable, then Welkin must also believe he was still living. Here? Where he could keep a few credulous servants in line with fear of what he might do to them?

Miranda began to jog through the house, stopping every few yards to call, "Alexi!" at the top of her lungs and listen for a reply. Only silence. No room she opened was occupied. No closet held a bound man; the dust in the attic had not been disturbed for years; the only sound in the cellars was the rustle of mice shocked by her light and noise.

She had been in the house at least two hours. The servants Welkin had sent away might come back at any moment. She had Hathden and Steth to think of: imagine losing one parent, his fate forever a mystery, and having the other jailed for the rest of her life, all within a couple of months! Hathden, yes, Hathden was close enough to manhood, but Steth was still more than half a boy.

As reluctantly as she had fetched her cloak, Miranda returned to the courtyard. The snow fell more heavily now, larger flakes that stuck to one side of the black column that had been the yard-thick trunk of an oak. Her footprints, and Welkin's, had been obliterated. She went quickly to the door in the courtyard wall and slipped out.

"Think, Miranda," she said aloud. *Don't go back to the same station.* She had a ticket from Rostt to Bierdsey. Getting on at the nearby station would surely make her stick in the trainman's mind: a scared blond woman with a ticket from the wrong place.

No, get on at Rostt. Welkin had lied about almost everything since the moment she had first met him, but he wouldn't lie about the road to Rostt being shorter than the track, would he? When she might so easily have looked at a map and be made wary by that lie?

She shouldn't put footprints on the drive, possibly to alert a returning servant. Sticking close to the courtyard wall, Miranda circled the house to come out on the side closest to Rostt. No one seemed to be around. She struck off across the lawn, sickly aware of the line of footprints stretching behind her, and went into the band of evergreens. The walking wasn't as hard as she'd feared. Thin dead branches crisscrossed her way, but the snow scarcely filtered through the needles above her. She broke through the branches and came cautiously out on the lane well beyond the end of Welkin's drive. Still no one. The only sound was the wind singing in the treetops. Here on the lane, everything was hushed.

"Extraordinary," someone seemed to whisper. Miranda stifled a sob and plunged on, running now. Not three hours ago she had descended from the train filled with hope. Now she had been stripped of that hope and become a murderer. It didn't seem possible.

She reached Rostt as dusk began to fall, tired, wet, and cold. The town was even smaller than Gwynnhead. Miranda met no one as she followed the lane, which had become the high street of the village. *Outcast,* she thought, looking enviously at the lighted windows as she tramped past thinking of her own placid home. *Murderer.*

The station was only a long stone platform with a small shelter where a schedule was posted. She had twenty minutes to wait. No one else was on the platform or in the shelter. Of two minds—to wait in the snow and dark or out of the snow in the light of a bare electric bulb—she stood at the edge of the shadow. It was snowing even harder than when she had left Welkin's house, finer flakes that stung her face as if in revenge. The wind had increased, sending veils of white through the light of the station. Miranda watched snow tumble into the footprints she had left on the platform and begin to drift them shut, like slowly closing mouths. The idea that she might actually, for a little while, get away with murder, might even get back to Gwynnhead and her sons, took root.

The train was a little bit late, but warm and dry. Fewer than half a dozen passengers sat in the car she boarded, drowsing or reading. Miranda spread her wet cloak across one whole seat and sank wearily onto the one behind it. The trainman, one she hadn't seen before, came by and took her ticket with a cheery remark about the weather to which she tried to respond in kind. When he moved on, she let her head sink back against the seat and shut her eyes. Her tunic. She felt the sprung seam at the back of her arm and decided it wouldn't show much. At the next stop, she tensed, but there was no hue and cry: no one got on. If lamps had been lit in Welkin's house, she could not see them through the wall of evergreens.

• • •

"There you are!"

Miranda opened her eyes. The man whose breakfast she had invaded stood in the aisle, rocking with the motion of the train. "I thought you were going afoot," he complained. "All four of us have been looking for you all afternoon."

"Have you?" Miranda said weakly.

He frowned. "Your tunic's torn."

"Yes," she said. "Comes of strain on the sleeve."

"Oh, that two-handed grab by the trainman, right? That was some dash you made," he went on. "I nearly ran under the wheels, trying to catch the train. Had to settle for hiring a gig. Didn't see you at the Province House?"

"Nor did I see you," Miranda said. Her voice seemed to come from somewhere very far away.

"Are you all right?" the man asked, with swift concern. "You look pale."

"I'm fine." As she turned her face to the window he dropped into the seat beside her.

"You're sure?"

Miranda let her head come to rest in the angle between the seat and the window. "I've given up, that's all," she said, again closing her eyes, only to see a dying man's lips shape a soundless word and wonder again what he had tried to say. The racket of the train seemed to make the marrow jitter inside her bones. "I'm going home."

CLUNN, AND HOME

1

The hunger that had driven her to the Railway Inn several hours ago had vanished, but in the station at Bierdsey Miranda bought two meat pies from the food vendor, one for the cat and one in case she should ever be able to eat again. Before crossing the lane, she checked the schedule posted by the ticket window: a train left for Clunn the next morning at seven.

"I'd like one ticket for Clunn, please," she told the seller.

"Return?"

Return! Miranda shuddered. *Never!* "No, one way."

She tucked the ticket into her purse, remembered to buy a newspaper for the cat's comfort from the boy outside, and trudged across to the inn.

"Lamb?" the landlord's wife called from the desk.

No, Miranda thought. *A lamb gets slaughtered, and today I've done the slaughtering.* She forced a smile and went over.

"Oh, dear." With brow puckered, Helsa searched her face. "It didn't work out, did it?"

"No." Miranda folded her arms on top of the tall desk, partly to keep herself upright. "Helsa, I'm giving up. I'm going home to my boys."

There was a long moment's silence. "Well, lamb, you did what you could, and a lot more than most wives would be able to."

I killed a man, Miranda thought. *I wouldn't have thought I'd be able to bring myself to that, when I opened that letter this afternoon.* "Maybe you should add up my bill," she said. "There's a train for Clunn at seven tomorrow morning. Oh, dear. Are the banks still open?"

"You'd have to hurry, lamb."

"Do you mind? I've bought the cat some supper—could you hold it for me until I come back?"

Helsa took the paper sack and the newspaper, and Miranda went back out into the snow. The bank was a fair distance, her boots were soaked and her feet icy; she was glad when she had cashed her letters of credit and could start back.

After a few yards a man fell into step beside her. Miranda looked up at him. "You again," she sighed. "Don't you ever rest?"

"I could ask the same of you," he pointed out.

She shrugged. "I had some business to do."

"Cashing in your credit."

"I have to pay for my lodging."

"I know. That's why I'm walking back to the inn with you. It's dark, if you haven't noticed, and a woman coming out of the bank alone at this hour might present a temptation to some. You've got me too tuckered out to run to your rescue."

"Oh." Miranda felt a small flame of gratitude begin to warm the chill that had settled inside her. "Thanks."

"Call it restitution for losing you earlier."

No, Miranda thought. *I lost you. And then myself.* They took the footbridge over the railroad tracks, descended to the platform, and crossed to the inn in unstrained silence. At the door, Miranda said, "Go home and rest. I'm not going out again today for anything. It's too nasty a night to be out watching over middle-aged sillies from the North Coast."

The friendly stranger smiled. "You're too nice a lady for Bierdsey, Mrs. Glivven. Take care of yourself." He went off into the snow, cloak wrapped tight, and Miranda pushed through the door. Helsa had the account added up, including tonight's lodging. She paid.

"Oh, and your pussycat's supper," the landlord's wife added, ducking under the desk to retrieve the bag and the paper. "Will you be down to dinner, lamb?"

"I—I don't know. I don't seem to have much appetite."

"Was the news bad?"

Very bad, Miranda thought. "It just wasn't really news. And I guess I want to see my boys and sleep in my own bed."

"That list you had didn't help?"

Can't you leave me alone? Miranda wanted to say. She shook her head and assembled a smile. "I'd better go feed the cat."

She was shaking when she reached the top of the stairs. Cold. Remorse. Fear. She missed the lock with her key, twice; slid the key home on the third try, used both hands to turn it, and stumbled into the room.

When she switched on the lamp, she found the cat sitting on the windowsill, looking out. As she took off her cloak it jumped onto the bed and stretched, ears back in a yawn.

"Supper, cat." Her voice was unsteady. She put one of the meat pies down and changed the newspaper, not bothering to read any of the new one. Back in the room after disposing of the old one, she sat on the bed and watched the cat eat.

"We're going home tomorrow morning," she told it. The cat glanced up at the sound of her voice and went back to the pie. Now, with a sting, the tears began. "Oh, cat," Miranda whispered. "I've killed a man." The cat kept eating. "He was power-mad and self-centered and he killed a woman and he was trying to kill me," she said, and thought, *but he was also pleasant and likable and very good at his job.* Aloud, she went on, "And I think he may have been the only one who knew what happened to Alexi." The cat, at this extended whisper, glanced over its shoulder. "So now we'll never know."

Somebody tapped at her door. "It's me, lamb," the landlord's wife called. Wearily, Miranda got up and let her in. "Look at you! You haven't even taken off those wet boots," Helsa fussed. She set a tray on the low chest of drawers. "I'll bet you never even ate your noon meal, that's how hard you go at your search. So I brought you some soup."

Miranda tried to smile. "Thank you," she said.

"It'll slide down easy," Helsa assured her. "I know you don't much feel like eating, and that's normal, lamb, with what you've been through. But you ought to try to put something in your stomach or you'll be faint before you know it."

The soup did slide down easy, and after it, the extra meat pie. But Miranda slept poorly that night, and when she slept, dreamed of crystal spheres that shattered with a puff of white smoke and a cloying odor, of bloodstains claiming coarse brown cloth thread by thread, of a man who gazed at her, baffled, and whispered, "Extraordinary."

Miranda had packed everything but her nightdress and the clothes she intended to wear on the train before going to bed, and had asked to be called at five-thirty. But it was almost six when Jorja knocked on her door.

"The mistress told me to let you sleep a bit extra," the maid explained. "And she's sent up your breakfast. You're not to think even once about the cost, she says. It's her treat."

Jorja carried the breakfast in on a large tray. Miranda scooped last night's soup tray off the dresser to let her set the new one down, thanked her, and looked with dismay at the four quilted caps keeping the food hot. How could she manage to down such a breakfast? But to her surprise, she ate every bit, except for a large sausage she fed to the cat.

She made the train to Clunn with at least a minute to spare. The sun had just risen. Overnight, the snow had stopped, and as the train moved north the light on the wide white fields became too bright to look at. Miranda leaned her head back, grainy-eyed. When they were well under way she tucked the cat's carrier under her seat and let the beast sit on her lap, hungry for a warm touch. She felt safe. With its deformed paws folded beneath it, nothing about the animal looked at all abnormal.

In time, boredom settled in. Miranda bought a lunch from a vendor who came through the train at a station midway from Bierdsey to Clunn: a thick roast beef sandwich, a boiled egg, and some tea. The cat pawed at her hand as she picked up the sandwich, so she pulled some of the beef out and set it down on the wrapping paper. Something about the beast looked different, although Miranda couldn't say what exactly. A little less catlike, somehow, even as it chewed at the beef with its cheek teeth and pawed again at her hand for more, like any other cat.

2

She descended from the train at Clunn to be met by two young men in Guard uniform. *They've found Jon Welkin,* she thought. *And somehow they know I killed him.*

"Mrs. Glivven?" one asked.

"I am she."

"Would you mind coming with us?" He looked down at her—Alexi's—suitcase, packed with her own case and everything belonging to both of them. "Here, let me take that."

A very polite arrest, she was thinking, when the other guard said, "Prefect Bikthen wishes to see you."

Her knees weakened with relief. She stopped to regain her strength, and the young guard simply waited. "Long train rides leave my mother stiff in the joints, too," he said sociably. *The man in Bierdsey,* Miranda was thinking. He must have telegraphed to Bikthen that she was coming by this train, and now Bikthen would want to know what she had learned. So far, she was safe. "The prefect's in the stationmaster's office," the guard went on. "So you won't have to travel all the way out to the Province House."

"That's very kind of him," Miranda managed to remark.

"You seem to be an important person." The guard looked her over as if wondering why. They had reached a solid wooden door in the stone wall of the station building. He rapped on it.

Landers Bikthen opened the door. "Ah, Miranda," he said. "I'm glad to see you."

"Hello, sir," she said.

"Landers, please! As I've told you before. Come in. The stationmaster has kindly permitted me to use his office for a few minutes." He glanced at the guards. "Wait outside, please?"

"I suppose someone telegraphed to let you know I'd be on this train," Miranda said as the door was pushed shut. Bikthen nodded. "One of the men you hired to keep watch over me in Bierdsey?"

"Correct, except that he wasn't hired for that—only given that assignment."

"Quite unnecessary."

"As I read their reports, both useful and dangerous."

"Possibly." The stationmaster's office was tiny, drab, and overheated, and furnished with a desk, two chairs, and one shelf on which a series of identically bound books stood: railway schedules for the whole country.

"Please sit down," Bikthen said, gesturing toward one of the chairs and, probably quite automatically, taking the one behind the desk and turning it to face her. "You were very busy in Bierdsey, judging by the reports my men sent. Now, tell me, what did you learn?"

Miranda stared at him. Exactly how much could she tell this man without finding herself in jail for the rest of her life, at the hands of guards who had once thought her a magician?

"More than the Guard did," she said at last.

"And that was?"

It couldn't hurt to tell him most of it, and he might yet be able to follow her leads to Alexi. "There's one night, at the beginning, still missing. I don't know where he stayed on the fifth of August. Beginning on the sixth, he stayed at an inn called the Blue Swan." Bikthen's eyebrows lifted: he must know the place, by reputation at least. "On the nineteenth of September"—the prefect didn't have to know about the search of Alexi's room, did he?—"he moved to a place called the Red Door Inn. On the twenty-seventh, he started to write me a letter, but he'd only got as far as the greeting when a man arrived at the inn asking for him. The innkeeper thinks it was someone Alexi knew."

Slowly, meticulously, Bikthen matched his fingertips and raised his hands to gaze at her over them, his elbows on the arms of the chair. Something about the gesture made her wary.

"They had a glass of ale together and then they left. Alexi never came back. That's all I found out."

"The twenty-seventh," Bikthen repeated. "The night of that meteor." He squinted into the distance for several seconds. "A most unusual phenomenon. Most unusual." His eyes strayed toward the cat carrier, which Miranda had set on the end of the desk.

"So I've gathered."

"No idea why he moved from one inn to another?"

"No. For a while, I thought—" Why did she always have the urge to blurt out the whole truth to this man?

"Thought what?"

She sighed. Rodde knew about the search, and so did the young maid; if Bikthen sent anyone asking, he'd learn about it anyway. "A couple of days before Lexi left the Blue Swan, the landlord's wife caught somebody in his room, apparently looking for a hair to use as some kind of pointer, if you can believe that. I thought she might have told Alexi, but it turns out she couldn't have, and no one else did."

"Not a hair to point with, Miranda." Bikthen sounded very serious. "Not if he knew where Alexi was. No, he wanted a hair to bind Alexi's will to his own."

The other use of a hair. Yes. She'd read about that in the library. But Welkin hadn't taken the offer of her own hair.

"Not that it would have done the slightest good, given a man like Alexi. Of course, he may not have known that." Bikthen leaned forward, now clasping his hands between his knees. "Miranda, I've got a confession to make." He sat biting his lower lip. "You're owed a confidence, I think," he said finally. "I've telegraphed His Grace the Governor, to suggest it, and he very reluctantly agrees."

Miranda swallowed. *He's going to tell me Alexi's dead, and he knew it all along,* she thought.

"What I have to say is hard . . ." Bikthen glanced again at the cat carrier. "Before I say it, I must have your promise never to discuss it with anyone."

Nervously, Miranda said, "Very well."

"There *are* magicians in this world, Miranda." The prefect's face lengthened. He looked at his folded hands. "The talent is rare," he continued with a sigh, "but it is real and it can be powerful. Further, it is necessary. We could not live as we do without it."

"*I* live without it," Miranda said. "And so do most other people."

Bikthen smiled sadly. "You may think you do, but you don't. Haven't you ever wondered why some professions have guilds? Why they keep secret?"

"To prevent too much competition, I suppose."

"That's what you were taught in school, no doubt. But no. It's because certain of their important processes require magical spells, which they are given an exemption from the law to use." The prefect waved a hand at the bare light bulb over their heads. "Don't you ever wonder where electricity comes from?"

"I know where it comes from. Coal, falling water, other energy sources."

"Ah. 'Other energy sources.' At least ninety percent from them, Miranda. Have you heard of mass-reduction chambers?"

"Of course."

"Don't you wonder what goes on in them?"

What a time for a science lesson! Miranda glanced anxiously at the window, where a wet snow had begun to slide down the dark glass. "At school they told us reducing mass releases energy."

"And so it does. Enormous amounts. But how do you go about reducing mass?"

Miranda shrugged. "I don't know. I'm not a scientist."

"No, Miranda, you're not a *magician*." He showed her his palm as she started to speak. "Mass is reduced by powerful spells. Scientists don't know how these spells work, any more than the magicians who cast them do—all anyone knows is that they do work and are useful."

The man telling her this might be Prefect of Clunn Province, but Miranda couldn't help tightening her lips with disgust.

"That's why I think it so interesting that Alexi vanished on the night a tremendous meteor is thought to have passed over Bierdsey. A meteor that never touched the earth, so far as anyone knows."

Miranda thought of the blackened, glassy walls of the courtyard of Welkin's house, the freshly painted window frames. A lightning strike, he'd said. Or something more sinister? She imagined a warm late summer's evening, a table under the broad crown of the white oak, a cold glass of ale set before each of two men. A house empty of servants, as it had been yesterday afternoon. And then Welkin had begun to speak, and his words had been in the Elder Speech.

She had searched his house for a man. *Zau akomt.* Didn't *zau* mean *pig*? He'd tried to turn her into a pig! Maybe she should have looked for a barn, instead.

Or maybe he had simply reduced Alexi's mass. To nothing. That was what the prefect meant by "interesting," wasn't it?

"You don't believe a word of this, do you?" Bikthen studied her face for several seconds before looking back at his hands. "That's the only reason I dared use you, Miranda. Disbelief isn't simply the absence of belief. It's not a deficiency, a lack of something. It's an *action.* When disbelief is as strong as yours, as you showed me the night I used the crystal to question you, it makes you *immune* to magic: as no one who believes, as no one who merely doubts, as nothing without a mind can ever be."

"Why are you telling me this?" Miranda asked.

Bikthen looked older than she'd thought him, somehow. "As I said, the talent is rare and can be powerful." He sighed. "Well, to be more accurate, the talent isn't so rare, but it is rare for it to be so strong . . ." He shrugged. "When it is, spells or no spells, the possessor becomes aware that he—or she—has some sort of control over events that others do not, and if he seeks out an education in magic, as can still be done if one goes carefully, he can become more than most of us can cope with. Once in a while such a man or woman may decide to use that talent against the government—or to try to control it."

That's what happened to Morten Shells, Miranda thought. *Welkin must have had one of his hairs. All those crack-brained ideas were Welkin's!* She started: where was her disbelief, her active disbelief? Gone, like a puff of white smoke.

"It's as if the person became drugged with his own ability," Bikthen was saying. "It's like strong drink, an addiction. . . . He begins to think he's invincible, and some-times such a person may become almost that strong. You see, if he can gain possession of something belonging to another with a strong talent, something that other one cares about deeply, he can use that to—how can I explain this?— to bleed away the other person's power for his own use."

Alexi's ring. But the library book had said, *Welkin* had said, *as long as the magician lives.* Miranda felt her hope revive. Was Alexi a magician? Was he still alive?

"In those cases we must go very cautiously." Bikthen seemed to search for words. "With the patience of a cat at a mousehole, as it were, and catch the one who is draining us at the ebb of his power . . . when sleeping, maybe . . ." He sighed again and looked at her. "We know a few great talents who we can trust, and when necessary we send one of them to hunt out the one with treason in his soul. Like most lightkeepers, Alexi was a strong magician. He was also one of our best hunters."

"I had no idea," Miranda murmured.

"Of course not. He could be trusted." The prefect seemed unable to meet her eyes. "The night of the fifth of August, he spent here in Clunn, being instructed by me in the task he was about to undertake."

"And you went to Bierdsey with him the next day, didn't you?"

Bikthen frowned at her.

"I saw your name in the Sun's guest list."

"We went by the same train, but not together. I had a secret task, too: to evaluate the state of Morten Shells's mind. I talked with Jon Welkin—a very disturbing conversation—and came home."

Another idea formed, another tiny corner of what she had become part of seemed explicable. "Did Welkin wear a moustache then?" Miranda asked.

"Last summer? No." Bikthen smiled slightly. "Jon's moustache comes and goes with the seasons. He grows one every fall and shaves it every spring, as regular as geese migrating. He might go by that, in fact. Why do you ask?"

"Because moustaches are so rare in Bierdsey. I was surprised to see his." Bikthen nodded, and Miranda, occupied with the implications of the seasonal moustache, absently nodded back. Yes. Welkin could easily have been the ordinary-looking man who had searched Alexi's room. The one Zara Rodde had to think about before she recalled who he was and went to the Province House to confront him, only to meet a swift death dealt with the nearest weapon to hand. A dangerous man.

Alexi had thought so, too. The moment the man had left town—the moment he had *read about it in the newspaper*—Alexi had changed inns.

"I have little hope for Alexi, Miranda." Bikthen looked away. "I must tell you that. I find it painful, not just that he failed, but that he is probably dead, or pent up in an enchantment that even he can't break." He shook his head. "I liked Alexi. He wasn't just an honorable and intelligent man, but one of wit and grace, as you know. I'd hoped you would lead me to the man he was hunting. I even thought I might have pointed you in the right direction, but it seems I was mistaken."

"You used me," she said. "You thought I could pull your chestnuts out of the fire, like the monkey who fooled the cat in the old story."

Bikthen winced, but he nodded.

"You sat on my bed and warned me that people might try to cheat me because I look unsophisticated, and all the while you were planning to use me yourself, just as surely as you used Alexi." Contempt had come into her voice. This was a provincial prefect. She didn't much care. "You told me to call you by your first name—me, a housewife from a small village. Did you think I'd be flattered, Prefect Bikthen? So flattered I wouldn't bother to think?"

"I—"

"Or did you just think I'd be too stupid, too naive, to see that you had some plan you weren't sharing with me?"

Now he set his jaw.

Miranda got up and leaned on the desk. "I knew right away, but I didn't care because I thought you might help me get Alexi back and I had no idea how much danger you were ready to put me in. Did it ever occur to you that I might be the only parent my sons have left? That Alexi and I are both single children, that our parents are dead, that if you'd gotten me killed there'd be *no one* to guide our boys to adulthood?"

"Miranda—"

"Has it ever occurred to you that maybe *you* are drunk with power, Prefect Bikthen? Has it?"

Bikthen lurched to his feet. "Shut up!"

She'd pricked him where he lived, Miranda saw, with a twinge of fear. She stood back.

"Believe me, Miranda, if I'd had the slightest doubt, if I'd thought for one instant that you had the least sliver of belief in magic, I'd have told you to take your cat and go straight back home to Gwynnhead and sit sniveling in your tower for the rest of your life!"

Sniveling! "Oh, you think I'd snivel, do you?" she snapped. "I guess I'm not quite as transparent to you as you are to me, then, am I?"

He came around the corner of the desk. "Listen to me, Miranda," he said.

"Another well-thought-out excuse, Prefect Bikthen?"

He grabbed her by the shoulders and shouted into her face, "Curse you, woman! Don't you see? *I* was the one who thought Alexi could find any rogue on earth, *I* assured the Governor he could take on any magician alive, *I* suggested sending Alexi to Bierdsey, and he was *my* friend! *I'm* responsible for whatever happened to him!"

Miranda stared into the hazel eyes so close to her own without saying anything, because nothing came into her mind to say. Bikthen closed his eyes. The anger drained out of his face. "I'm so sorry," he said. The words sounded forced out of a throat too tight for speech. "Oh, Miranda, I am so sorry."

Miranda put a hand on his arm. He still held her shoulders and his face was still close; she could feel the warmth of his body across the small space between them.

Bikthen's eyes opened. He tilted his head, looking at her mouth as if he might kiss her. *I'll bite him,* Miranda thought. But he only sighed, let his hands drop, and stepped back with shoulders sagging.

"You'd better go home," he said. "There's a storm coming up from the south."

"There's no train for Gwynn-on-the-Main until tomorrow morning."

"No, but there's a northbound express that goes through. I can request a special stop for you."

"That would be a help."

Bikthen pulled out his watch and glanced at it. "Where did the time go? We'll have to hurry—it comes through in twelve minutes." Miranda picked up the cat carrier and reached for the suitcase.

"Here, let me get that," Bikthen said. He hoisted the case and carted it to the door.

"Prefect Bikthen?" Miranda saw him wince and try to hide it. "Landers, then. Did Alexi know that disbelief in magic brings immunity to it?"

"Of course he did. Why do you think he never tried to convince you?"

"A long time ago . . ." But not very vigorously, and not for very long, Alexi had argued against her skepticism.

"Too many dangerous people in Alexi's life, Miranda," Bikthen said softly. "He always tried to protect you. I—" He took a deep breath and pushed the door open with his shoulder. "I promised him I would, too. That's why I took four good agents to Bierdsey with me. Not," he added acidly, "because I thought I'd need them to deal with the man you found for me."

One of the guards stepped forward to take the suitcase from him. "Here," Bikthen said to the other one, reaching into his purse and bringing out a fistful of coins. "Go buy half a dozen meat pies."

"Sir," the guard said.

"And hurry. They're for Mrs. Glivven, and she's got a train to catch."

The guard departed at a dead run.

"Meat pies?"

"You'll need something to sustain you on the journey. It might be slow, if the storm's bad. I'll telegraph for someone to meet the train. Is there anyone from Gwynnhead who would be willing?"

She gave him Andreu's name. The headlight of the north-bound train began to gleam along the tracks beside her. *I might make it,* she thought. *I just might make it home.*

3

Very few people shared this car. The trainman came through and looked at her ticket. "Oh, yes," he said. "You must be Mrs. Glivven. We're stopping at Gwynn-on-the-Main for you."

"That's right."

"I'll give you ten minutes' warning. Be ready to go; we'll lose five minutes just slowing down for you and with this weather it's going to be hard keeping to schedule as it is."

"Thank you," she said.

"We do what the Prefect of Clunn Province tells us to do," he told her, with a glance at her plain clothing and the worn gloves she still held on her lap. But he moved on without asking more questions or objecting to her having the cat carrier on the seat beside her.

A sound came from the carrier. Miranda leaned down to listen. *Zheee,* the cat moaned. She opened the top of the case to look in: the cat looked up at her. *Zheee,* it breathed. *Zhee . . .* and now she thought she heard the faintest of d's at the end of the word. She did not doubt that it was a word, something that struck her as odd only several minutes later.

Zheeed.

"*Zheeed,*" she tried with her own mouth. Not a word. But if her mouth were a cat's?

"Feed?" she asked, after a few seconds of experimenting. "You want me to feed you?"

The cat nodded weakly.

This, too, she accepted. She unwrapped one of the meat pies Bikthen had supplied and dropped it into the case. Only when she had closed the top did the whole episode strike her as extremely peculiar. She opened the carrier again and looked at the cat.

It was changing, without doubt. The ears seemed a tiny bit misshapen, more rounded than they should be. And wasn't it somewhat larger? What was happening to the poor beast?

Vexelen, she heard in her mind's ear. Welkin saying, "*Vexelen, Mirant.*" *Change, Miranda.* But it wasn't quite "*Vexelen, Mirant,*" she heard, now. It was "*Vexelen, Achlexan.*"

"Extraordinary," she said. The cat glanced up at her. The pupils of its eyes were elliptical, but now she noticed that they did not come to points at the ends. She was sure they had before. She'd have noticed that they didn't sometime in the past few weeks, wouldn't she? Or Hathden or Steth would have pointed out such an abnormality?

Understanding began to dawn at last. She watched the cat devour the meat pie. "Alexi?" she said.

The animal in the case looked up from the pie. She could swear it smiled before it went back to eating.

"Alexi?" A nod? Was that a nod?

Miranda sat straight in her seat and looked about. Her back was against the end of the car. One man sat three seats ahead. About halfway down the car, a family—mother, father, four small children—talked quietly among themselves. The smallest child had been crying a moment ago.

Her heart began to beat heavily. Welkin had agreed to see her: not because Bikthen had asked him to, but because he wanted to find out how much she knew. He had offered to scan Alexi's letters: not to help her identify the places he described, but to see whether any of them gave him away. He had been pleasant and courteous, ready to relax and let her go about her futile search until she got too discouraged to go on, until she had mentioned that she was traveling with a cat.

If I hadn't said I had to feed my cat, she realized, *I would still be looking, and Welkin would still be living.*

But why a cat? Why bring on himself that tremendous discharge of energy, threatening his house, destroying a tree he had valued, surely endangering his own life, when he could have turned Alexi into something man-sized and docile and avoided all that?

"I must be mad," she said aloud. The . . . cat . . . glanced up with silver-gray eyes. Now she was sure it smiled. A rush of excitement went through her.

"Did Jon Welkin cast a spell on you?" she whispered.

Again, that nod.

Alexi? Truly her Lexi? Her eyes stung with tears. "But why are you changing?" she asked, still in a whisper.

He tried so hard to say something. Miranda couldn't make it out. One word sounded like "kill," but surely that was her guilt speaking?

No. She remembered the door of Welkin's study, impossible to open, then opening of itself after the man died. A spell did not long outlast the one who cast it. Probably the intensity and duration of the spell affected how long it lingered. Alexi was changing because Welkin was dead. Was he asking if Welkin was the man she had confessed killing?

"Yes, I killed him," she whispered. "I didn't mean to, but I did."

The pie was gone to the last crumb. Alexi—if this was Alexi, if she wasn't half-crazy after the last two days, if Bikthen hadn't put some insanity into her mind with his glittering crystal—licked his chops with a very catlike swipe of a thin tongue and folded his legs under him. He no longer looked comfortable that way.

Miranda leaned her head against the back of the seat, watching the snow glide past, tears gathering in her eyes. The regular dip of the telegraph lines between poles alarmed her: surely Welkin had been missed and his body found by now. At any station, the train might slow, the brakes hiss, two or three guards in uniform come into the car and seize her. Just let her get home, just let her explain, and Hathden and Steth could be trusted to feed their father, give him meat for bones growing back into their human form. If she could just get home.

At last she fell into an uneasy sleep, lulled by the click of the wheels over the rails beneath her.

Light snow was falling when Miranda stepped onto the platform at Gwynn on-the-Main before dawn, the fringes of the blizzard Bikthen had warned her about in Clunn. He'd been as good as his word, at least: as the train groaned back into motion, old Andreu came up to her with a grin and a hug she tried to return. "Oh, I'm so glad to see you," she said. "But I've rousted you out of bed so early! I'm sorry."

"Glad to come get you, M'randa. Those boys of yours have missed you, but don't be s'prised if they deny it. Still got that troublesome cat?"

"In the carrier," she said. "I'm not letting it out until I get into the house!"

"There's good sense," Andreu agreed. His team was stamping in the cold, snorting the snow out of their noses and shaking their heads.

"A bad storm coming, for sure," the old man remarked, tossing the suitcase into the bed of his wagon. "Horses always know. And the gulls were tight to the water all yesterday." He went on chattering buoyantly, not seeming to notice the effort of Miranda's replies. As they topped the rise before the causeway she saw the beacon light shining. She felt a leap of joy mixed with fear: how was she to explain herself to her sons?

Andreu carried the heavy suitcase up to the tower door while Miranda clutched Alexi's prison to her chest and struggled up the steps. The snow had thickened and the wind risen, snatching her breath out of her mouth. She tried to hand Andreu a large banknote, but he put his hands behind him. "Take it," she said. "Prefect Bikthen told me to give it to you, for your trouble coming to fetch me."

Andreu shook his head. "Don't make a thief of me, Andreu! Take it."

Hathden opened the door as Miranda tucked the money into Andreu's outer cloak pocket. "I thought I heard voices," he said. "Welcome home!" While he was hugging her, Andreu went down the steps. She called a thanks after him.

The sitting room had not changed. It looked a little larger, after the cramped sleeping room in Bierdsey, but it was the same familiar room.

"Steth! Get up, you lazybones!" Hathden yelled. "Mother's home!"

GWYNNHEAD

1

"What's that?" Steth asked sleepily, escaping Miranda's embrace with the skill of long practice.

"A cat carrier."

"Oh, did you bring that yellow cat back home with you?" He looked at the carrier with more interest.

"Yes." Miranda shooed a curious Mrs. Putz away and opened the top of the carrier. The animal had changed still more over the train journey from Clunn: fueled with all six of the meat pies Bikthen had bought, it had grown much larger. The eyes that looked up at her had rounder pupils than before, and the face seemed flatter, more like a long-haired cat.

Hathden peered into the carrier. "What's the matter with it?" he asked.

Miranda sighed. "A long story. Let's lift it out and see how it is, first, and then I'll tell you." She slid her hands down the sides of the carrier and clasped them around the cat's—Alexi's—body. Goodness, he was hot! A fever?

"It's so big!" Steth exclaimed. "That's not the same animal. It's not even a cat."

"No." Miranda took a deep breath: what she was about to say would be hard. "It isn't a cat." She sank into her easy chair by the window with Alexi on her lap. "Sit down, boys."

Steth promptly collapsed cross-legged on the floor, then drew his knees up under his nightshirt, but Hathden remained standing near the carrier.

"This is important," Miranda told them. "So listen. All your lives I have told you that magic, all practice of magic, is a ruse and a delusion." Steth nodded solemnly. "Until last night, I fully believed that to be true. I was wrong."

Steth made the expected nose-wrinkle of derision. Hathden only nodded slightly and sat on the edge of Alexi's chair. Miranda took another deep breath.

"I have every reason to believe this animal we thought was a cat is really a man. Now he's coming out of an enchantment, and I'm almost certain it's your father." The beast nodded, as did Hathden; Steth's face became a blank of incredulity.

"He needs to be fed," Miranda said. "He's eaten enormous amounts over the past few hours. And he's not just growing, he's changing. A lot, as you can see." She looked again at the creature on her lap: the forepaws that had caused her such trouble were altering, too, the inner toe splayed away from the others and all five of them a little less curled into the neat paws of a cat.

"*Zheeed,*" Alexi moaned.

"He's hungry again," Miranda said. Hathden went out to the kitchen and returned with a large bowl of milk. He knelt beside her to hold the bowl until Alexi had lapped it clean and rested his head on his . . . hands, Miranda supposed she should call them. Mrs. Putz walked away with her tail in the air.

"You think Father was enchanted, and that's why he stopped writing?" Hathden said. "All that long while ago?"

"It took him a long time to come home from Bierdsey." Miranda tried to imagine what it could have been like, to be so small, so insignificant, trying to find his way north, not even able to stand tall and see landmarks. She shook her head. Inconceivable. But even ordinary cats had been known to make such journeys.

"I'm hungry," Steth said.

Miranda stood and put Alexi down where she had been sitting and went out to the kitchen. Hathden had been cooking oatmeal when she and Andreu had arrived. The pot was standing on the stove, the porridge getting too thick. She stirred a little more water into it and put it back over the heat.

"What does he most need to eat, do you think?" Hathden asked, coming after her.

"Protein, I would guess," Miranda said. "And calcium for the bones, and he'll need energy, so plenty of carbohydrates." She looked at the unshuttered window. Light had come, but the snow was even thicker than before.

Hathden followed her gaze. "We won't have school today," he said. "Nobody will cross the causeway in this. Later, I'll see if I can get to the store."

Hathden returned from the store in early afternoon with as much food as he could carry. A gust of wind came through the door with him, laden with tiny flakes that melted in a shower of fine droplets as they hit the warm air of the house. "Sit by the heater," Miranda told him as he stamped the snow from his boots. "I'll put the food away."

"I want to check the beacon."

Miranda felt the blood drain from her face. "Why, wasn't it working when you came up the hill?"

"Oh, yes." Hathden went to the door in the sitting room without explanation, closing it behind him. The sound of his steps faded up the stone spiral. When he hadn't come down in half an hour, Miranda went after him.

"Hathden?" she called, from halfway up the stairs.

"Up here."

She went the rest of the way up. Hathden was leaning on the broad windowsill, much as he had been the day he had announced that the light was now his to keep. Struck by his slumping pose, Miranda thought, *It was his manhood come early, and now he'll have to give it up.*

"I have to talk to you," she said.

"Don't tell me. The light still belongs to Father." He kept his back to her. "I'm glad, really, but—"

"But you can't help being disappointed," Miranda said. "That's not what I need to tell you, though. We can talk about it later, if you want."

Hathden sighed, still looking out the window at the storm.

"Come here?" Miranda sat on the top step, cold as it was. The steps had been thoroughly swept, she noticed for the first time: Hathden took pride in his new work.

Hathden crouched on the step beside her. "What?"

"I'm in some danger," she told him. "Please, don't tell Steth, not yet. The Guard may come for me when the storm's over, if the causeway's clear."

"The Guard!" Hathden gaped at her. "Why?"

"Shh." She wiped tears away with both palms and whispered, "I killed a man in Bierdsey."

He stared. "You?"

Miranda told him about Welkin as briefly as she could. The story seemed to take a very long time.

"Then that's why Father's coming back to us," Hathden pointed out when she was done. "Without the man dead, he'd have been a cat for the rest of his life."

"Jon Welkin could have been persuaded somehow to remove the spell, I'm sure," Miranda said. "I don't think he was heartless. If I'd had the sense to see what was happening, if I hadn't had such a strong disbelief—"

"You'd be a pig," Hathden said. "No help to anyone. Two particularly tender hams and some meaty bacon, probably."

"No." Miranda decided to ignore the rudeness of the comment. "He thought I was a magician. He'd have wanted me alive."

"But he'd still have been senior assistant to the Prefect of Bierdsey Province. And he'd still have been making the man do stupid things to get him retired and take his place."

"Yes."

"And no matter how good an administrator he'd have been, no matter how good a Governor he *thought* he'd be or even wanted to be, it's still not right to twist others to your purpose."

"No," Miranda said.

"Mother, if this Jon Welkin had become Governor, how long do you think he'd have worked for our good?" Hathden asked. "A man willing to steal any kind of power from anyone else by any means he could? A man who killed at least one person and enchanted at least one other when he was threatened? And even if you'd convinced him to let Father out of his spell, how long do you think he—or you—would have lived?"

What was she to say to that?

Hathden answered his own question: "Not long."

"He's still dead," Miranda said. "And I'm still the one who killed him." She could feel the square shaft of the poker pressed against her palms, feel the tautness of her belly muscles as she had pushed it home. She rubbed her hands together.

The door at the bottom of the steps opened. "Mother?" Steth called. "Are you going to stay up there all day? Because this animal is asking for food again."

"I'll be right there." Miranda stood up. To Hathden, she said in an undertone, "I'm trusting you to do what's right, if they come to take me away."

He looked shocked and hurt. "Of course."

2

Two days later, the storm died. The point of land the tower marked had been windswept almost to the bare ground, except for a tall drift on the lee side of the house, but the town of Gwynnhead was choked with snow and the causeway made impassable with frozen seawater. To Miranda, this was a double-edged blade: she had a few more days free of worry about the Guard, but where was she to get enough food for Alexi?

On balance, she was relieved the day the causeway reopened and the village grocer had been resupplied. Her sons were to stop on the way home from school for more food, under a strict injunction to say nothing about their father.

The knock on the door was a few minutes early.

"Why can't they open it themselves?" Miranda muttered testily, annoyed at being interrupted in massaging Alexi's aching muscles. The knock was repeated. "Oh, all right!" She hurried from her bedroom to the front door and snatched it open. Landers Bikthen stood on the step.

"Oh," she said.

At the end of the lane by Evelyn's house was a four-man enclosed sleigh. Two uniformed men stood beside it. Bikthen turned and waved once and they climbed back in.

"May I come in?" the prefect asked.

"Oh. Certainly." Miranda stepped back and let the man walk past her into the house. She glanced again at the sleigh at the bottom of the hill and shut the door.

Bikthen was removing his gloves. She took his fur-lined cloak from him and lifted it onto a hook beside her own. "Please sit down," she managed to say. "Can I get you some tea?"

"Thank you," Bikthen replied. "That would be welcome."

Miranda stopped in the kitchen to put the kettle on, then slipped down the hall to shut Alexi into their room. When she returned to the kitchen, Bikthen was standing in the doorway. He tilted his head at her but said nothing. "It will just take a few minutes," she told him nervously. "Please, make yourself comfortable, if you can."

"I'm comfortable," he said.

Flustered, she spooned tea into a pot, set it on a tray, got two of her best cups out of a cupboard, remembered saucers and went back to the cupboard for them, all the while feeling Bikthen's gaze on her. The water took forever to boil. At last she poured it over the tea, saying, "I hope you like raspberry; that's all I've got," and remembered to fetch the strainer out of the drawer.

"I'll carry it," Bikthen offered, picking up the tray.

"I see you have some guards with you," Miranda remarked as she led him into the sitting room.

"An unfortunate necessity."

Please, not before the boys come home, she thought, biting her lips. "Aren't they cold?"

"The sleigh's heated." He set the tray on the table she pointed to. "Sit down, Miranda. Stop fussing."

She sat down and poured out tea, remembering to use the strainer on the second cup.

Tomtom came strolling into the room and sat down to look at the visitor, his white nose and paws gleaming.

"A handsome beast." Bikthen sipped at the steaming tea. "Ah, wonderful! What happened to that beautiful golden cat of yours, Miranda? I hope you haven't lost it."

"Oh, no."

"Where is it?"

"It's around somewhere. Maybe outside."

"Strange things have been happening in Bierdsey in the week since you left." Bikthen set his cup on his saucer and cocked his head at her. "I wonder if you could help me understand them."

"Me?" Miranda set her own cup down and wished she hadn't as it chattered against the saucer.

"Morten Shells has suddenly regained his old vigor— quite a stunning transformation, according to all reports. There's an exceedingly junior assistant named Navocque making all kinds of bizarre accusations against Jon Welkin, and a Captain Lafass of the Municipal Guard has some odd things to say of him, too."

"Really," Miranda said.

"Welkin himself is dead."

"My goodness." Miranda swallowed to settle her voice. "Such a young man."

"Dead under unusual circumstances, Miranda." Bikthen gazed at her steadily. "He was murdered in his own study at home."

She couldn't quite meet his eyes. "Is that right?" she said. "How very odd."

"He had ordered his servants out of the house for the

afternoon; something he'd done several times before. And he was found stabbed with a poker from his own fireplace, wearing clothing belonging to one of those servants. Evidently a prolonged struggle had taken place. A blue wool cloak identified as having been owned by a man gone missing three years ago was hanging from a cloaktree in the study."

Miranda wondered whether she dared pick the cup up again.

"Fragments of glass on the hearth seemed to be from a crystal ball, of the type containing a charm that destroys inhibitions when released," Bikthen went on. "If Welkin shattered it, he may have been the agent of his own death. What do you think, Miranda?"

After a few seconds, she drew a shaky breath. "Why would so intelligent a man as Welkin do that?"

"Just what I wondered," Bikthen remarked. "On deliberation, I'd guess it more likely that someone who had no idea what the ball contained threw it at him in an attempt to defend herself."

She gazed at him stonily.

The back door opened. "Mother?" Steth yelled cheerfully. "Hathden's stopped at the library. I've got as much food for Father as I can carry."

"Just put it down," she called. "I'll be right there."

"Hathden will bring some, too," Steth replied, still from the kitchen, "so we won't be running out so soon. Did you know there's a big sleigh in front of David and Evelyn's house? Who do you think is visiting them?"

"Running out of food for Father?" Bikthen repeated. One corner of his mouth twitched. "Don't you and your sons eat?"

Miranda closed her eyes. When she opened them, Steth was standing in the kitchen doorway, looking stricken; Bikthen had matched his fingertips and was leaning back in his chair gazing at her with an expression of amused satisfaction. He glanced at her son. "You would be Steth, I think, isn't that right?" he asked. "I'm Landers Bikthen, the Prefect of Clunn Province."

Poor Steth had gone white. "Hello, sir," he said. His voice was hollow. He forgot to bow.

"Your mother and I are having a small discussion, Steth," Bikthen said. "Do you mind leaving us alone?"

"Right away, sir." Steth backed into the kitchen. Miranda heard the latch of the door to his room click a moment later. She turned her gaze to Bikthen.

"Miranda. I want to see that cat," he said. "Now."

"I—I'll see if it's in the house." She stood up. An effort. "But if it's outdoors, I'm afraid it doesn't come when it's called."

"I'll wait. I have plenty of time. It's bound to get hungry sooner or later. Isn't it?"

Miranda fled to her bedroom. She leaned the door shut and rested the back of her head against it for a moment. "Alexi," she whispered.

Alexi sat up: he now resembled a cross between a cat and a monkey with a shortened tail. In the six days since they had returned home he had grown to the size of a year-old child. "Ah?" he half said, half mewed.

"Landers Bikthen is in our sitting room," Miranda gasped. "He wants to see the golden cat. Now."

"Ah k'm." Alexi slid down from the bed and painfully rabbit-hopped toward her. He held his arms up to be carried.

Miranda scooped him up. "You want to see him?"

Alexi nodded.

"Alexi, he'll know I killed Jon Welkin!"

He nodded again.

"He's got the Guard with him. They'll put me in jail!"

Alexi shook his head. "P'ahmith, no."

"You promise me, no?" He nodded.

Stiff-kneed, to keep from falling, Miranda carried him into the sitting room.

"Ah, Alexi!" Bikthen got to his feet. He was smiling. "You can't imagine how relieved I am to see you!" Crossing the room, he took Alexi's hand, which by now resembled that of a raccoon. "Can they feed you enough?" he asked anxiously.

Alexi shook his head.

"Well, I came prepared for that. Just a moment." He went to the front window and looked out. After a few seconds he made a gesture to someone outside and turned back to the room. "Sit down again, Miranda, please?"

Now they will come to arrest me. She perched on the edge of her chair, with Alexi on her knees, as Bikthen resumed his own seat.

"How did you know?"

Bikthen smiled broadly. "I was sure the cat was Alexi when I first saw you at Clunn, even though you obviously hadn't the slightest idea. That's why I wrote you the letter of conduct. I've been thanking fate for old lady Mirk and every bee in her venerable bonnet ever since."

She had not been asking about the cat, but Miranda frowned. "Why did you think the cat was Alexi?"

"He was so clearly a magicked cat. Extraordinarily daring, to turn a man into something so small as a cat. I've never heard of it being done in modern times. But it explained everything—everything I knew about at the time."

"Was it the toes?" Miranda asked, bewildered. "But normal cats are occasionally born with extra toes."

"No, not the toes," Bikthen said. "His teeth. He has only four incisors in each jaw. Normal cats have six."

Miranda looked at Alexi, who looked up at her and spread his lips. Four tiny, tiny incisors spaced widely between the sharp canines. She would have to take a closer look at one of the real cats, if the prefect allowed her time for good-byes. *Where's the Guard?* she wondered. *Why don't they come?*

"Now, that is what I simply cannot understand," Bikthen mused aloud. "Why a man as cautious as Jon Welkin would take the risk of turning Alexi into a cat, when something larger would have been so much simpler and safer. It seems wholly out of character."

"Ah zhozz," Alexi said.

Bikthen frowned. After a moment of trying the sound silently in her mouth, Miranda said, "You chose?" Alexi nodded.

"Oh, I see," the prefect said. "He started the *vexel*, and you altered it? Why?"

"Boom," Alexi said, very clearly. He gazed expectantly at the prefect. Something thumped against the front door, but no one knocked.

"You wanted the explosion?" Bikthen looked out the window. "Ah! You thought it would kill him and release you immediately?" Alexi nodded. "But he controlled it well enough that he wasn't even injured." Alexi nodded again. "That's the undamaged spot in the courtyard of his house, I take it?"

Miranda hadn't noticed one, but she held her tongue. She might well have missed a patch of dead grass under the snow.

"And the rest of the energy? I've heard what it did to the walls of the courtyard of his house, and there was a report of a bolide that passed out to sea over Bierdsey that night. He directed and dissipated it?" Alexi nodded.

Bikthen's eyebrows jerked. "He must have been much stronger than anyone thought! That much mass converting could have blown the countryside apart for miles around."

"Zo." Alexi's thin tongue flicked over his lips. "Thl-lo."

"Oh, the change was slowed down! Yes, you'd have given off an aura at first. . . . And I suppose that gave him enough warning for a containment spell. . . . And if the energy burned off over a matter of minutes? Yes? That would reduce the strength needed. Well, that explains that," Bikthen said with evident gratification. "Did he put most of the energy into the other universe?"

"What other universe?" Miranda demanded. *Where are those two men?* She heard more sounds on the doorstep. *Why don't they knock?*

"A theoretical energy drain," Bikthen was explaining. "In order to account for the way energy behaves in our own universe, physicists have postulated that it is connected to another universe and that energy moves back and forth between the two—or more. And to explain why nothing else moves between universes, the theory is that atoms are too large to fit through the connections. I don't pretend to understand the mathematics, but apparently it is sufficient. There's no proof, of course."

"Ah." Alexi tapped his chest with one hand and gestured with the other.

"Oh, you *both* worked the transfer spell?" Bikthen paused for Alexi's nod. "Now I see. You didn't want to destroy anything but Welkin, and he defended himself." Again, Alexi nodded.

"I think Alexi chose to be a cat because he knew you would take him in," Bikthen went on. Miranda looked at the creature in her lap, who nodded vigorously. How close she had been to shutting him out forever she swore never to tell him. "Well, thank you, Miranda. That clears everything up."

"Everything but Welkin's death," she said tentatively.

He smiled at her. "That, too. You needn't worry, you're quite safe. You recall the man who got on the inbound train at Province House to find you already aboard, with your cloak and boots soaking wet?" Miranda felt her courage evaporate, as if from her skin. She nodded. "He seems to be the only witness who can connect you in any way with Welkin that afternoon," Bikthen said, his voice soft. "But you can count on his silence. He's a hunter, too."

Miranda shrugged unhappily. "But an investigation might—"

"Obviously, you could plead self-defense if you had to," Bikthen pointed out. "But do you really think you could ever be brought to trial? With all that would be made public? Never. And no one in authority would want to accuse you, even if that were not the case. Think of yourself as having performed a public service, Miranda. I don't think we would ever have found another method of controlling a magician as strong as Jon Welkin. And think of what his death means to Alexi."

"Zheeed," Alexi said, as Bikthen stood.

"In a moment." Miranda got up and put him on the chair where she had been sitting. Bikthen was already lifting his cloak from the hook.

"That thump should have been the largest cheese the

market at Clunn had to offer," he said, opening the door. "Ah, yes. And a drum of powdered milk." He bent and with his own soft hands spun the knee-high drum into the house on its bottom rim. "There. Mix a cup of the powder to a quart of water, I think—it should say on the side. Alexi will need the protein and calcium."

Miranda nodded. "I'd thought of that. It was getting to be a problem."

"So I imagined. Good luck, admirable Miranda." Bikthen paused and looked intently into her face. "Try not to think too harshly of me, will you?"

Before she could reply, he whirled and started quickly down the outer steps. In the room behind her, Alexi groaned, "Zheeed."

"Just a minute," Miranda said over her shoulder. Cloakless, she ran down the outer steps.

Bikthen stood on the step of the sleigh, ready to lever himself into the high back seat. "Please," Miranda said breathlessly. He looked down at her. "Don't ever send him out to hunt again. Promise me that?"

The prefect shook his head. "That's his choice, Miranda," he said gently. "It always has been."

3

The next few weeks were a blur. Impossible to keep secret the huge amounts of food going into her house, even with Evelyn's help. Visitors she seldom saw came to call and sat looking distractedly about, while Miranda tried to present a normal face to a world that knew perfectly well that the Prefect of Clunn had come personally to talk to her.

The moment a visitor left she would go to the bedroom to check on Alexi, rub his aching muscles, brush away the golden fur he was shedding, feed him, feed him. Oddly enough, he never excreted anything: as a cat, he'd had a normal digestive system, but now every atom was going to transform him from that cat into a man twelve times its size.

"M'anda," he said clearly, after a fortnight or so. "M'anda, I love you." She pulled him into her arms—he was now about the size of an eight-year-old—and laid her cheek against what was almost a human cheek. "Doon kye," he said. "Don't cry."

He seldom spoke more than a word or two at a time, and those with great effort. Miranda thought it might be because of his teeth, still cat teeth, so tiny in his enlarging mouth. One day he came to her with three of them in what was nearly the palm of a human hand, a palm in which lines were forming exactly like the lines she had once known so well. The next day the edge of a human incisor showed in his gum. She rejoiced.

With more flexible hands, Alexi began to write notes. Miranda would find them, laborious little messages in a version of his old easy script that looked so tense it wrung her heart. Often they began or ended in the middle of a sentence:

. . . had to see you, she found in her chair. *Came home. Later I will tell you.* Or on her pillow: *Saw you go into library and waited for you to come out. Couldn't believe you didn't know me. . . .*

She bowed her head and wept. How could she have not known him? She had almost forgotten what it had been like to be certain of how the world was made, that everything followed the natural laws taught to her in school.

Soon Alexi joined his family at the table for suppers. One day Hathden mentioned that he'd like to stay after classes the next day to complete a project for his history teacher and asked Miranda if she'd be at home to tend to the light.

"Switch?" Alexi said.

"It's broken." Miranda silently passed mashed potatoes to Steth. "Hasn't worked for almost two months."

"Fix," he said.

"Can't figure out how," Hathden told him. "Andreu had a look at it, and so did Master Craffid, but neither could see how it was supposed to work. Master Craffid thinks a piece is missing."

Alexi nodded. "Fix," he repeated. After supper he sat a long time at the kitchen table, carefully printing something on a piece of paper. "Come, help fix," he said to Hathden when he was done, tugging his son toward the tower door. "You read."

Miranda followed them to the door and stood at the bottom of the stairs, hearing Hathden's voice stumble through the words of a charm in the Elder Speech. Several minutes later her husband and son came down, looking pleased with themselves. The next day when she went up to light the beacon, the stairwell brightened as she climbed: the lamp had turned itself on. Reaching the top of the steps, Miranda examined the automatic switch. The little leaves had opened to the widest circle. A faint hum told her the gadget was working. "Like a charm," she muttered with bitter humor, and went back down the stairs.

The Feast of the Equinox arrived. Miranda set out the traditional white candles, and Alexi and Hathden and Steth helped to bake the traditional sweet pastries. That night she made love with a man still part beast. Afterward she held him tightly, stroking the thin fur that lingered on his back and aching for the day he would be wholly himself. The candles had burned to the sockets and the pastries had long since been eaten before the last golden fur rubbed off his shoulder blades and Alexi was fully human. She loved him more than ever, although he was never again quite the same Alexi who kissed her good-bye on a summer morning and went off to do a preposterous job.

But then, she has never been quite the same Miranda. It's not simply that the force of magic struck her so hard or that the legacy of the Glivvens was revealed as something stranger than she could have believed on that far off summer day. She dreams, sometimes, of a crystal globe that shatters with a puff of white smoke and a sweet, cloying odor. Or, alone in the house and going quietly about her chores, she may hear someone whisper, "Extraordinary!" and wonder what that final, unvoiced word might have been. Glancing at Alexi's wedding ring, she may momentarily see it on a different hand. Or she may glimpse a man with a dark moustache, his face shadowed by the hood of a blue wool cloak, where no such man can possibly be.

Often, when the wind is off the sea and the sky lowering, she stands listening to the secretive creak of the gulls and the arcane reply of the ocean, and wonders about those others who might have been released by Jon Welkin's death as Alexi was: huge friendly dogs, perhaps, or pigs or other beasts; men or women who began the long change back from beasthood with no one to comfort or feed them, and died of disenchantment. On one of those days she unbolted the automatic switch and threw it into the mumbling water below. But there is nothing she can do about the charm against the wind: the one that keeps the tower, and therefore her life, from toppling, no longer able to withstand the force of the elements.

Everyone has charms against fate's mischiefs, Miranda often thinks. She wishes only that she still could choose her own.

Shadow Novels from
ANNE LOGSTON

Shadow is a master thief as elusive as her name. Only her dagger is as sharp as her eyes and wits. Where there's a rich merchant to rob, good food and wine to be had, or a lusty fellow to kiss...there's Shadow.

"Spiced with magic and intrigue..."–Simon R. Green
"A highly entertaining fantasy."–<u>Locus</u>

__SHADOW   0-441-75989-0/$3.99
__SHADOW HUNT   0-441-76007-4/$4.50
__DAGGER'S EDGE   0-441-00036-3/$4.99

And don't miss other Anne Logston adventures...

__GREENDAUGHTER   0-441-30273-4/$4.50
Deep within the Mother Forest, Chyrie, an elf with the gift of animal-speaking, must embrace the human world to fend off barbarian invaders...and save both worlds.